SOLOMON'S EXECUTIONER

STEVEN TURK

ARIETE

ARIETE

ARIETE PRESS

Copyright © Steven Turk 2013
All rights reserved

ISBN–13: 978-1491296585
ISBN–10: 1491296585

Printed in the United States of America

FOR MY SON, NATHAN

CHAPTER 1

July 13, 1997

Greta Bauer lived the littlest of lives growing vegetables in a garden by a woods. The last home along the cinder alley, her tiny cottage had been white with bright green shutters when she moved in but was now weathered and gray like the others. The few shutters that remained hung askew like crooked teeth under a roof ridge that sagged in an ominous, wry grin.

Dressed in dark, shapeless clothes and a sweat-stained, brown fedora drawn low over her gray hair, it was hard to tell that the stooped, leathery-faced figure was even a woman. For as long as most people could remember, she was simply the "vegetable lady" who pulled her ancient Radio Flyer wagon through the neighborhood offering potatoes, carrots and other vegetables from dusty gunny sacks and dented pails. The rusting wagon was nearly as tired and worn as she but provided the benefit of an incessant squeak that advertised her approach to potential customers.

There was no room for negotiating with Greta. Her response was to simply turn away and pull her wagon screeching further up the street.

She rarely spoke. When she did, her words were slurred in a heavy accent made even more unintelligible by a perpetually swollen, lower lip the color and texture of raw liver. It caused her to drool uncontrollably, so it was not surprising that young children hid behind their mothers clutching tiny fistfuls of dress or housecoat whenever she was summoned to a kitchen stoop or a back yard gate. As the children grew older, they would make sport of taunting her from hiding places in trees and garage rooftops.

For the bravest, it was a right of passage to sneak into Greta's garden late on summer nights to steal a watermelon. But even that was discouraged for most after several children playing in the woods reported seeing her plucking baby rabbits from their nest and twisting their tiny necks one-by-one. The details of the incident grew more distorted with each telling and soon became part of the neighborhood lore that kept Greta isolated.

On this Saturday like all the others, Greta Bauer was busily digging potatoes in the waning light of day when a vague, uneasy feeling washed over her. She scanned the woods for signs of the rowdy teens that sometimes harassed her and did not see the man watching her through a narrow opening in the trees–so close he could hear her grunt and wheeze. His chiseled face, square-jaw, even the oval of his shaved head merged seamlessly with the darkening woods under a muddle of green and black face paint matching his camouflage clothing. Motionless, he was all but invisible save for the curious color of his eyes; limpid and green as tiny puddles of olive oil. Even as a frenzy of sunset mosquitoes flitted around his head and probed the flesh of his face and ears and sweat soaked neck for a meal of blood, he didn't move.

The man was the only person on earth who knew exactly who Greta Bauer was. Even though she was no longer the burly, arrogant young woman in the black and white picture he carried in his backpack, there was no mistaking her. He also knew precisely what he had to do to her that night after darkness settled over the woods and she was in his control inside the secluded cottage.

He had read about it and planned it with great care. Even better, he had practiced the entire procedure on a pig.

The last of the light was nearly gone when he watched Greta straighten and pull the loaded wagon squeaking across the alley to a spigot in the cottage yard where she washed the dirt from the vegetables.

The slow ache began to climb from his neck to the back of his head. It was nearly time.

He patted the outer pocket of the backpack resting at his feet for the long, curved sheath that held the razor-sharp knife, then felt around inside for the hammer, coil of rope, latex gloves, duct tape, the small device to which a tiny disposable propane cylinder was attached, the small rubber ball and, most importantly, the hand-held taser.

His head throbbing now, he drew a deep breath then exhaled heavily–cleansing himself. As the pain grew in intensity, he began to separate himself from it by allowing his thoughts to descend into that place inside he had created when he was a boy. A sanctuary where he could watch his other self emerge–the powerful self who feared nothing and no one. The self who righted wrongs and protected him.

His face was expressionless now. His green eyes cold and empty. Even as the woods around him became more alive, everything grew increasingly dreamlike.

As if through a gauzy veil, he watched the shadowy swirls of starlings turning overhead, heard the croaks of the bullfrogs and the brittle screech of the tree crickets as if his ears were stuffed with cotton. He was no longer inside himself, but floating, hovering. He had surrendered control completely to the other self.

Gradually, the old woman became barely visible to him in the dying light and finally disappeared completely in the darkness. He pulled on the latex gloves while he waited in the quiet for the cottage door to slam and the light to appear in her kitchen window, then cautiously emerged from the ragged thicket and stole his way to the cottage.

The old woman had just sat down at her small kitchen table with a cup of tea when she heard the crunch of footsteps in the cinders outside.

"Gott damn kids come to schteal from my garten," she cursed, slamming the cup down, heaving her squat bulk from the chair and lumbering onto the porch. Just as she was about to grab a hoe to chase them off, a powerful arm wrapped tightly around her neck from behind and two metal probes pressed hard into her throat. In the next instant, she felt the excruciating pain of 150,000 volts shoot through her body for three seconds. It was as if she were hit in the head with a hammer. A burst of air filled her lungs. A thin halo of smoke rose from her hair. Her muscles stiffened and locked. Her withered nipples hardened, then finally her entire body went limp and she descended into darkness.

Her living nightmare would soon begin.

CHAPTER 2

It was beginning to rain when rookie patrolman, Patrick Snell, was dispatched to Greta Bauer's address in response to a routine call. A woman who regularly bought vegetables from the old lady was concerned that she hadn't been seen for some time either in her garden or carting her produce through the neighborhood.

The watery hiss of the patrol car tires on smooth asphalt changed abruptly to the crunch of cinders when Officer Snell turned into the alley and drove along the rows of old houses. He slowed at the vegetable garden and pulled to a stop along side the cottage. Everything was quiet and still except for the lazy rhythm of the rain on the roof and steady beat of his windshield wipers.

Snell called in a welfare check to report that he had arrived at the address and was going to see if anyone was home. He stretched a nylon rain cover over his uniform hat, got out and pulled on his raincoat as he dashed to the shelter of the porch. After knocking on the door several times without a response, he walked around to the side of the house through the knee-high grass and peered into the first window. It was dark and difficult to see through the rusted screen and grime-caked glass. When his eyes adjusted, he could make out a kitchen sink under the window and something large and bulky hanging from the ceiling.

Snell pulled the flashlight from his belt and aimed the beam at it but still couldn't tell what it was. It appeared to be nearly seven feet long and partially draped in something. He swept the light over the form and froze when suddenly two bulging eyes stared back at him from a swollen, bluish human head topped with ragged tufts of gray hair. He scanned down further and saw that the flesh had been cut away from the torso exposing layers of yellow fat and dark, red muscle underneath.

Snell bolted backwards from the window as if he were kicked by a horse, dropping the flashlight in the wet grass. He fell to his hands and knees, retching and vomiting violently until he was emptied out and the only sound was of rain pelting his back. He climbed to his feet, steadied himself and swallowed hard to relieve the burn in his throat. He retrieved the flashlight and shown the now trembling light back into the kitchen.

"Sweet Jesus, how could anyone do that to another human being?" he wondered out loud as he examined the gruesome corpse more closely before shining the light around the room. Calmer now, Snell circled the rest of the cottage peering in each window as rain poured off the roof onto his hat. When he saw nothing else unusual inside, he made his way back to the cruiser and gathered himself for a minute before picking up the microphone to radio in his report and request assistance.

"Dispatch, this is car 29. Officer needs 1078 at 398 Getten Lane. There's a body. Strung up. Hardly looks human."

"What is it?" asked the dispatch.

"Hard to say. It looks like it's been skinned."

CHAPTER 3

"Good morning, Eau Claire," the alarm clock radio blared. "It's six a.m. Time to rise and shine. Gonna be a hot one today." Michael Donovan opened one eye and fumbled clumsily with the volume knob then rolled toward his wife. "You awake, Tess?" he whispered.

"No. I'm sleeping, can't you tell?" she replied sarcastically.

"Then why aren't you snoring?" he taunted, gently prodding her with a thick finger.

"Very funny."

"How about some coffee?" he said. "I'll make us a pot."

"Don't you go near that coffee pot, Copper," she said, throwing off the rumpled sheet. "If you do I'll report you to the Food and Drug Administration for manufacturing toxic substances. I'll make it."

Theresa Donovan gave him the nickname "Copper" both for the color of his wavy red hair and because he's a cop. She had called him that ever since they saw a rerun of the old Jimmy Cagney movie, "White Heat" years before when they were first dating. In the movie, Cagney's character pulls out a gun and shoots several rounds into the trunk of a car at an unfortunate policeman inside whom he calls "a copper".

"You know, maybe it's time to change your handle from Copper to Silver," she said, throwing on her robe and inspecting his wavy, graying mane.

"Great. Me and The Lone Ranger's horse," he muttered.

"Yeah. I wouldn't want to insult The Lone Ranger's horse. We'll stick with Copper then. Now about that coffee," she said.

"You never put enough coffee in your coffee. It tastes like tea," he complained.

"It'll be perfect, I promise," she quipped. "You take your shower and get dressed. Time to chase the bad guys."

Donovan finished showering and paused to study the familiar face in the bathroom mirror. The hot water gave his fair Irish skin a pink glow and left his jowls looking like they were dusted with cinnamon. The copper color of his carefully groomed mustache was gradually surrendering to the same grizzled iron gray as his hair.

He remembered the little boy who used to stare back at him. The one who worried he'd never grow into his big teeth and dreamt of being a policeman just like his dad.

Donovan lathered up and shaved, combed his hair and brushed the impishness back into his wiry, brick orange eyebrows.

He could smell the coffee when he tramped down the stairs and stopped at the landing mirror to knot his tie.

Hearing him, Tess Donovan looked up from the newspaper spread out on the kitchen table and sipped her coffee. "Only eight months to go as of today," she called, pushing her reading glasses higher on her tiny, freckled nose.

"I don't want to talk about it," he said, appearing in the kitchen doorway. He poured the fresh coffee into a mug that read, 'Instant Detective. Just add coffee'.

"Retirement isn't a death sentence," she said.

"I know," he said, wanting to stop the conversation. He didn't want to deal with a future empty of meaning.

"You just gotta find a hobby besides fishing or you'll spend all your time up north and I'll never see you again. How about taking up woodworking?"

"I'd cut off a hand or something," he grumbled.

"Gardening. You could grow roses."

"They remind me of funerals."

"Start a new career then. You'll only be fifty-five."

"Whoever came up with the idea of forcing cops into retirement should be shot. I'm in the prime of life!"

"Open a bookstore. You love books," she countered. "Look at

the piles of them in that knotty pine cave you call a den; crime novels, training manuals, law books, criminology, forensics. There's enough there to open your own store now."

"It isn't the books, Tess. It's the wisdom and knowledge they contain," he replied with feigned haughtiness as he lifted his pinky and sipped his coffee.

"I know. You could write a book," she exclaimed.

He laughed.

"What's so funny?" she asked.

"The only part about retirement that appeals to me is not having to write anymore; no reports, no more forms. My writing days will be behind me. Besides, who would want to read about the least exciting law enforcement career in history."

"You could promote it as a sleep aid," she chided.

"Not funny, Tess."

"I'm sorry," she said, setting down her cup and wrapping her arms around his waist.

"I wanted to make a real difference. I wanted some excitement," he said somberly. "Now I'll finish a long, mediocre career with a whimper. Do you realize I never used my gun? Not once in all these years did it even come out of my holster."

Tess squeezed her arms tighter. "I don't believe that's a bad thing, Copper. Remember, no one ever shot at you either."

There was a second of uncomfortable silence as Donovan absorbed the unintended but unpleasant jab of memory that his father, Sgt. Daniel Donovan, was killed in the line of duty when Copper was in high school. He quickly recovered to avoid any notion that Tess had stung him. But, they both knew.

"Of course no one ever shot at me! The strippers I bust for selling a little on the side don't have anyplace to conceal a weapon," he replied. "And the perverts don't want to conceal anything at all. I suppose the eight year old I took in for threatening a crossing guard with a toy gun might have some possibilities, but you know how the courts indulge minors."

"I wish you wouldn't talk like that. You've been a good cop. Decorated for saving lives. You've taken a lot of bad guys off the street and helped make Eau Claire a nice place to live," she said.

"You should work for the chamber of commerce," Donovan replied, tousling her mop of graying, black hair.

"Well, it's true," she replied.

"I hoped for more," Donovan sighed. "Is it too much to ask for another John Dillinger to come along? Or maybe a Bonnie and Clyde."

"Be careful what you wish for," she chided.

"They just don't make criminals the way they used to," he replied.

"Seriously, Copper, I worry about what will become of you. You have to find another interest."

He kissed her cheek and paused at the kitchen door before leaving. "All I know how to do is chase bad guys and you. So I guess that'll just leave you when they put me out to pasture."

"You could do worse," she hollered as the door closed behind him.

Twenty minutes later, Donovan followed Brian Scully's red Porsche into the police station parking lot. They began working together when Scully was promoted to detective a year earlier.

"Morning," said Donovan as Scully squeezed his beefy frame out of the small Porsche. "You look like shit. Late night?"

Scully flashed a smirky grin and they walked together into the building. "You're just jealous," he said.

"When are you gonna settle down and stop chasing women?" jabbed Donovan good-naturedly at his thirty-two year old partner.

"I was settled down. Didn't work out," Scully replied.

"You just need to find someone like Tess and start again. Someone to take care of you. Laugh at your jokes and keep you warm on winter nights."

"A nice Catholic girl to get the skid marks out of your underwear is more like it," said Scully with a laugh as he popped a stick of his trademark Juicy Fruit gum into his mouth. He claimed it reduced his appetite.

"You could do worse than Tess," Donovan replied irritably.

"I do worse–frequently. Luckily, I usually can't remember their names. Besides, can you imagine a nice girl like her with someone like me?"

"Got me there. You are a self-centered pig," said Donovan in exasperation.

"But a well dressed pig," Scully replied, pausing to inspect his reflection in the glass entrance door. He tugged on the French cuffs of his tailored shirt until a half inch of white shown perfectly even from both sleeves of his size 54 blue blazer. Donovan paused and shook his head at Scully's familiar primping ritual.

"I'll give you that - but under the Ralph Lauren Big & Tall threads you're still a pig," Donovan said dryly.

"What can I say?" said Scully, holding the door open.

"How 'bout 'oink'," said Donovan.

After the morning briefing in the squad room, the detectives settled into the routine of reading reports from the night before and making phone calls in the small office they shared. It had been a busy night for the Eau Claire Police as it often was when the weather was hot. Still there was nothing that grabbed the detective's attention.

"Couple of bar fights," said Donovan. "Fender benders. DUI's. Looks like the weenie wagger was at it again. Whipped it out in front of a woman in the produce section at the Super Valu. Report says she only provided a sketchy idea what he looked like. She mostly remembered how big he was."

"Too bad we can't do a line-up of dicks," quipped Scully. "We'd finally nail that showoff."

They were finishing a second pot of coffee as a slow-moving storm crawled toward the city from the west. Donovan looked out the office window at the darkening sky. "Your pretty little car is going to get all wet, Brian," he said.

Scully was about to respond when the desk sergeant poked his head in. "You fellas need somethin' to do?"

"Whacha got, Lloyd?"

"Looks like our quiet little town has a murder. A grisly one, at that."

CHAPTER 4

Donovan felt his excitement growing as the two detectives pulled out of the parking garage in their undercover gray Ford Crown Victoria. "Looks like you're finally going to have a shot at something worthy of True Crime magazine," quipped Scully as they fell into the procession of screaming police cars rushing to the end of an alley on the other side of town.

Donovan didn't respond. He listened intently to the lively chatter on the police radio until they arrived at the address. It was already crowded with police cars animated with wildly flashing red and blue lights. Donovan's heart pounded. He felt a tingle of excitement race through his body as they pulled to a stop.

"You the first uniform on the scene?" he asked the young patrolman who met him when he got out of the car.

"Yeah. Got a call about twenty minutes ago," Snell replied. Scully fumbled for the release button on his black umbrella. "It looks like the vic's an elderly woman named Greta Bauer. Neighbor lady called in because the old gal hasn't been seen in several days either selling vegetables or going to mass every morning."

"Been inside?" asked Donovan, so focused that he appeared to be oblivious to the rain.

"No. Just looked through that window when no one answered the door and saw the body hanging there. Then I called for backup. These guys just got here," Snell replied, referring to the two other uniformed police posted at each end of the property.

"So you're not certain no one else is in there?" asked Scully from under his umbrella.

"I checked the other windows while I waited for backup before going in. Didn't see any other vics or any sign of a perp."

"That's the window where you saw the body?" asked Donovan, pointing.

"Yeah. It's the kitchen."

Lightening cracked overhead and rain pelted down as Donovan and Scully slogged through the tall grass surrounding the little cottage. Scully tried to share his umbrella but could not keep up with his partner's determined charge to the kitchen window. Donovan scanned the gloomy interior with his flashlight until the beam fell on the hanging corpse.

"Holy shit," whispered Donovan, barely audible above the amplified drumming of the raindrops on the umbrella. Scully's eyes widened. He stopped chewing his gum.

"I want a perimeter around this entire area," barked Donovan, moving away from the window and gesturing in a circle to the uniforms. "Including that garden and the wooded area behind it. I don't want anymore trampling around here than necessary to secure the area."

Scully chewed his Juicy Fruit faster now. Donovan moved closer under the umbrella so Scully could hear him above the rapid-fire raindrops. "You ready?" he asked.

They returned to the Crown Vic to grab rubber gloves and paper shoe covers then climbed onto the tiny porch and put them on.

"Remember the old saying, be careful what you wish for?" asked Scully.

Donovan ignored him and pushed the slightly ajar door forcefully with a single gloved finger. It groaned and swung open. Instantly the suffocating, putrefied stench of rotting flesh filled their nostrils.

Scully gagged. Donovan reached inside and felt the wall next to the doorway for a light switch and flipped it on. A bare bulb over the sink threw a harsh light into the kitchen revealing the old woman's naked body hanging in the center of the room over a circle of dried blood and excrement. Flies, angry at being disturbed, swarmed around the corpse.

Donovan and Scully stopped short to study the grotesque scene. The old woman's hands had been tied together behind her back with a length of heavy plastic rope. It was neatly knotted and strung up over one of the exposed ceiling joists dislocating both of her shoulders. "Jesus," whispered Scully. "That musta hurt."

Her feet, also tied, were secured to a large spike driven deep into the kitchen floor. Whatever was jammed into her mouth was held there by gray duct tape wrapped tightly around her head. Her cheeks swelled like grayish-blue balloons. Streaks of dried blood ran down her wrinkled forehead from her butchered scalp, painting her face a grotesque dark red. Dead, gray eyes bulged as if in surprise. Or, more likely, thought Scully, as if frozen in terror.

"Holy shit. Didja ever see anything like it?" said Donovan, moving closer.

"She's been skinned all right," whispered Scully, fighting back the urge to gag.

"Some sick son-of-a-bitch knew what he was doin'," came a familiar raspy voice from behind them. "Like a butcher or maybe a hunter who's pulled the hide off his share of deer."

Scully and Donovan turned in unison to see the ponderous bulk of Chester Case, the County Coroner, standing in the doorway. A stunned look of disbelief was on his sweaty, round face as he waddled into the kitchen.

Case held a handkerchief over his nose and circled the hanging body, careful not to step in the dried, dark puddle under it. The flesh from the woman's thick torso had been neatly cut horizontally across her rib cage under her large, flaccid breasts and continuing completely around her back. The skin had been carefully separated from the layer of tissue underneath and pulled down to her hips, leaving it to hang to her knees–a grotesque skirt of heavy, fatty folds.

"Look at her eyes," said Donovan. "I didn't know eyes could open that wide. She must'a been terrified."

Scully was losing his fight not to vomit and hurried outside for fresh air. Donovan hardly noticed. He was still as a stone statue as his eyes wandered over the gruesome scene. His mind raced through the accumulation of everything he had learned from twenty-five years of law enforcement classes, training, procedural manuals, and forensics texts as well as reading the shelves of crime related books in his personal home library. Even a vague awareness of the countless murder mysteries he had ever read worked its' way into his consciousness. He pushed these thoughts away and ordered his mind.

Chester Case watched Donovan's face become curiously expressionless as the transfixed detective focused his attention; first on the body, then slowly on everything else in the room. Now he understood what they meant when other cops in the department referred to his old friend as a "buff". Michael Donovan was completely in his element.

After several minutes, Donovan finally said solemnly, "Chester, you were in the Navy right?"

"Yeah. Right out of high school," Case replied.

Donovan was staring at the perfectly executed knots in the ropes that held the victim's hands and feet. "Did they teach you knot tying?" he asked.

Case moved closer. "That's a bowline. Good for mooring a small boat to a pier. It's a little complicated. Don't see it much. Of course most people can't tie a knot to save their butts."

"Let's make sure we save that rope without untying it," said Donovan, scribbling in his notebook.

C'mon, Donovan. I know my job," Case replied testily. "That's standard procedure. I'll have to cut it from the beam, but it'll be intact on the body."

"Sorry, Chester. I just want to make sure everything we do is by the book," Donovan replied apologetically.

Scully returned and the detectives went through the small cottage opening drawers and closet doors while Chester Case bagged the victim's hands to protect any DNA evidence that might be found under the fingernails. Over the next several hours, the crime scene was examined, photographed and dusted for fingerprints. Finally, the body was cut down and Greta Bauer's remains were lowered into a body bag held high by several pale, nervous policemen wearing latex gloves and facemasks.

Chester Case zipped the bag closed and looked up at Donovan.

"What the hell do we have here, anyway?"

"Shit. I don't know. But we best keep it quiet or we'll have an all out panic going on," said Donovan, gritting his teeth as he looked around the now crowded kitchen. "Okay, everyone. And I mean everyone. We don't want this going any further until we get a handle on it. Understand?" Anyone asks you, you don't know anything."

The rain had stopped by the time the gurney carrying Greta's body was carried outside. Following close behind, Donovan and Chester Case were surprised to see that the small crowd milling around behind the bright yellow crime scene tape had grown to a mob. Even more surprising were the satellite trucks that were parked all around the site.

Word of the murder had spread like wildfire throughout the small town and had already reached the Twin Cities a hundred miles away. Television stations representing every major network joined the local stations and launched squadrons of television crews with gorgeous, young reporters flashing perfect teeth onto the I-94 Interstate across the St. Croix River for the hundred mile drive east into Wisconsin.

Cameramen hurried to capture the scene of the gurney carrying the body bag being wheeled across the alley and slid into the coroner's van. Reporters scrambled frantically to set up remote reports with its flashing lights in the background as it pulled away.

In a glare of lights, a pert, young blond reporter, trying gallantly to appear serious and authoritarian, talked into the camera in carefully measured words. "Police have said only that an elderly woman, the apparent victim of a homicide, was found in her home in this quiet neighborhood in Eau Claire, Wisconsin. Although authorities have not confirmed her identity, WCCO News has learned from neighbors that the home is the long time residence of a woman named Greta Bauer. The elderly Bauer grew vegetables and sold them door-to-door here but otherwise kept to herself. None of the neighbors we talked with knew of any reason why anyone would want to murder this harmless old woman.

"We are also following up on rumors that Bauer may have

been tortured before she died but so far authorities are not talking. Her body has been removed from the scene and is being taken to the morgue where Eau Claire County Coroner, Chester Case, will conduct an autopsy to determine the cause of death."

"We have been informed by authorities that a statement by a spokesperson for the Eau Claire Police will take place within the hour. Channel 5 will interrupt programming to bring it to you as it happens.

"Sheila Feller, Channel 5, KSTP News reporting live from Eau Claire, Wisconsin."

Donovan and Scully sat in their cruiser with the engine running and the air conditioning on full blast when the familiar voice of the Police Chief Clarence Krumenauer came over the radio.

"Donovan."

"What's going on over there? Every newsy from here to Poughkeepsie wants to know what's going on," barked the chief.

"The old woman was apparently tortured before she died. Strung up like a deer," said Donovan.

"Tortured?" asked the chief.

"Skinned from her chest to her waist," Donovan replied.

"Jesus. Any witnesses? Anything?" Krumenauer asked hopefully.

"Not so far. We have uniforms knocking on doors in the neighborhood and combing the property. The coroner just removed the body and we're going back in to see what we can find. There's a little parlor, a bedroom and a bath. Seems to be a cellar beneath a trap door in the kitchen. The whole place is full of junk."

"I doubt the perp is local," said the chief. "We'd probably know if we had a sicko like that running around. Sounds like a sicko."

"Let's see what turns up, chief," said Donovan. "Look, news trucks are all over the place. They'll want a statement. Wanna stonewall until we know more?"

"Too late," Krumenauer replied. "There's already talk of some kind of Satanic ritual. Ed Gein's name has even come up."

"So the word's out on that?"

"I'm afraid so."

"So what's the plan?" asked Donovan.

"Let's just put what we know out there. Answer questions honestly but refuse to go further," the chief replied. "Give 'em the facts. Don't pass along your personal opinions. Don't comment on the wild speculation they're sure to toss at you."

"Okay, chief," said Donovan, pressing the end call button.

"Who's Ed Gein?" asked Scully immediately.

"Ed Gein. A wildly insane serial killer from the 1950's. One of Wisconsin's own. He's been dead for years."

"Why Gein?"

"He liked to skin his victims. Ate 'em, too. Least parts of 'em."

"Could be a long day," said Scully, unwrapping another stick of gum and filling the car with its distinctive, sweet smell.

"Damn. I hate this television stuff and the reporters with their stupid questions," Donovan grumbled. He began writing furiously in a notepad to organize what he would say. "Go out there and tell them we'll make a statement in a few minutes, will ya, Brian?"

Ten minutes later Scully had cordoned off an area outside the crime scene. It was quickly surrounded by cameras and reporters stabbing microphones at Detective Donovan as he approached.

"I am Detective Michael Donovan of the Eau Claire Police Department. Now, here's what we know so far. The victim's name is Greta Bauer. We're not certain of her age, but believe her to be in her 80's. She had lived alone in this home for several years and supported herself by selling the vegetables she grew in her garden. Didn't even have a telephone.

"Her body was found after a concerned neighbor called to report that Bauer hadn't been seen in the neighborhood for several days. An autopsy will be performed to determine the cause of death after which we will provide you with more information. Thank you."

Donovan started to walk away when one of the reporters called out, "Is it true she was tortured?"

"I don't know."

"Can you comment on the rumor that she was skinned?"

"Some skin appears to have been removed from her torso. Yes."

"She was tied up? Bound and gagged?"

Donovan was surprised by the amount of information that had already leaked out and looked angry as the rapid-fire questions continued faster than he could answer.

"Is it possible the victim was used in a satanic ritual?"

"I don't know anything about that sort of thing."

"Did she appear to be sexually assaulted?"

"Look," said a frustrated Donovan. "I can only comment on what I know to be true at this point. The victim was found tied both hand and foot and suspended from a joist in her kitchen. I can't tell you that she was tortured or sexually assaulted. I don't even know how she died. Some skin appears to have been cut away. That's it. No more questions. Thank you."

Donovan ignored the continuing chorus of questions and walked back to the car with Scully. "How the hell did all that shit get out so fast?"

"I don't know," Scully replied. "I doubt it was a cop. Maybe someone from the coroner's office. People love to talk."

Just then Police Sergeant Axel Lund called from the porch. "Lieutenant Donovan! We may have found something."

CHAPTER 5

"Now what?" Donovan wondered out loud.

Lund walked briskly toward them carrying a wooden box. "There are a few photographs, old letters and some other official-looking stuff in here. Looks like most everything's in a foreign language. I think it might be Polish or something. I don't know."

Donovan took the box from the Sergeant and set it on the hood of the car. The musty smell of old paper and dust filled his nose. He sneezed several times as he sorted through the documents. Inside a large manila envelope he found an odd assortment of official-looking documents and a handful of black and white photographs. He hastily shuffled through them then set the box in the backseat of the cruiser.

"Is it Polish?" asked Scully.

"Not sure. I think so," Donovan replied.

"Lud knows Polish, right?" asked Scully. "Maybe he can tell us if any of the stuff gives a next-of-kin."

Otto Ludwikowski was a semi-retired cop who still worked occasionally when extra help was needed for security or crowd control. Lud had been one of Donovan's father's best friends and had taken him under his wing when the younger Donovan was a rookie.

"Yeah. I'm pretty sure he knows Polish," Donovan replied. "Let's have him take a look. He lives close to here."

They called ahead and Ludwikowski was waiting just inside the garage when the Crown Vic pulled into the driveway. He was sitting in an old lawn chair next to a metal bucket that was filled with sand and mounded with cigarette butts. His baggy gray pants were peppered with cigarette burn holes.

"So this is your reward for a lifetime of crime fighting, eh

Lud?" Donovan chided as he got out of the cruiser.

Lud laughed. "Yup. And the only paperwork I do these days is wiping my ass. What's up, Mikey?"

Lud listened intently as Donovan described the Greta Bauer murder. Scully grabbed the box from the car.

"We don't have a next-of-kin on the victim and were hoping you might spot something in here that will tell us," said Donovan. "We think it's in Polish."

Lud nodded agreeably and said, "C'mon."

They followed him into the house where his wife was in the kitchen adding ice to a pitcher of Kool-Aid. "You boys thirsty?" she asked.

"Hi, Inga," said Donovan. "Meet my new partner, Brian Scully. I'm drier than a popcorn fart."

"Good," Inga Ludwikowski laughed as she took three glasses from the cupboard. "Otto's got to have his black cherry Kool-Aid. Along with those damn cigarettes, it seems to give his life meaning."

The old cop ignored the remark and rummaged through the box for anything that caught his eye. Setting the letters aside, he removed the large manila envelope, spilled the photos out onto the kitchen table and arranged them into neat rows as they all watched; baby pictures; formal family photos populated with overweight women, severe, long-bearded men and unhappy children posing stiffly in their Sunday best. A photo of a striking young woman in blond braids wearing a blouse and a pleated skirt with knee high stockings caught everyone's eye.

"Is this the victim?" asked Lud.

"Don't know," Donovan replied. "That picture's pretty old."

"What about these other documents?" asked Scully.

"The ones in English are U.S. Immigration documents admitting Greta Bauer into the country. The rest are German and Polish. I think–but, I'm a little rusty. Can you leave this stuff and let me go through it?"

"How long will you need it?" asked Donovan.

"Give me a day or two if you can. There's a lot here for your murder book," he said.

"What on earth is a murder book?" asked Inga.

"That's what we call the collection of documents around a case. Kind of a paper trail," Donovan replied.

"I'll call you first thing if I find anything that I think you'd want to know about," Lud said.

"This is pretty hot, Lud. I might have to find someone not so rusty," said Donovan.

"Sure. Sure. I understand, Mikey. But, you know I like to keep my hand in if I can. Maybe you could leave it until you find someone," Ludwikowski replied.

"Sure, Lud. Appreciate the help." He and Scully drained their glasses, thanked Inga and returned to police headquarters leaving the box behind. They recognized several of the news crews and satellite trucks that were setting up in front of the station as they parked the Crown Vic in a department spot behind the station. Reporters surrounded the car immediately.

They got out and Donovan put his hands up in mock surrender as they peppered him with questions.

"I don't have any new information for you right now. We're waiting to hear from the crime lab people and the coroner. Soon as we hear anything we'll let you know," he said as they pushed their way through the small crowd.

Inside, the chief was just hanging up the phone. "This is nuts," he said. Must be a slow news day. You wouldn't think the murder of an old lady by some whacko would cause such an uproar."

"It's the ghoulish aspect," said Donovan. "Same reason horror and slasher movies keep selling tickets."

"I suppose," the chief replied. "Got anything new?"

"We've got Otto Ludwikowski going through a box of pictures, old letters and stuff we found in the Bauer's root cellar. They're in Polish so we thought Otto might help. Might be something there. They go back to the forties and fifties. I doubt they'll turn up anything, but you never know. It would be nice to find a next of kin."

A young woman stuck her head in the door. "Chester Case is on line two, chief."

The chief picked up the phone. "Hi, Chet. I've got Donovan

and Scully here. Gonna put you on speakerphone."

"Have you finished the autopsy?" asked Donovan.

"All but the lab work. Some of that will take a little time," said Case. "We want to be very thorough."

"Got a time of death?"

"The vic was pretty far gone as you know from the God awful putrefaction. The hot, humid weather aided in the decaying, but I'd say she was dead for several days, at least," said Case.

"So the corpse is significantly colonized by necrophagous insects?" asked Donovan. Scully and Chief Kremenauer looked at each other in mutual amazement at Donovan's depth of knowledge.

"Blow flies. Lots of 'em," Case replied.

"Any other trauma? Defensive wounds?" asked Scully.

"Found a couple of things. First, I think the perp used a stun gun to subdue her. We found two dried, purplish, rust-colored abrasions on her neck."

"Sounds like this guy was really prepared," said Scully.

"What else?" ask Donovan.

"Well, he cut off her hair with a knife or something. Big chunks here and there with a number of lacerations to the scalp."

"Why the hell would he cut off her hair?" asked Donovan without expecting a response as he jotted in his notebook.

"And she was branded," said Case.

"Damn. You mean the old gal was tortured on top of being skinned?" asked Donovan.

"It's a number. Like a, you know, a serial number or something. On her abdomen. We didn't see it until we put her skin back in place. It starts with an A. A-1-8-7-3-3."

"Any ideas?" asked Donovan, jotting the number down in his note pad.

"Not a clue," said Case. "It appears to have been made by branding iron. The letters are clean and sharp. Exactly a half-inch tall.

"Any defensive wounds?" Scully repeated. "Stuff like that?"

"None that I can see. If she managed to scratch the perp, it's difficult to tell. There's enough dirt under her fingernails to start a small farm. And she wasn't sexually assaulted," the Coroner added.

"She probably didn't know what hit her until it was too late".

"So you can't tell us anything in other words," said the chief.

"I can tell you her last meal was bread and beans."

"Well, keep us posted, Chet," said the chief.

"There's one more thing," said the Coroner, pausing uneasily. "It looks like the perp cauterized some of the blood vessels to keep her from bleeding to death before he was finished with her."

"Holy shit," said Donovan, looking up at Scully who had accelerated his gum chewing.

"That means she was still alive during the skinning. At least for a while."

CHAPTER 6

Donovan and Scully picked up coffee and donuts for the uniformed officers still on the scene and returned to the cottage in the early evening. The television trucks and bystanders were gone by now, but two patrol cars remained. The rookie officer, Patrick Snell, stood watch over the cottage while a Sergeant and two other uniforms combed the woods.

"Take a break!" Donovan called into the trees. Minutes later they were gathered around the Crown Vic drinking coffee and munching donuts while they talked.

"I'm not sure, but it looks like someone spent some time sitting in one spot in there," said the Sergeant, pointing to the area of the woods he had just left.

"What makes you think so?" asked Scully.

"There's a spot where the grass is matted down. You can see the garden and the cottage from there without being seen. And there are still traces of a couple of footprints. They're mostly gone, but it looks like they could have been from work boots or something else with a heavy tread. I cordoned off the area just in case."

"We'll take a look at it," said Donovan. "Anything else?"

"Not that I saw."

Donovan and Scully tossed the remains of their coffee and followed the Sergeant to a small clearing a few yards from the garden strung with bright yellow tape.

"I suppose a deer or something could have bedded down here, but they don't wear boots," said Scully.

"We'll get the crime scene guys back here to take a look," said Donovan. "Good work, Sarge."

"Let's walk up the alley and knock on a few doors before dark," said Donovan to Scully when the two detectives returned to the cottage. "Then grab a bite and put our pointy heads together–see what we can make of this."

The first house they came to was a tired two-story that had been converted to a duplex. The front porch was cluttered with broken junk and what appeared to be motorcycle parts. Before Donovan could knock, the curtain on the window was pulled aside. A tattooed man in his thirties wearing a wife-beater undershirt looked out. Scully flashed his badge and the door opened.

"Someone killed the vegetable lady, huh?" the man said more than asked. He stepped onto the porch being careful not to let his softly growling German shepherd out.

"Yes, sir," Donovan replied, taking out his notebook. "I'm Detective Donovan and this is Detective Scully. We're talking with the neighbors to see if anyone has any information that might help in our investigation. Could I have your name, sir?"

"Jerome Pettit."

"Lived here long, Mr. Pettit? asked Donovan. He made note of Pettit's work boots.

"Couple years, now."

"Did you know the victim, Greta Bauer?" asked Donovan.

"Not really. The old gal kept to herself. Never talked much. Just worked in her garden and sold her vegetables door-to-door. Went to morning mass rain or shine. Helped her dig up a big rock once. Sometimes they popped up in the spring with the thaw."

"Did you see any unusual activity at her house in the last few days. Any people you didn't recognize? That sort of thing?"

Pettit thought for a minute before answering. "I work nights at a bakery. I'm asleep in the daytime so if something went down then, I probably would have slept through it."

"Could have been anytime, Mr. Pettit. The victim had apparently been deceased for a while," said Scully.

"Well, my dog was making a commotion when I left for work a few nights ago. Had to put him inside. Don't know if that means anything. He goes ape shit when there's somethin' in the woods over there," Pettit said pointing. "I figured it was a stray or a deer or somethin'."

"What night was that?" asked Donovan.

Pettit thought for a minute, popped a Pall Mall into his mouth and lit it with a well-worn Harley-Davidson Zippo. "Musta been a Saturday night. Yep. Saturday before last."

"Do you remember what time?" asked Scully.

"Ten thirty or there about," Pettit replied. "That's when I leave for work."

"But, you didn't see anything? Is that right?" asked Scully.

"Too dark at that time of night," Pettit blew smoke from the side of his mouth.

"Any vehicles that didn't belong?" asked Scully.

"Not that I remember," said Pettit.

"Did Bauer have many visitors?" asked Donovan.

"Not that I ever saw," Pettit replied. "She'd chase a kid outa her garden now and then, but that's as close to a visitor that I ever saw."

"Are you aware of anyone in the neighborhood who was close to Greta?"

"Nah. Like I said, she kept to herself."

The detectives continued up the alley knocking on doors. Most who answered had rarely or never even spoken to Greta Bauer. All were terrified that something so heinous could happen right next door.

It was getting dark when they returned to the cottage. They posted a "Crime Scene - Do Not Enter" notice on the back porch door, released the remaining patrol units then drove across town to grab something to eat.

The Athena Café was a small eatery where local cops congregated. It was owned by a diminutive Greek immigrant named Angelo Stavros. Annoyingly gregarious with an ego to match his oversized jet-black mustache, Stavros provided uniformed policemen with free coffee and occasionally meals when they were on duty. It wasn't surprising that the place was never robbed. He greeted Donovan and Scully at the door and ushered them to a booth in the back.

"What can I get you officers?" he asked. It had become needless to offer menus they had long since memorized.

"Butter Burger and fries," said Scully.

"Those things are going to kill you," said Donovan, ordering a salad.

"But, they're so good," Scully replied. Scully was particularly fond of the Greek's burgers. A half-pound of beef liberally sprinkled with Lawry's Seasoning Salt and topped with a dollop of butter. Even the homemade bun was grilled in butter.

They talked about what they knew and didn't know about the murder until Stavros brought their food. Donovan was taking the first bite of the salad when his cell phone rang.

"It's Otto," he said. "Otto, whacha got?"

Scully tried to read the notes upside down that Donovan was jotting in his notebook. He finally gave up and took a mouthful of burger.

"Thanks, Otto. While I've got you, did you happen to see the number A18733 on any documents?" asked Donovan.

"Not that I recall, Mikey," Otto replied. "But, I'll go through them again. I wasn't looking for a number."

"Call me if you find it anywhere, will ya? We'll be over in the morning."

"Otto found an Immigration and Naturalization permit and some other government documents admitting Greta Bauer into the United States on March 3, 1951," Donovan said after ending the phone call.

"Any next of kin?" ask Scully, wiping butter from his chin.

"There's a return address in Krakow, Poland on the personal letter that we can look at. I'd be surprised if it will lead us anywhere, but you never know."

The television crews were setting up for live report on the 10:00 o'clock news when Donovan and Scully returned to headquarters.

"Jesus. Don't these people have homes?" grumbled Donovan.

Scully eased the cruiser through the throng of photographers and reporters and pulled into the parking lot.

"The chief still here?" Donovan asked the desk sergeant on duty who nodded and went back to tapping on his keyboard.

"I'll talk to the chief," said Donovan. "You get on the Internet and do your computer geek thing. See if anything turns up for that number. Maybe it's a winning lottery number."

"Didn't seem lucky for the old gal wearing it," Scully replied, turning to walk down the hall to their office.

"Brian," Donovan called as an afterthought. "Let's post this on the NCIC. But, keep it to the Mid-States for now." The Mid-States Organized Crime Information Center (MOCIC) is one of six regional databases on which information is shared between police departments.

"Phone still ringing off the hook?" asked Donovan, sticking his head in the chief's doorway.

"Like a damn fire alarm," Krumenauer said. He held up a stack of yellow message notes.

"I figured."

"You up to talking to the press again, Donovan? You did good today."

"Do I have a choice?"

"No," the chief replied flatly.

"I already told them everything except about the number," Donovan replied.

"Well, just go over it again. But, let's continue to keep the number to ourselves for now."

Donovan washed up, combed his hair and put on the fresh white shirt he always kept on hand. The parking lot was suddenly filled with blinding television lights when he pushed through the doors.

"I really don't have anything to add to what I told you this afternoon, but I know that the community is pretty shaken up about this and I want to reassure them that, based on what we know so far, we believe it is unlikely that the person who committed this horrible crime is even in the area. This was not a random act. It appears to have been carefully planned and methodically executed. We ask that anyone who has any information that might help us to please step forward. It could be almost anything from observing an unfamiliar individual acting strange to a vehicle where it didn't belong. Anything."

CHAPTER 7

Good morning, Eau Claire. It's 6:00 a.m. Up and at 'em!" blared the all–too–cheery voice on the radio. Donovan practically leapt out of bed.

"You seem energized," Tess observed. "A good murder must put a spring in your step."

"Beats chasing weenie waggers," he observed wryly.

"Want breakfast?" she asked.

"You go back to sleep. I'm meeting Scully for breakfast. Plan the day before going in."

"Well, be home for dinner, ok? You're grilling," she ordered.

Donovan arrived at the Athena early and slid into the booth as the Greek was pouring Scully his second up of coffee.

"You're up with the chickens," he said to his partner.

"Couldn't sleep. Been up for hours. I keep seeing that old lady's skinned body hanging there," he replied, rubbing his eyes.

"Can't take it home with you, Brian. It'll fuck you up," Donovan scolded mildly.

"That sounds a little strange coming from the biggest buff in the department," Scully replied.

They ordered breakfast and talked while CNN reported the news on the little television perched atop the Athena's old Coke machine.

"I was thinking, let's split up and cover the homes in the neighborhood. See if anybody saw or heard anything. Cover more territory that way," said Donovan.

They finished their breakfasts and an hour later Scully was walking east up Madison Street while Donovan knocked on doors on the street that ran along the opposite side of the woods from the crime scene.

Of the people he interviewed, none could recall anything unusual until he came to an elderly man sitting in a lawn chair on the front porch of his 20's style bungalow. He introduced himself as Fred Albert. Both a belt and suspenders held his baggy pants up around his substantial girth. Tobacco juice ran down the corner of his mouth and his arthritic, gnarled hands rested on a wooden cane planted between his feet.

Donovan introduced himself.

"This about Greta?" the old man asked.

Donovan's heart leapt. "Did you know her, Mr. Albert?"

"Bought produce from her for forty years. Can't figure why anybody would want to do her like that," Mr. Albert said, spitting a long stream of tobacco juice over the porch railing.

"So you don't know of anyone who would want to harm her?" asked Donovan.

"Not a one," replied the old man. "There was no reason to dislike her. Come to think of it, there was no reason to like her either I suppose. She just worked her garden and sold her vegetables making as little contact with other people as possible. Some folks believed she was a few bricks shy of a load, but I knew better."

"Why do you say that?" asked Donovan.

"Oh, I dunno. Years ago she used to talk more. Seemed to know more than she let on. But, that's just my hunch," he said.

"Do you recall seeing or hearing anything unusual in the neighborhood recently?" asked Donovan.

"I've been thinking about that," the old man replied. The only thing I thought a little odd was one night a week or so ago."

"What was that?" Donovan asked.

"I doubt it was anything important," said Albert.

"You never know, sir," Donovan replied.

"I didn't see anybody, mind you. It was just a van parked right over there for a few hours," he said, pointing to a spot across the street along the woods.

"What kind of van?" asked Donovan.

"White one. The delivery kind. You know, doors that open along the side. And it was there the day before, too. But, not for long."

"See anyone in the van?" asked Donovan.

"No. I didn't see it come and I didn't see it go," said Albert. "I'm a night owl so I know it was still parked there long after dark."

"What seemed odd?" asked Donovan.

"Well, look at it over there. Nothing there. Nobody parks there except to change a tire or check a map or something. That whole block is mostly woods," he replied. "Nothing there but squirrels and rabbits, but ya can't hunt 'em cause it's in the city limits."

"But, the van wasn't unusual in any way except that it was parked where there isn't a house or anything?"

"Sounds stupid when you put it that way," said Albert. "It was just odd, that's all. Nobody ever parks there. I spend a lot of time sitting right here and I can tell you, no one in my recollection has ever had reason to park there. Especially for hours."

Do you know the make? The year?" asked Donovan taking notes. "Did you get a look at the license plate?"

"Just an old white van," Albert replied with a shrug. "You know, a panel truck. The kind without any windows on the side. Ya know? Nothing unusual except where it was parked," he replied. "Didn't think much about it at the time, so I never thought to look at the license plate. But, I did keep an eye on it out of curiosity. That's about all there is to do at my age when you live alone and can't get around."

"Think about what day it might have been, Mr. Albert," said Donovan. "It could be important."

The old man knit his forehead and stared off into space for several seconds before suddenly lifting his eyebrows. "Lawrence Welk!" he said and spit another stream of tobacco juice over the porch railing.

"Lawrence Welk?" Donovan repeated.

"They show reruns on the television set every Saturday night and I remember going inside to watch. Gave up waiting to see who would come for the van to watch the bubble show," said Albert, referring to the iconic background bubbles that were a signature of the orchestra.

Donovan jotted down 'Lawrence Welk' next to Mr. Albert's name, address and phone number already written in his notebook and thanked him for his help.

"Right about there, you say. That's where the van was parked?" asked Donovan, edging toward the porch steps and pointing.

"Both times," said Mr. Albert.

Donovan walked across the street and up along the edge of the woods to the spot. He saw nothing unusual. The asphalt and the concrete curb and gutter street there were clean as a whistle. Not so much as a gum wrapper or a cigarette butt.

"Hey!" the old man bellow from his porch. Donovan looked up to see him signaling with his cane to move to the right. He moved in that direction several feet further until the old man nodded approvingly. The street there was just as clean but now Donovan saw what could be an opening into the woods. Little used, but possibly a path of some sort. He followed it a few feet into the dense green foliage. It reminded him of the woods where he played war and cowboys and Indians with his childhood friends. He paused after perhaps fifty yards where the path diverged in two different directions.

Taking care to walk around the areas that might contain a footprint, Donovan followed the branch of the path that seemed most likely to lead toward Greta Bauer's cottage. After walking for several hundred feet, he saw the yellow crime scene tape and recognized the opening where the grass was matted that the patrolman had pointed out to him the night before. It had been too dark to see the path then but was clearly visible in the light of day.

"Maybe you're right, Mr. Albert," he said out loud to himself.

Scully was waiting when Donovan returned to the Crown Vic. "Anything?" he asked.

"Might have a possible type on the vehicle," Donovan replied. "And I want to seal off the entire wooded area. It's worth a closer look."

"I'm on it," said Scully reaching for the radio.

CHAPTER 8

Greta Bauer's remains were cremated and her cottage was boarded up at the end of July. By then the untended vegetable patch was overrun with weeds and rabbits. The "murder book" that had quickly swelled with police reports, coroner reports, forensic data, and crime scene photos at the beginning of the investigation had not grown perceptibly thicker. No responses had come in from to the posting on the regional crime center database. And a careful search of the path that Donovan discovered through the woods came up empty. The investigation had grown cold.

The Police Department in Krakow, Poland provided nothing more about the victim. No next of kin could be identified. The return address on the letters found in her root cellar was now an empty lot and there was no record matching the name of the sender. The content of one letter contained news that someone named Beata Klaff had died. The letter was dated March 1957 and no record of her life or death was found.

The remaining items found in the box offered nothing more to go on. Although they were able to make a partial cast of the boot print found in the woods, it would take weeks to identify the manufacturer if at all and then they still had no way to link it to the perp.

No fingerprints or hair samples were found and the significance of the number burned onto the old woman's abdomen was still a mystery.

After the cremation, Donovan and Scully, along with a half dozen of the vegetable lady's customers, attended a small graveside service for her at Lakeside Cemetery where the city provided a burial plot. Donovan carefully surveyed the small group gathered there. All were sober-faced, middle-aged women who were there either out of curiosity or a sense of duty. He couldn't tell.

An elderly priest from St. Patrick's Catholic Church read from the same prepared funeral service liturgy he had probably read a thousand times before. Ruddy cheeked with gray hair that needed cutting, the old man concluded by noting that he had not personally known Greta Bauer and asked if anyone at the graveside would like to speak about her as a person. When no one did, he mumbled a final prayer and the little group of mourners returned to their cars to go their separate ways.

Donovan and Scully were walking to the Crown Vic when Scully noticed a man climb into a white van parked under a stand of trees in the distance. He pointed him out to Donovan.

"Seems to be in a hurry," said Scully as the van's tires kicked up dust and rocks and took off toward the cemetery entrance.

They hurried to the cruiser, but by the time they negotiated their way out of the line of other cars boxing them in, the van was long gone.

"That was a Ford Econoline," said Scully, the more knowledgeable of the two on the subject. "Late 80's I'd guess. Maybe newer."

"Plates. Did you see a plate?" asked Donovan.

"No. The tree was in the way," Scully replied.

The detectives returned to the cop shop where Scully dug up a photograph of a white Econoline similar to the one they saw at the cemetery. "Let's go back and show this to Mr. Albert. See if it helps his memory."

Fred Albert was a long time answering the door and apologized. "I move pretty slow these days," he said. "Would you like to come in?"

"No, thank you, Mr. Albert. Sorry to bother you," said Scully. "This will only take a minute." He pulled a picture out of the inside pocket of his blue pinstripe suit coat. "Does this look like the white van you saw the night Greta Bauer was murdered?"

The old man took the photograph and studied it. "Could be,"

he said. "But, I can't say for certain. Those old vans all look alike to me."

"But, it could be?" asked Donovan.

"Yeah. It could," he replied.

They checked the DMV database for white Ford Econoline vans with an Eau Claire area owner address. There were well over a hundred.

"It's a long shot, but we don't have anything else to go on. Let's see if any of the owners have priors," said Scully, showing the printouts to Donovan.

They divided the list of white Econoline owners and began the task of searching the database of known criminals in the Eau Claire area.

"Remember to look for anything that could relate to that number", said Donovan. "I suppose we should take a look at any with commercial licenses although the van we're looking apparently didn't have any kind of business name painted on it."

It was the kind of slow, tedious police work that Donovan usually found boring, but this time it was different. This was the opportunity he had waited for his entire career. A chance to shine.

Scully was just returning to police headquarters when the streetlights came on. He had checked out the vans on the list that were owned by local businesses to see if any were without signage or markings of any type. When Scully dropped in his desk chair Donovan looked at his watch for the first time all day. He was half way down his half of the list and had printouts on two individuals who had had minor scuffles with the law—neither of which looked promising. "Got anything?" he asked.

"Not a thing until I stopped at the All Seasons florist on the west side," Scully replied.

The thought of food and home left Donovan instantly. He looked at his partner from under raised eyebrows. "Well?" he asked.

"They have two white Ford Econolines. One with the usual

signage. You know, logo, phone number. That sort of thing. That's the one they use to make deliveries around town. The other has no signage on it at all. It's kind of beat up so they don't want their name on it. Bad image and all."

Donovan felt his frustration growing but remained silent.

"I asked the owner if it was in use yesterday at Lake Side Cemetery. He thought it was and checked his schedule. Sure enough he had sent one of his guys there to tend the flowers on several graves for families who contract with them for regular maintenance. Mostly people who live out of town."

Donovan looked disappointed. "Let me guess, it was there at the time of Greta Bauer's service."

"Afraid so. But, he didn't have a clue why it might have been parked across the street from Fred Albert's home. He did say that he hires high school kids now and then for extra help when the shop is busy and you never know what they're up to."

"Did you get their names anyway? The kids." asked Donovan.

"Yah. There were just a couple. I checked them out and they're squeaky clean," Scully replied.

Donovan took off his glasses and rubbed his eyes. The hunger and tiredness returned. "Let's start again in the morning. Something Chester said stuck with me," he said. "Let's see if we have any deer hunters on this list."

Scully was already navigating the Internet when Donovan arrived at 6:30 the next morning. "You're in early," he said.

"Just wanted to get started on the deer hunting angle," Scully replied without looking up from the computer. "I'm on the Wisconsin Department of Natural Resources website. Take a guess how many deer hunting licenses were issued last year."

"Not a clue," Donovan replied, pouring a cup of coffee.

"Nearly a half million," Scully said. "477,318 to be exact and one hell of a lot of them in our area alone."

"Now the question is; how many of these intrepid deer slayers drive white vans?" asked Donovan, taking a sip.

"Shouldn't be too tough to find out," Scully replied just as Donovan grimaced and spit the coffee back into his cup.

"By the way, that coffee is from yesterday," said Scully with a wide grin.

"Thanks for the tip," Donovan growled.

"Tell you what," said Scully, looking at his designer watch. "The DNR doesn't open for another hour at least. I'll spring for breakfast."

The Athena Cafe was busy serving breakfast as usual when they arrived. The counter was lined with men sitting by themselves either reading the morning paper or watching the news on the television. The tables and booths were populated with regulars arguing about politics or the disappointing performance of the local semi-pro baseball team at Carson Park the night before.

Donovan and Scully slid into an empty booth–the little Greek owner brought coffee without being asked. "Nice and fresh," he said, setting the steaming cups in front of them.

They ordered, drank their coffee and talked about how to approach the day's research.

"Think this deer hunter angle is too much of a long shot?" asked Donovan.

"What else do we have? We have to go with what we've got even if it isn't much," Scully replied. "But, with so many deer licenses issued, it'll be easier to find out which white van owners bought them than to check which hunters own white vans."

"Makes sense. And if it's all we have, I want to cast a wider net and expand our list of owners into the surrounding counties. It should still be manageable," Donovan replied.

Their breakfasts arrived and they ate in silence for several minutes. "How's Tess? Still making big plans for your retirement?" asked Scully in an attempt to change the subject.

"Now she wants me to write a book about my life of crime fighting," he chuckled in reply.

"Whoa. That would be a real thriller," teased Scully, pushing the last of a cheese omelet onto his fork with a slice of toast."

Donovan nodded in agreement, but was thinking to himself that Greta Bauer's murder might make a damn good story.

CHAPTER 9

They had eleven names when they had finished cross-indexing the list of white van owners in a five county area against the list of deer hunters who had purchased licenses last season. Of the eleven men, three had criminal records with offenses ranging from minor crimes like petty theft and vandalism to serious offenses that included assault and battery, and armed robbery. The first two were quickly eliminated. One was serving five to ten years in Waupun State Prison; the other had died from a drug overdose.

"That leaves an ex-con named Elton McClure," said Scully. "Dishonorably discharged from the Marine Corps–history of violent behavior. McClure served time for a particularly brutal assault on a woman and was paroled last November. The victim was so beat up that she nearly died from her injuries."

"Nice guy," said Donovan. "Do we know where he is?"

"Last known address was a trailer park in Chippewa Falls. Before that he was in and out of the Mendota State Hospital," Scully said.

"Let's make a courtesy call to the Chippewa police and see what they have on Mr. McClure; tell them we'd like to snoop around a little. See if we can learn anything," said Donovan.

Twenty minutes later, the Crown Vic cruised over the aging Chippewa River Bridge and navigated through the tidy business district to the police station on Island Street.

"What brings you to our fair city?" asked the desk sergeant when Donovan presented his shield.

"We're investigating a murder in Eau Claire," Donovan replied.

"The Greta Bauer thing that's been on the news?" the sergeant asked.

"You got it. We're following up on a long shot and want to see what you guys have on him," said Donovan.

The sergeant buzzed the chief and walked Donovan and Scully down the brightly lighted, institutional beige colored hall to his office.

Chief Darrel Hind was a middle-aged man with a shaved head and fitted shirt stretched across a slight paunch. He got right to the point. "What can we do for you, detectives?" he asked, gesturing for them to sit.

After giving him the background of their investigation, Donovan said, "We'd like to know more about a man named Elton McClure. At one time he lived in Chippewa Falls –we'd like to talk with him."

Chief Hind picked up the phone and pushed a speed dial number. "Lois, will you please bring in anything we have on one Elton McClure?" he said.

Minutes later, a slender blond wearing too much make-up and a too-revealing blouse entered the office and handed Hind a file about two inches thick. He opened it and studied the contents; court records, prison records, arrest reports and wants and warrants. "Elton McClure is well known to us," he said. He has a long record with this department and been a guest in our holding cell on several occasions."

"Anything recent?" asked Scully.

"Looks like he spent the Fourth of July weekend with us. He decided to put on his own pyrotechnic show and was arrested for disturbing the peace. He likes things that go 'boom'."

Donovan made notes.

"We have his last known address as the Stardust Mobile Home Park," said Hind, closing the file. "That's just up highway 29 near Lake Wissota."

The detectives accepted an offer to set up in an empty office to go through McClure's file and the use of the copy machine. They were nearly finished an hour later when Lois appeared in the doorway.

"I thought you should see this," she said, flashing the copy of a citation in the air. "Elton McClure got a speeding ticket a couple of weeks back."

Donovan took the ticket and examined it closely. "He was stopped July 13th at 3:15 a.m. traveling north on highway 53 just inside the city limits. He was driving a white Econoline van. Doing 78 in a 55 zone."

"Arresting officer was Ike Patrow," said Lois.

"He on duty by any chance?" asked Donovan.

"Nights. He's off now, but I can call him," she said.

"Would you mind?" asked Donovan. "I'd like talk to him."

Lois returned a couple of minutes later. "Ike is on line three," she said, gesturing to the phone on the desk.

"Officer Patrow, this is Detective Michael Donovan, Eau Claire P.D. Sorry to bother you on your day off."

After telling him about Elton McClure and explaining the reason for the call, he asked, "You stopped a white Econoline van early Saturday morning two weeks ago. It was driven by our guy. Do you recall?"

"Oh, I remember Elton," said Patrow. "Said he was on his way home from a friend's house in Eau Claire. Nothing unusual. Pretty routine speeding stop. He appeared to be sober. I just wrote him up and sent him on his way."

"Did he appear to be agitated or anything at all?" asked Donovan.

"No more than anyone else caught speeding," Patrow replied.

"Is there anything else at all that you can recall?" probed Donovan.

"He was alone. The van was a piece of shit. I was surprised he would push it that hard," Patrow recalled. "He had priors but wasn't a wise ass or anything. Very respectful. Didn't say much."

Donovan ended the call, the detectives gathered up the copies they had made of various documents and were back in the Crown Vic driving north through the busy Lake Wissota recreational area crowded with marinas, resorts, root beer stands, steak houses and roadside taverns that all seemed to display neon signs offering Lenienkugel's Beer, the local brew.

The Stardust Mobile Home Park was a labyrinth of unpaved roads crammed with dozens of mobile homes and crudely built storage sheds in various degrees of disrepair. Rusting pick-up trucks and beat up cars seemed to be everywhere.

Scully pulled the cruiser to a stop in front of number 327. They knocked on door of the singlewide trailer. A woman in curlers and a cheap housecoat appeared smoking a cigarette. When she saw Donovan's badge, a look of surprise came over her and she clutched the coat tightly together around her neck. She identified herself as Shirley Pickett–she had lived in the trailer for over a year.

"Did you know the former resident, Elton McClure?" asked Scully, taking notes.

"No. I still get mail addressed to him now and then, but I think he's long gone. I've heard the neighbors mention him," she said pointing to the mobile home next door. "They said he was a bad actor. He in trouble with the law?"

"No, ma'am. We just want to talk to him," said Scully. "Can you give us the neighbor's name?"

"Babcock. Terry and Toni," she replied.

"That their truck?" asked Donovan, pointing toward a bright red Nissan pickup.

"Yeah. They're probably home. Neither one of them work full time."

The detectives climbed the shaky wooden steps alongside of the neighbor's trailer and knocked, ignoring the plastic sign that read; 'DON'T COME A KNOCKIN' IF THE TRAILER'S A ROCKIN'.

A man about thirty with a long, unkempt ponytail opened the door. Donovan flashed his badge and introduced himself. "Okay if we ask you a few questions, Mr. Babcock?"

"About what?" Babcock answered warily.

"How long have you lived here?" Donovan asked.

"Couple years or more," he replied.

"Did you know the former resident of the trailer next door," Donovan asked, nodding behind him.

"Elton McClure? Sure, I know Elton. Is he in trouble again?"

asked Babcock.

"We just want to talk to him. He hasn't been charged with anything. Do you know where he lives now?" asked Donovan.

"Last time I saw him he said he was living in a hunting shack north of Ladysmith," said Babcock.

"That's a big area. Can you be more specific?" asked Donovan.

"Tell you what," said Babcock. "You get to Ladysmith and stop at a bar called the Willow Dam Inn. Ask for Bud. Bud Merek. He's the owner. He'll either tell ya or show ya how to find the shack. I doubt you'd find it on your own. It's all back roads through a piney wood that lead nowhere. No good for nothin' 'cept huntin'."

Donovan phoned the Ladysmith Police to tell them they were coming and followed highway 178 as it wound its way north along the Chippewa River past tiny summer cabins dotting the shore. They crossed over the old iron bridge into the town of Cornell and continued north through the thickly wooded pine forest past resorts on the Holcomb Flowage with names like Big Swedes's, Paradise Shores and Ted's Timber Lodge. Little more than an hour later the Crown Vic passed through the small town of Ladysmith and turned into the parking lot of the Willow Dam Inn. Scully pulled the cruiser to a stop next to an ancient Chevy parked by the two story outhouse they had been told to look for when they stopped for gas on the other end of town.

"Well, I have to admit, it's an attention getter," Scully chuckled as he eyed the double deck tower with matching crescent moons cut into the doors. The location of the women's outhouse beneath the men's spoke volumes about the Willow Dam Inn as did the worn and grimy hand-carved wooden penis that served as a door pull at the entrance. The interior of the tavern was dark and smelled of stale beer and cigarette smoke. Atop the long bar was a line of upturned barstools in various states of disrepair.

"Did you ever see anything like it?" asked Scully, looking up at low ceiling beams cluttered with an endless assortment of oddities; a menagerie of mangy mounted animals including a two-headed bobcat, a fur-covered pike and an albino fawn complete with pink eyes. Next to it, surrounded by a collection of old shotguns was a

NO HUNTING sign peppered with at least a hundred-bullet holes.

"Isn't that one of your girlfriends?" jabbed Donovan, pointing to a garish, inflatable sex doll that lay suspended on it's side with a long neck bottle of Leinenkugel's beer lodged in her plastic mouth. The obscene figure seemed to have a position of honor among the countless other curiosities.

The place seemed to be empty until the quiet was broken by the clang of a pipe wrench that came flying through a door behind the bar and landed on the concrete floor. A string of curses followed that would have made a sailor proud. "God damn it! You piss brained, ball busting mother fucker!"

The detectives were looking at each other approvingly when a cadaverous man with a full red beard appeared in a doorway. He was wrapping a rag around his hand.

"Ah, customers. My lawful prey!" he said, flashing a nearly toothless smile.

"Is your hand all right?" asked Donovan.

The man made a fist and stroked the air in front of his fly as if masturbating. "Yep. Still works," he laughed.

"Are you Bud Merek?" asked Donovan.

"Last I looked. Who wants to know?" he asked, now slightly wary.

"I'm Detective Donovan and this is Detective Scully with the Eau Claire police. We were told you might know the whereabouts of a man we want to talk to as part of an investigation."

"What'd he do?" asked Merek.

"He hasn't been charged with anything," said Scully.

"Name is Elton McClure. We understand he has a hunting shack up here somewhere," said Donovan.

"Sure, I know Elton. He's a rough customer," said Merek.

"Have you seen him lately?" asked Donovan.

"Doesn't come in here much and that's just fine with me. He's dumber than a brick and got a chip on his shoulder the size of a fence post. But at least he's figured out he's better off living alone in the woods away from people–gets in less trouble that way."

"Can you tell us how to get to his cabin?" asked Scully, taking out his note book.

"That's tricky unless you know these parts," Merek replied. "There's roads that go nowhere. Roads you wouldn't know was roads and roads that'll have you going in circles until you run up your own rear end. It'll be easier to show you."

"Do you have the time now?" asked Scully.

Merek grinned mischievously. "Sure. I'll take you as far as the road Elton's shack is on. Then you're on your own," he said. "I don't want anymore to do with that crazy bastard than I have to. And I'll thank you not to tell him I helped you."

"We appreciate your cooperation, Mr. Merek–we'll keep you out of it," said Donovan, handing him his card. "Just in case."

Merek locked up the tavern and they followed him outside.

"Try and keep up. I ain't got all day to play cops and robbers," he said with an impish grin, climbing in his Chevy and revving the engine.

Scully drove and followed him onto the paved, two-lane road that ran past the tavern. Merek maintained the speed limit for five minutes, signaled and turned right onto a gravel road that cut through the dense forest. Scully was enjoying the scenery when suddenly the Chevy took off like a sprint car. Rocks flew into the Crown Vic and filled the air with road dust so thick it became difficult to see.

"That bastard is crazy," said Scully, backing off.

"Don't lose him," laughed Donovan. "I thought you knew how to drive, Mr. Porsche. Or is that cute little car just for show?"

"Well you can explain it to the chief. You know how he hates dinging up his cars."

"I'll handle Krumenauer," said Donovan.

Scully grinned and stomped down on the accelerator. Even as the powerful engine roared to life, the dust thrown up by the Chevy was getting farther away. "What the hell does he have in that old piece of shit?" Scully wondered aloud.

Soon the cruiser was completely engulfed in a thick, brown cloud forcing Scully to slow and finally stop. When it cleared enough to see again, the detectives found themselves staring down a long empty road. Scully continued for several more minutes and skidded to a stop. "He must have turned off," he said turning the cruiser around to backtrack. They soon found the side road where they glimpsed the Chevy far off in the distance racing over an old bridge.

"Catch him," Donovan laughed. Scully floored the accelerator of the 250-horse power engine and by the time they reached the bridge, the cruiser was going nearly 90 miles per hour. Scully didn't notice the rise in the road where it met the bridge deck until it was too late. Without warning, the cruiser launched into the air nearly clearing the entire span and landing hard on the other side with a resounding crash.

"It's a damn good thing this baby has a heavy-duty suspension," laughed Donovan, running his tongue over his teeth to feel if any were chipped.

Scully was determined now and didn't slow. He caught up with the old Chevy in time to see Merek shoot his arm out the window, brake hard and accelerate into a perfect slide onto another side road.

"That bastard is screwing with us!" said Scully.

"He screwing with you," laughed Donovan.

They continued like this turn after turn. Scully was almost certain they crossed the same bridge twice but said nothing. Several side roads later, they came upon Merek parked by a narrow opening in the trees. He was leaning against the Chevy smoking a cigarette and waving gleefully.

"Thought you'd never get here," he said, approaching the driver's side of the Crown Vic.

"You're crazy, you know that don't you?" said Scully.

"Everbody's somethin'," Merek replied with a huge gummy grin showing through his beard. "Elton lives down that road," he said pointing, "So this is as far as I'm going. You'll see the shack about a half-mile in. It's the only one."

"Do you know if he's armed?" asked Donovan.

"Does a bear shit in the woods?" Merek scoffed. "He's a hunter. Of course he's armed."

"How are we going to find our way out of here?" shouted Scully as Merek was getting back into his Chevy.

"Just turn around and stay on that road until you run into the blacktop," said Merek. "It's a straight shot."

"You mean you've been running us around in circles for grins?" barked Scully angrily.

Merek just smiled. "One more thing. Watch out for snares and animal traps. Elton uses them for his hobby."

"What hobby is that?" ask Scully.

The last thing Merek said as he put the old Chevy in gear and drove away was "taxidermy".

They could hear Merek's fading laugh as Scully guided the cruiser into the narrow opening. "I'll be a son-of-a-bitch," Scully chuckled nervously as tree branches snapped and thwacked the car. "He really got us good."

They continued through the gauntlet of trees for about two hundred feet when they came to several large boulders blocking the way that sat under a massive logging chain paddle locked to fat oaks on either side. A handmade sign warned; "THIS IS PRIVATE PROPERTY. ABSOLUTELY NO TRESPASSING."

"Guess we'll have to hoof it," said Donovan resignedly. "Bring the shot gun. I have a bad feeling. And don't slam the door. No point announcing we're here."

It was hot and eerily quiet in the woods. Only the occasional complaint of a lone blue jay or the rustle of a squirrel scampering unseen through trees could be heard. They waved away squadrons of angry black flies circling around them and slowly moved along the curve of the road. Scully was the first to see the small cabin rising from the tall grass ahead in an opening. The simple, unpainted shack had rough sawn board and batten siding, a steep, tar paper roof with a broad eave on one side protecting a neat stack of split oak from the rain. Surrounding a sagging door and two small windows, the entire front of the shack was covered in a bizarre collection of animal skulls and deer antlers. Most bleached white from years in the sun.

"Elton's shack gives me the creeps," whispered Scully.

"I know what you mean. I'm beginning to rethink retirement."

"Where's the van? There's no van."

"Maybe it's around back. Maybe he got rid of..." Donovan's reply was cut off by a gravely voice shouting from somewhere ahead.

"Turn around and leave now. Can't you read the sign? This is private property."

"We're police officers!" yelled Donovan. "We just want to talk to you."

The squawk of a blue jay broke a long silence as they waited for a response.

"Did you hear me?" yelled Donovan.

Silence.

"Cover me," said Donovan. He stood, holding his detective shield high as he slowly approached the cabin. Scully stood behind a tree and held the shotgun poised to shoot.

"I'm Detective Donovan of the Eau Claire Police, Mr. McClure," He could hear his own heart beating as he listened and waited. Nothing. After calling again with no response, he walked around the side of the cabin and caught his breath. There, suspended from the thick limb of a tree by a heavy nylon rope was a partially butchered deer. The tongue hung garishly from the side of the mouth and the carcass, emptied of its internal organs, was splayed wide and held open by a stick to reveal the pattern of white ribs intersecting the hollow of deep red meat.

Part of its hide had been cut away and was pulled down. A frenzy of feeding flies buzzed noisily around the exposed meat.

Donovan froze. The memory of Greta Bauer's flayed torso hanging in her kitchen returned so powerfully that even the stench of putrefaction seemed to fill his nostrils.

"It's just a deer carcass," he said to himself, fighting the urge to vomit. Heart beating faster now and hyper alert, his eyes darted around as he moved closer to a battered picnic table sitting next to the deer. On it lay a skinning knife and a sharpening stone.

Donovan collected himself and continued to plod around the rear of the cabin. Not knowing what to expect now, he peered warily around the corner to see the back door open wide and a white Ford Econoline van parked nearby.

Donovan took a position against the cabin next to the door, swallowed hard and called out again. "We're police officers, Mr. McClure! Come out where I can see you. We just want to talk with you. Come out now and nobody gets hurt," he called.

No answer. Donovan peered into the cabin and, seeing it was empty, raised his Smith and Wesson ready to shoot and went inside to look around. Satisfied it was empty, he worked his way back outside and swept the gun along the woods hoping to make certain McClure was no longer around as he approached the van. Several lengths of PVC pipe were tied to a roof rack. He looked in a dirt-streaked window. The interior was littered with an assortment of tools; a box of PVC pipe connectors, a pair of sawhorses, extension cords, a spool of nylon cord, boxes of nails, a five-gallon gas can and various carpentry tools. Hanging from a hook on the opposite side of the van was a roll of gray duct tape.

It was deathly quiet now. The only sound was the wind passing through the trees. Donovan relaxed slightly, lowered his weapon and called for Scully to join him.

"He took off out the back when we identified ourselves as cops," said Donovan as Scully appeared. "Could be anywhere."

"What's around the other side?" asked Scully.

"He's a poacher. He was in the middle of dressing out a big buck when we interrupted him," Donovan replied.

They walked behind the shack and looked around then Scully went to the truck.

"See the duct tape?" asked Donovan.

"Yeah," Scully replied. "Think it's the same stuff we found on the vic?"

"Not sure, but the van is the right color and our boy seems to be pretty good with a knife. Let's look around some more," Donovan said. "Watch out for snares and stuff, Okay?"

They split up. Donovan walked the tree line on the north side while Scully walked the south. After a few minutes, Donovan heard Scully whistle and hurried to join him at the entrance to a well-worn trail into the woods.

"McClure!" he yelled. "You in there?"

The only sound was the rustle of leaves.

"Give me a minute then follow," said Donovan, stepping into the shade of the winding path. It was cooler in the dense woods as he moved cautiously along scanning the trees in every direction,

"McClure! We just want to talk," he repeated over and over.

The path split into several directions when he was about 500 yards in. He paused to wait for Scully when he heard the brittle snap of a twig off to his right. Crouching low, he signaled the general direction of the noise to his now visible partner. Suddenly, there was a flurry of footsteps racing through the forest and both detectives sprinted toward it through branches that seemed to reach out from all sides slapping and scratching their faces and hands.

"I can't... do this... got to... rest," said Scully, stopping and gasping. While they both gulped air hungrily, the loud crack of a rifle echoed through the trees and bark exploded on a nearby oak.

Instantly, the detectives dropped to the ground and found themselves in a bed of sandburs. "Shit," said Donovan as the sharp, spiny burs stuck through his clothes and imbedded themselves painfully in his hands.

"Son of a bitch," said Scully, his heart beating wildly now. "That bastard is trying to shoot us!"

They went silent and waited for more gunshots to direct them where to return fire. When none came, Scully pumped a shell into the chamber of the 12 gauge shot gun and rose to a knee.

"Stay low," said Donovan. "I'll swing around and see if I can drive him out of his hiding spot toward you. Okay?"

"Be careful, partner," Scully wheezed.

"Count on it," said Donovan, jumping to his feet and dashing through the trees. Instantly, the report of two more shots signaled McClure's location. Scully fired off a couple rounds in the general direction to provide some cover.

Within seconds, the silence was broken once again by the sound of McClure running through the woods.

"He's taking off again," yelled Donovan, running in the direction of the footsteps. He saw a flash of camouflaged pants, a wife beater tee shirt and a mass of thick, curly brown hair sticking out from under a battered baseball cap.

"Stop right there or I'll shoot!" he called.

Suddenly, McClure found himself face-to-face with the barrel of Scully's shotgun. "Take another step and I'll unload this thing into your sorry ass," Scully growled.

Frantically, McClure turned to run, tripped on an exposed tree root and dropped to the ground like a sack of rocks. The rifle flew from his hands–before he could recover it, Donovan burst through the brush and was on him, driving a knee into his back and knocking the breath out of him.

Scully stepped down hard on McClure's outstretched arm as he reached for the rifle, cuffed him, lifted him to his feet and held him while Donovan frisked him and emptied his pockets. He found a small amount of cash, a pocketknife, a couple of stove bolts, three joints and a book of matches from a bar in Eau Claire called The Joynt. Scully read McClure his rights as the three of them walked back through the woods and down the long drive way. Scully put McClure into the back seat of the Crown Vic while Donovan called the Ladysmith police on his cell phone. "Elton McClure is "cuffed and stuffed," he told them.

"He's what?

"McClure is in custody and we're bringing him in."

Donovan turned to McClure who sat scowling behind the cage in the backseat and said; "Pretty big fuss to make over a little pot and poaching."

"Fuck you," said McClure. "I'm just trying to get by same as everyone else. If you mother fuckers would leave me alone, I'd be fine. Besides, there are more deer around than this piss poor excuse for a forest can support."

"That doesn't explain why you'd risk getting killed or killing a cop over some lousy misdemeanors. Doesn't make any sense," said Scully.

Scully backed the Crown Vic out of the woods to the dirt road. He drove in the direction that Bud Merek had indicated and ten minutes later they were pulling onto the paved highway that led into town.

"The trip out was easier than going in but not nearly as much fun," Donovan said.

Scully laughed.

Two uniformed officers were waiting when Scully pulled into the Ladysmith Police Department parking lot. "Cuffed and stuffed. That's a good one," said one as he led the way inside where McClure was booked and placed in a holding cell.

"What do we have here?" asked Captain Earl Hoffsteader, the officer who seemed to be in charge. Hoffsteader was a veteran cop with a crew cut, ruddy cheeks and a gut that spoke of too many years sitting in a cruiser and too many donuts.

Donovan brought him up-to-date. "We're out of our jurisdiction, but all bets were off when he fired at us. In addition to attempting to shoot a couple of fine police officers, you can charge him with possession, resisting arrest, possession of an unregistered firearm, parole violation and poaching. That should be enough to give us a closer look-see inside that shack. We already know at least some of what we'll find inside the van."

"We'll send a unit out there," said Hoffsteader.

"Can you wait for a search warrant? We have a lot more riding on this than a little pot and poaching. I wouldn't want to compromise our investigation," said Donovan.

"I suppose. In the mean time, let's begin interrogating McClure. Elton is well known to us."

McClure was still handcuffed and fidgeting nervously when the key rattled in the lock of the holding cell door. He was taken to the small interrogation room where Donovan, Scully and Hoffsteader waited.

"I can't say it's good to see you again," said Hoffsteader, removing the cuffs. "We were thinking you finally had your act together and here you go hunting deer out of season and taking pot shots at our out-of-town guests. Among other things."

"I thought they were trespassers. No one said anything about a search warrant. I got the right to protect my property."

"You don't have the right to kill someone."

"I wasn't trying to kill 'em. Just get 'em ta leave. My shots never came close. Just ask em'."

"Maybe you're just a lousy shot," said Scully.

McClure sniffed indignantly. "You'd both be dead now if I wanted to kill you."

"As dead as the deer you poached?" jabbed Hoffsteader.

"You look the other way at poaching all year round, Earl. Some of us have to hunt if we're gonna eat. I get tired of squirrel."

Hoffsteader let it drop and avoided eye contact with the detectives.

"Tell me, Elton. Do you get down to Eau Claire now and then?" asked Donovan.

"Once in a while. Most everyone does. Why?"

"Were you there two weeks ago?"

"Two weeks ago?"

"Saturday. July 13th."

"How the hell do I know? I can't remember where I am every minute."

"Answer the question. Were you in Eau Claire on Saturday two weeks ago?"

"I don't know. And so what if I was?"

"I get the feeling you have something to hide, Elton. Why do you suppose I feel like that?" asked Donovan.

McClure shrugged.

"Look Elton. Why don't you just own up to it," said Donovan. "We know you were there. You were stopped for speeding in Chippewa Falls on your way home."

"So this is all about a fuckin' speeding ticket?"

"What were you doing in Eau Claire, Elton?" asked Scully.

"Hanging out on Water Street. See if I could pick up a college chick in one of the bars."

"Did you?"

"No. Stuck up bitches think their shit is good to eat."

"Did anyone see you there? Anyone who could vouch for you?"

"No one who would admit it," he snorted.

"Why's that?" asked Scully.

"Let's just say I'm not part of their crowd."

"Sounds like you had a bad night, Elton. Is that why you were angry?" asked Donovan.

"Who says I was angry?"

"You tell me," said Donovan.

"Look, I sold a little pot on Water Street to some students from the University. Did some little shit get caught smoking and rat me out? Is that how it is?"

"We don't care about a little pot," said Donovan.

Donovan stood slowly, put both hands on the table and leaned in close to McClure's face. "Does the name Greta Bauer mean anything to you?"

"Who the fuck is Greta Bauer? Never heard of her."

"Greta Bauer is a little old lady who someone killed and skinned like that deer that's hanging behind your cabin right now," said Scully.

"Jesus, that's pretty gross. You think I did that? Why the fuck would I do that to an old lady?"

"Why would you attempt to shoot two police officers to avoid a fucking fine for poaching? You're on parole, Elton. Just having a gun in your possession puts you back in prison," Donovan said.

"I want a lawyer," McClure replied setting his jaw. "You fuckers ain't gonna hang an old lady's murder on me."

"The murderer drove a white Ford Econoline van, Elton. Just like yours," said Donovan.

"And he was very handy with a knife. Just like you," added Scully.

"I might have poached a deer, man, but I didn't kill no old lady."

"Maybe you did both, Elton."

"No way man."

"Let's change the subject. Are you good with numbers, Elton?" asked Donovan.

"Whatya mean?"

"Remembering them. Like what was your prisoner number when you were in the joint?"

"Which time?"

"Let's start with the last time."

"168620," Elton recited.

"How about your social security number?"

"484-77-4638. What is this bullshit? Why don't you just look 'em up in my records?"

"What does the number A18733 mean to you?" asked Scully. Both detectives watched McClure's expression for any hint of recognition.

"Nothin'. Should it?"

"You tell us."

"Don't mean nothin' as far as I know."

"You're a taxidermist, right?" asked Donovan.

"I fart around with it now and then."

"Do you sign your work?"

"What? Are you fuckin' nuts? How would I sign a dead animal?"

"You tell us," said Scully popping a stick of gum in his mouth.

"I'm done talking", McClure replied, crossing his arms over his chest defiantly. "I want a lawyer. You fuckers are nuts."

CHAPTER 10

The Athena Cafe was more crowded than usual the next morning and the little Greek was excitedly barking orders to his waitresses. The detectives took the last booth and ordered.

" Do you think McClure's our guy?" asked Scully, pouring cream and heaping sugar into his coffee.

"I dunno."

"The history of violence. The van. The trip to Eau Claire the night of the murder. The skinning knife. The tape and polyethylene rope in his van. That doesn't convince you?"

"It's all circumstantial. I'd feel better if we had some physical evidence that puts him at the scene."

Donovan's cell rang. It was Earl Hoffsteader.

"They've got the search warrant," he mouthed to Scully. "We'll be there in a couple of hours, Earl."

Donovan and Scully followed a caravan of Ladysmith patrol cars led by Captain Hoffsteader back to McClure's property.

The boulders were rolled into the brush and the logging chains cut away to clear the narrow opening to the long driveway. They wound their way to the clearing and parked next to the shack.

Hoffsteader directed a search of the van and the area outside. Donovan and Scully walked to the rear of McClure's shack and went inside.

"Jesus. How can anyone live like this?" asked Scully, surveying the primitive, cluttered surroundings. Spikes of light spilled in through bullet holes in the walls and a mouse scurried into a hole in the wood plank floor.

A filthy mattress on a crude, wooden platform took up one corner over which a green Coleman propane lantern hung. Next to an ancient cast iron cook stove sat a small table with a single chair under one of the two windows. Roughly made shelves were lined with canned goods, bags of flour, sugar, a box of stick matches, coffee and a few cooking utensils. They were not surprised to find a pile of well-worn porn magazines in a stand by the bed.

Scully paged through one of them. "Pretty rough stuff. Apparently our friend Elton is into S and M."

Donovan picked up a dog-eared issue of *Bondage and Discipline* with a cover showing a woman in a dog collar tied to a rack. A large red ball was held in her mouth by leather straps. He opened it randomly; winced and tossed it back on the stack.

"This stuff is sick."

Much to Donovan's disappointment, there was no sign of a taser anywhere. No instruction manual. No batteries. They moved outside. The deer carcass was now teeming with flies laying eggs in the rotting flesh.

"Let's ask Hoffsteader if someone can cut this thing down and bury it," said Scully waving them away. "But, we have to be sure to save the knot in the rope. See if it's a match."

Scully tagged and bagged the skinning knife that was on the picnic table. It would be checked for traces of human blood.

"That's a nasty looking thing," said Scully, examining the knife's ergonomic, T-shaped handle and razor-sharp, semi-circular blade. He held the plastic bag closer to inspect the cutting hook on the tip. "It could open you up like a zipper."

There was no evidence of a taser found in the truck, but the spool of polyethylene rope and the roll of duct tape were bagged as evidence. Hoffsteader appeared as they were placing the samples in the trunk of the Crown Vic.

"If it's okay with you, we'll take this stuff back to Eau Claire and send it to the State Police Crime Lab in Madison for analysis," said Donovan.

"Fine, as long as I get copies of everything," Hoffsteader replied. "But, first follow me. We've found something."

Donovan and Scully followed him into the pines for several hundred feet until they emerged into the bright light of a clearing. There stood an orderly forest of perfectly cultivated marijuana. Row after row of the lush green plants, some as tall as ten feet and topped with massive buds, were neatly bisected by a network of PVC pipes and soaker hoses. A gas powered pump drew water from a nearby stream.

"Elton seems to have quite a green thumb," said Scully. "Any idea what it's worth? We don't run across growers in Eau Claire on this scale."

"We've caught our share over the years around here. Our rule of thumb is your average plant produces about a pound of weed. That'll sell on the street for about $4,000 if it's any good," Hoffsteader replied.

Scully popped a Juicy Fruit and scratched his head. "Well, say there's over a hundred plants here. That could be close to a half a million bucks."

"It's not hard to understand why Elton didn't want anyone trespassing," said Donovan.

"Still doesn't clear him. But, it sure could be a game changer."

McClure was taken from his cell and brought back into the interrogation room. During several hours of questioning, he owned up to cultivating the pot but stuck to his story of being innocent of the old lady's murder. After passing a polygraph test with flying colors he was returned to his holding cell.

Ladysmith police officers showed his mug shot to employees at every gun shop and sporting goods store in the area. Although a few thought they recognized him, all were certain they had not sold him a taser. A check of the Public Library in Ladysmith and several other towns also came up negative when they asked about McClure using their computers to access the Internet.

"Thanks for your help, captain," said a frustrated Donovan. "It isn't looking like we got ourselves a murderer, but you can nail McClure seven ways from Sunday on other stuff."

CHAPTER 11

"Let's take the scenic route back," said Donovan. "I need some think time."

Scully drove west on US 8 from Ladysmith then south on WI 40 to Bear Lake where he turned west and meandered through the twisting miles of lake country. They were just crossing the bridge over Lake Chetek when Donovan's cell rang.

"Donovan."

"Lloyd," said the familiar voice of Sergeant Lloyd Carlson. "Just got a call from a police detective in Joplin, Missouri. He thinks he might know of another executioner victim."

"Light 'em up," said Donovan. Scully hit the flashers and lights and stepped on the gas. Traffic was light when they turned onto US-53 and what little there was gave the cruiser a wide lane to pass. In less than an hour they pulled into the police station parking lot.

"What's up?" Donovan asked the desk sergeant.

"You might want to call this guy, Mike," he said, handing Donovan a square of pink paper on which was written Detective A. Corwin, Joplin P.D. and the phone number.

Donovan punched in the number on his phone and was soon listening to a deep, raspy voice with a slight Missouri drawl.

"Andy Corwin."

"Andy. This is Detective Donovan of the Eau Claire P.D. in Wisconsin. I'm returning your call regarding a murder in Missouri that could be tied to the one we're investigating."

"Yes. But, it isn't a Missouri case," Corwin replied.

"What do you mean?"

"I was driving through Oklahoma. I stopped for coffee somewhere in Choctaw County and was reading a local newspaper. There was a story about a John Doe murder there. The vic was branded with a number just like the one you posted on the crime center database. I remembered it because I thought it was so unusual."

"Do you remember anything else from the article? A name I could contact?"

"Sorry. I just remember it was Choctaw County. You might want to give the authorities there a call."

Donovan jotted the name in his notebook and found the number for the Choctaw State Police. He introduced himself to the officer on the phone and explained he may have some information about their John Doe.

"I'll check around and have someone get back to you."

Donovan's phone rang five minutes later.

"Detective, my name is Orville Thompson. I'm the coroner for Choctaw County in Oklahoma. I got a message that you might know something about our John Doe murder."

Donovan punched the speakerphone button so Scully could hear and gave the coroner the investigation background. "So," concluded Donovan, "it appears your John Doe has same number branded on him as a vic we have here."

"A18733?" asked Thompson.

"That's it. Perfect half-inch letters branded across the abdomen. Neat as could be," Donovan replied.

The coroner was quiet for a minute. Donovan could hear the shuffling of paper.

"Our guy was branded on his forehead," said Thompson. "But, the rest is right. Half-inch numbers–very neat. What else you got?"

Donovan recounted the Greta Bauer murder in great detail.

"Gotta be the same perp," Thompson said.

"When did John Doe get it?" asked Donovan.

"We estimate the date of death as the third or Fourth of July. He was badly decomposed."

Donovan sat up and flipped open his notebook. "Go on."

"The victim was an elderly male. Found naked as a jaybird. What little hair he had to begin with was whacked off with a knife or somethin'. Let's see. He was tied spread eagled in a barn on an abandoned ranch in the middle of nowhere. His mouth was taped shut and, like I said, he was branded across his forehead. Identical number, A18733."

"Does the number mean anything to you?" asked Donovan.

"No, sir. Not a thing."

"How was he killed?"

"It's a strange one. Our medical examiner's best guess was that chloroform was injected into his heart. But, the autopsy also showed he had been injected with an assortment of chemicals in his arms, legs–even his eyes. Probably before he died. Stuff like bleach. Ammonia. Dye. Maybe some sorts of cleaning compounds."

"Something like that," said Donovan. "You'd think it would have been picked up by the news. I never heard a thing about it.

"Oh, I suspect it only made the local papers here. We're out-of-the-way and pretty used to branding in these parts, Detective. I suppose the sheriff figured some sicko just got his hands on a vagrant."

Where's the body?"

"Cremated. We have his autopsy and investigation records, of course. But, when the remains went unidentified and unclaimed for thirty days, we had the body cremated."

"Wish you hadn't done that."

"We're a very small county with limited resources," the coroner replied defensively. "We simply don't have the money to keep a body for more than thirty days."

"Sure. I didn't mean to imply anything. Can you fax us copies of everything you have?"

"Got the file right here. I'll get it right out to you. Pictures, too."

Donovan took Thompson's contact information and gave him the police department fax number.

"That's number two," he said when he hung up.

"Yeah," said Scully. "This could be big doin's."

Documents from the Office of the Choctaw County Coroner were streaming out of the fax machine by the time they finished briefing Chief Krumenauer. Pages of police reports, a certificate of death, autopsy files, the medical examiner's toxicology report, fingerprints and, finally, a series of harshly grained, black and white photos of the victim's slender body on the morgue table. A close-up of his head clearly showed the identical brand that was now so familiar.

Donovan's "Murder Book" was growing again.

"Confirm the same perp?" asked the chief after Donovan and Scully had time to review the printouts.

"It's our boy," Donovan replied.

"Better prepare a statement for the newsies and schedule of briefing. Looks like we might have a serial killer on our hands."

At 6:15, just in time for the evening news, Donovan stood on the lawn in front of the police department surrounded by lights and reporters.

Tess shut off the vacuum when she heard the phone ring. "Turn on the news, honey. We have another one."

"Oh, my God. Who is it this time?"

"Watch the news. I gotta run."

Tess flipped through the channels until she saw BREAKING NEWS crawl across the bottom of the screen as reporter gave the details;

"Police in Eau Claire, Wisconsin announced minutes ago that they have just learned of another victim that may be linked to the killer of local resident, Greta Bauer, the elderly woman whose partially skinned body was found in her home just a few days ago. The latest victim is an unidentified elderly man in Oklahoma. Reporting live from Eau Claire, Wisconsin is our own Sheila Brovan."

The picture changed to an attractive young woman holding a CNN microphone.

"On the heels of the gruesome murder of an elderly woman in this small, quiet Wisconsin town, Eau Claire Police Detective Michael Donovan told reporters just minutes ago that he had received a phone call from the Coroner's Office in a remote area of Choctaw, Oklahoma. In the call, Choctaw Coroner Orville Thompson provided information regarding an unidentified man who was murdered sometime over the Fourth of July weekend that may link it to the unsolved murder of Greta Bauer here several days later. Here, in its entirety is Donovan's briefing."

The picture changed to Michael Donovan surrounded by microphones. Tess watched nervously. She knew how it irritated Copper when reporters ran out of intelligent questions and continued 'just to hear their own voices on television'."

Tess crossed her fingers and listened.

"I'll take questions, but please don't ask me to speculate on things I would have no way of knowing. It will only add to the frenzy of an already charged situation."

"Why can't you tell us what links these killings to the same murderer?" came the first question."

"We'll make that public in due time. Right now we feel it could compromise our investigation," said Donovan. It was a pat answer to the question he knew was coming.

"Was the cause of death the same?" asked one reporter.

"No, but there were some similar characteristics. According to the Choctaw Medical Examiner, this victim was injected with various substances including bleach, ammonia, dyes and cleaning solutions. More than likely, however, it was chloroform injected directly into his heart that ended his life," said Donovan, reading from his notes.

"What characteristics were similar?

"At this time I can only tell you that they were both elderly and their hair had been cut off."

"Were the victims related?"

"Not that we know of."

"Is there any reason to believe that the Oklahoma victim was a naturalized citizen like Bauer?" asked a reporter.

"Without any identification it is impossible to tell," Donovan replied, trying not to appear irritated but astounded that anyone could think a dead, naked person without any identification whatsoever could be identified.

"Will the body be exhumed for closer examination?"

"The John Doe was cremated in accordance with Choctaw County policy after it was unclaimed or identified within thirty days. However, we have complete reports from the Choctaw County Sheriff's office, the medical examiner, autopsy findings and complete post-mortem photos."

"Will you travel to Oklahoma as part of the Bauer investigation?" asked a reporter.

"That hasn't been determined."

"Do you expect that other victims will be revealed now that the two murders have been linked and are receiving national attention?" asked a reporter.

"What's your name?"

"Jim Pecca, WCCO News."

"Well, Jim, I don't have a crystal ball. Answering questions like that requires a crystal ball. So why don't you just make your own guess. Now does anyone have a question that doesn't require a Nostradamus to answer?"

Properly admonished on national television, some of the reporters grew quiet. Most, unfazed by Donovan's scolding, continued the rapid-fire inquisition.

Donovan grew increasingly agitated and abruptly ended the questioning. "That's all we have. When we learn more we will share it with you. Thank you."

Scully walked with him back inside the station. "You can't let 'em get under your skin, partner," he said. "They're just doing their jobs."

"Me too," Donovan replied. "Me, too."

"About time they found that asshole," said a man to no one as he watched the WGN Morning News bulletin some 280 miles away. "Finally," he thought, "they're taking notice."

He particularly enjoyed the police detective's comment about Nostradamus, but was dissatisfied with the superficial way the murders were described–they were much better than that. A distorted smirk appeared on his hard, angular face as he dropped his yellow green eyes from the ancient television and returned his attention to the map of Chicago that lay next to him on the bed. It was carefully folded to display a section of north side. Various locations were indicated by neatly drawn circles with hand-written notations of the driving distances between them. Arranged around the map was a thick red file folder and various photographs of a vacant industrial building, a small parking lot behind a tavern and several telephoto close-ups of a thick-set older man in a Cubs baseball cap raking the front lawn of a tidy, middle class home.

CHAPTER 12

October 1997

It was mid afternoon when Notre Dame kicked off to Navy. Although the score had shifted back and forth, Donovan barely noticed the television. Outside, the October sky was turning a threatening, leaden gray. By the beginning of the fourth quarter it began to snow. He brought in an armload of oak from the woodpile and got a warm blaze going in the den fireplace. He could hear Tess in the kitchen fussing with a new recipe for chicken Marsala. It was a perfect Saturday afternoon he thought as he propped his feet up on the ottoman.

Donovan had spent the afternoon rereading selections from several books that were now stacked neatly on the end table next to his reading lamp. The subject of each was a different serial killer.

"Copper," came a sweet, lilting voice from the kitchen.

"I'm not going to the store again, Tess. Two trips per recipe is my limit. I don't care what Julia Childs says you need. Substitute an onion or something."

Tess appeared in the doorway. "With an attitude like that I'll substitute the plumber for my husband next time my plumbing needs attention."

Donovan laughed. He looked up to see her saunter toward him carrying a Waterford crystal tumbler with two fingers of 18-year-old Bushmills Irish Whiskey–neat, just the way he liked it.

"Wanna wear it or drink it?"

He grinned. "You're too good to me."

"Tell me about it," she said imperiously. "What have you been reading?"

Donovan lifted the book in his hand titled *The Butcher of Plainfield*. "Trying to get in the heads of a serial killers.

"Fascinating."

"You might like this one. It's kind of a cookbook. About Ed Gein. He liked to cook and eat his victims - or a least parts of 'em."

"Julia Childs for cannibalistic serial killers? I'll pass," she said, returning to the kitchen.

Donovan sipped his drink and went to the desk for a legal pad and a fountain pen. He liked fountain pens. The character of the line and the watery blue ink seemed to help him refine his thinking and give his words more importance.

On the top left of the page in large neat letters he wrote SERIAL KILLERS and next to it CHARACTERISTICS. Then, one at a time, he listed the names of the serial killers who were the focus of the books in front of him; Ted Bundy, Son of Sam, Jeffrey Dahmer, Ed Gein, Albert Fish, The Green River Killer and John Wayne Gacey. Next to each he made notes on what was known about them. Last on the list he wrote "X" to represent the killer he was pursuing.

Next, he wrote SANITY. Historically the courts had ruled that most of the serial killers were sane enough to be convicted and were frequently executed. On the other hand, Ed Gein, the Wisconsin farmer who exhumed bodies as well as killing several people, was wildly insane and remained institutionalized for the rest of his life. Although Gein skinned his victims, the skinning of Greta Bauer was not the same. Gein kept and often ate body parts, made furniture, even clothing from the skin. Greta Bauer's flaying seemed ceremonial or ritualistic.

RAGE was next on the list and it forced Donovan to wrestle with the facts. It would be easy to consider "X's" murders as acts of rage. After all, one was skinned, the other, according to the Choctaw County Sheriff, was killed by toxic injections. Rage, he decided, would result in quicker, more violent murders. "X" appeared to want his victims to suffer although the two victims were murdered in different, yet equally methodical manners.

For example, some of Greta Bauer's blood vessels were cauterized presumably in an attempt to reduce the bleeding so that she would suffer longer. It seemed to Donovan that both murders indicated a high level of intelligence. Each was well planned, efficiently executed and the threat of discovery was minimized.

Donovan studied the list of killers again and spelled out GEOGRAPHY in the blue ink. With the exception of Ted Bundy, whose choice of locations coincided with his changes of address, the others were killed within a specific area near the perp's home. Donovan speculated that "X" was not a resident of either area in which he committed the murders. That means that either his employment involves travel, that he is an itinerant drifter or he has the financial means to move around at will. Donovan didn't believe a drifter would have the wherewithal to commit these carefully planned murders so "X" must have a home base somewhere.

He knew that a serial killer's first murder most often occurred in the area in which they live. The profiling experts refer to it as their comfort zone. So, if Greta Bauer wasn't his first victim, it might indicate that he was right in surmising that "X" was not an Eau Claire resident. Still, it seemed unlikely that "X" was a Choctaw resident either. Perhaps the first victim has yet to be discovered.

CALLING CARD. Donovan knew from his reading that it was not unusual for serial killers to want their string of murders linked together. When they did, the notoriety of the killings grew exponentially in the public eye. Jack the Ripper wrote letters to the London police, Son of Sam not only wrote notes admitting his string of killings in New York City, he announced when the next one would take place. Ted Bundy bit his victims leaving unique impressions of teeth marks that were traceable to him.

Clearly the flagrant branding 'calling card' indicated 'X' wanted credit for his deeds. Moreover, he wanted the world to know about them. But, why? Donovan was convinced it had something to do with the significance of A18733.

ELDERLY VICTIMS. Why old people? Could it be that 'X' had built up hostility and aggression since childhood toward his parents? That would explain the advanced years of the victims and that they were of both genders. Or maybe, Donovan thought, they were simply easy prey. Could their age have been a mere coincidence? He doubted it.

METHOD - While the actual methods of each killing were both ghastly, each was distinctly different. In one case it was from shock or bleeding to death from being flayed. In the other case, the injection of a deadly fluid. Still, the known method of subduing each victim was identical; tasered, stripped naked, bound with identical polyethylene rope using the same knots, and gagged with a rubber ball held in place by identical duct tape wrapped around their heads.

TROPHIES - Ed Gein and Jeffrey Dahmer kept bodies and body parts of their victims. Rodney Acala, the serial killer thought to have murdered hundreds of young women over a thirty year period, collected their ear rings. 'X' appeared to have a thing for hair. Donovan puzzled over this one time and again. Why hair, he thought as sipped his almost forgotten whiskey.

KNOW VICTIMS? - Some serial killers chose their victims randomly, others stalked them. Donovan thought it was clear that 'X' knew about his victims. The level of planning required specific knowledge of their habits. However, because they were geographically diverse, it seemed unlikely he actually knew them.

Finally, he wrote FREQUENCY and next to it - regular pattern. <u>Likely to kill again</u>.

CHAPTER 13

Milos Dulecki strolled into the cool evening air from the heat and the stench of the factory and smiled. He had finished his regular shift plus two hours of overtime at Broadmore Tire and looked forward to a cold beer at Polaski's Bar on his way home.

"Have a nice weekend, Milos," said the guard as Dulecki passed the factory security shack.

"You too, George," replied Dulecki, pulling a Chicago Cubs baseball cap down on his thick gray hair.

"You must be getting close to the big day."

"Yah! Three more months and you won't be seeing my sorry ass around here again," Dulecki called with a slight Eastern European accent. "Thirty-two years of this is plenty. I'm goin' fishin'!"

He hiked across the nearly empty parking lot and climbed into a green Buick Century sitting by itself in a far, dimly lit corner. He tossed his lunch pail in the back and lighted a cigarette with his last match. As he did, his face glowed in the binoculars of the man waiting in a white Econoline van on a dark, side street. Dulecki fired up the Buick and sped from the parking lot. The van followed him at a distance as he drove past abandoned warehouses and factories to Polaski's.

A barstool propped open the back door and boozy laughter, the brittle click of pool balls and the lonely twang of jukebox country drifted into the parking lot as Duclecki pulled into his preferred spot in a dark corner by the dumpster. He believed his car was less likely to get creased or dented there. As usual, he left the windows open and the doors unlocked–nothing to steal anyway.

Two minutes after he was inside, the white van backed into the adjacent spot so that the van's sliding door was next to the Buick's driver's side.

The driver shut off the engine and felt the first ache climb up the back of his neck. The muscles in his jaw throbbed and his shaved head began to sweat as he waited in the darkness to drift away as his other self took control.

"Gotta cold one back there, Al?" Dulecki asked, sitting in his favorite spot by the row of beer taps.

"How ya doin', Milos?" Polaski asked, retrieving a bottle of Budweiser from an ice-filled cooler. Dulecki took a long drink, swiped a book of matches off the bar and lit another cigarette.

"When are you going to put a smoke eater in this dump," chided Dulecki. "It's damn near winter and you have the doors open."

"Customers like the fresh air."

"Bullshit," said Milos, looking around at the handful of customers scattered at a few tables or shooting pool.

"Besides my electric bill is already too high."

"Ah! You're just cheap. You could pinch shit out of a buffalo nickel."

Polaski laughed.

"You might want to put a light in that parking lot, too. Can't see a damn thing out there it's so dark. If I break my neck I'll sue you for every dime you got."

"That and ten cents will buy you a cup of coffee," Polaski countered. They both laughed.

Dulecki didn't feel the usual easy comfort of the bar tonight and drained the bottle faster than he normally did.

"Get you another?"

"No, gotta get home. My twins are coming for dinner tomorrow with their tribes of little ones. Need all the rest I can get. See ya."

He paid and walked back to his car, a little surprised to see a white van parked next to it that wasn't there before. He climbed in without another thought and slid the key into the ignition. In that instant, he saw a movement in the corner of his eye. Before he could react, his neck was wrapped in a powerful arm reaching over from the back seat and he felt a blinding pain shoot through his body. He gasped for air. Struggled to breathe–wanted to pull at the arm but could not move. Seconds later he settled into unconsciousness.

CHAPTER 14

October 24, 1997

Brian Heath and his younger brother, Duane, slung their BB guns over their backs and shimmied up the narrow opening between two decaying factory buildings on Chicago's north side. The day was warming and their t-shirts were damp with sweat by the time they crawled through the broken window onto the catwalk high up over the factory floor. The pair often broke into the abandoned steel plant to shoot pigeons, but something was eerily different this time. A strange stillness and an odd odor hung in the air.

"Peeyu! What stinks?" asked Brian, crinkling his nose.

"Pigeon shit."

"Worse than that."

The boys worked their way toward the ladder leading down from a gantry crane that spanned nearly the entire width of the factory. The massive machine that once moved huge steel plates and I-beams now sat idle–nearly white with layers of bird droppings.

Duane paused to plink at a roost of pigeons, sending them fluttering overhead just as Brian started down the ladder. He was half way to the bottom when he froze.

"What's that?" He pointed to an oddly shaped form sprawled far below on the concrete. Brian leaned out from the catwalk for a closer look.

"Is it some kind of animal?"

"I think it's dead body."

"If it is, it doesn't have any clothes on."

They both climbed down to the factory floor and edged toward it.

"Holy shit," whispered Duane. "It is a naked, dead guy."

Milos Dulecki's bent and mutilated body was badly decomposed when the Chicago Police found it. He had apparently been spread eagled between four huge bolts that once anchored a machine to the floor. Short lengths of neatly knotted rope dangled from his wrists and ankles. Remnants of the rope also remained on the bolts. His hair had been hacked off and a rubber ball was stuffed in his mouth, held there by duct tape wrapped around his head.

Dulecki had been listed as a missing person since the police investigated the report of an abandoned car nearly two weeks earlier. The Buick Century registered to him was found in a North Side tavern parking lot. The windows were down and the keys were in the ignition. A lone shoe was found on the floor near the gas pedal–the shoelace still tied. Police learned that Dulecki had been employed at the Broadmore Tire Factory for over thirty years. He didn't gamble and drank little more than a beer or two after work. He had no criminal record, not even a speeding ticket. Dulecki was active in the St. Stanislaus Kostka Polish Church. By all appearances, he lived a quiet life with his wife in an Oak Park suburb.

His disappearance was a complete mystery.

Police at the murder scene quickly determined that Dulecki hadn't been robbed. Although his clothes were shredded and tossed about, his watch was still on his wrist, his identification and credit cards were in his wallet along with twenty-three dollars and a few worn pictures of his family. Also found was a book of matches imprinted with Polaski's Bar where he was last seen. The forensics team that cleared the scene found several boot prints in the grime and pigeon shit and dust leading to and from a door that had been forced open. Two trails of heel marks indicated that Dulecki had been dragged. There were no latent fingerprints or physical evidence.

Police interviewed the distraught family as well as Dulecki's neighbors and co-workers, but no leads developed and no motive could be determined. The Cook County Coroner's autopsy report indicated that every major bone in Dulecki's arms and legs had been completely fractured by blunt force trauma. Most likely by repeated blows from a heavy club or baseball bat – snapped in two like the branches of a tree. Each broken limb was then methodically bent at such severe angles that the body appeared to have extra knees and elbows. The jagged end of a fractured femur protruded from the broken skin of one thigh and the humeri of both arms stuck out.

Less noticeable at first were the multiple broken fingers on each of Dulecki's thick, workingman's hands.

Even more puzzling than the brutal injuries and gruesome manner in which the body was arranged were half-inch numbers burned into his forehead with what police believe was a branding iron – A18733.

CHAPTER 15

Donovan rummaged through the chaos of morning papers left behind at the Athena and plucked out an early edition of the Chicago Tribune. He scanned the front page of the first section and Scully perused the sports while they drank coffee and waited for their breakfasts. Donovan was several pages deep when saw a small headline that stopped him dead in the middle of his egg white omelet.

MURDER VICTIM FOUND TORTURED AND BRANDED.

The naked body of a Chicago man was found yesterday in an abandoned city industrial building, the victim of an apparent murder. After notifying family members, Chicago police identified the victim as Milos Dulecki, a 68 year-old tire plant worker just weeks from retirement. Dulecki had been reported missing by his wife last week when he failed to return home from his work shift. His body was found by two young boys in the vacant Northside factory on Bartlett Street. An unnamed source inside the coroner's office reported that it appeared that the victim was naked and had been branded. Virtually every major bone in his arms and legs were broken. Police refuse to provide further details until an autopsy is completed. However, they did confirm the branding.

"What's most puzzling is the number," said a police spokesman. "Some kind of alpha numeric code – A17833 was burned into the victims forehead with what appears to be a branding iron."

"Read this," said Donovan.

Scully set down his knife and fork, pushed aside a stack of buttermilk pancakes and licked the pancake syrup from his fingers. While he read, Donovan reached into his suit coat for his notebook.

"You don't even have to look," said a wide-eyed Scully. "It's the same number."

"Well, I guess Elton's off the hook for sure now," Donovan replied.

They each left a few dollars on the table and hurried outside to the Crown Vic. Minutes later they were on the phone to the Chicago Police Department.

"My name is Detective Michael Donovan with the Eau Claire P.D. in Wisconsin. Can I speak with the detective in charge of the Milos Dulecki murder investigation. I have information."

He clicked his pen excitedly as he waited.

"This is Detective O'Neil, can I help you?"

Donovan introduced himself and rattled off the basics of the Greta Bauer and John Doe murders including that both victims had the same number as Dulecki burned into their skin.

"What do you have so far?" he asked O'Neil.

"Vic's name is Milos Dulecki. Sixty-eight years old. Lived with his wife in a small house on Chicago's near north side. Worked at the Broadmore Tire Company for thirty-two years. No criminal record. Paid his bills. Immigrated from Poland in the late forties."

"It sounds like someone really worked him over," said Donovan.

"Big time. Lot of rage involved. His body was found by a couple of kids in an abandoned steel fabrication building. Had so many broken bones he was like a rag doll. Mouth taped shut. Naked as a jaybird. Tied up. Hair chopped off. Even more strange was that number burned into his head. What's that about?"

"I don't know," Donovan replied. "The number. The naked thing. The chopped off hair. Greta Bauer was older, too. Polish by birth and emigrated to the U.S. around the same time. Don't know about the John Doe in Oklahoma."

"All three murders were brutal," added O'Neil. "But, still it's the identical number burned into them that's the clincher."

"Look, my partner and I want to come down," said Donovan. "There're plenty of flights from Minneapolis," said O'Neil. "Get on one. I'll pick you up at the airport."

Five minutes later, Donovan was in Chief Krumenauer's office.

"Chicago's not far," complained the chief. "Every dollar we spend on expenses is one less dollar for new patrol cars."

"Okay. We'll drive," said Donovan. He knew how Krumenauer loved his patrol cars.

Donovan called O'Neil back and got directions to the Near North Side Precinct. "It's normally a six hour drive, but I think we can clear the way and be there sooner," said Donovan.

He called home to tell Tess.

"It's all over the news," she said. "I thought you'd be calling. Looks like your wish for a big time crime is coming true."

"It sure does."

Less than five hours later, Donovan and Scully pulled into a visitor's spot at the police precinct on Chicago's Larrabee Street. They asked for O'Neil and were directed to a dreary conference room with a small, gunmetal gray table and half a dozen more or less matching chairs. Before they could sit, the door opened and an imposing, athletic-looking plainclothes detective came in carrying a file folder.

"O'Neil," he said, extending his hand. "You made good time."

"I'm Officer Donovan. This is my partner, Officer Scully."

O'Neil sported a Marine-style haircut and was neatly dressed in a crisp white shirt and tie. He tossed the file on the table. "Have a seat," he said. Donovan took the case file from his briefcase and sat.

O'Neil went first. He reviewed the investigation and brought them up-to-date.

"Any leads to go on?" asked Scully.

"We found the victim's car parked behind a bar he frequented. The keys were still in the ignition. We figure the perp was waiting in the back seat. Pulled the old guy right out of his shoes. Or at least one of them."

"Apparently he was tazed. There are marks on the neck.

After he was zapped, we figure the perp took him to the abandoned factory and killed him there. Looks like nearly every bone in his body was broken. His hair was chopped off. And, of course, there is the brand. The numbers."

O'Neil fanned through several eight by ten photographs on the table and selected one. "Of course there are the numbers," he repeated, putting it on top of the pile.

Donovan and Scully leaned in closer to study the photograph of Milos Dulecki's forehead. "Except for where it is on the body, it looks the same," Donovan replied, pulling out a photograph of the number burned into Greta Bauer's abdomen and setting it alongside.

"The "A" and the numbers are identical. Same size, same everything."

They compared a photo of the footprints found at the factory with the impressions from the boot casting made near Greta Bauer's garden. To no one's surprise, they also appeared to match.

"Well, here's what we know," said Donovan. "Both victims emigrated here from Poland in the early 50's. And both were fairly on in years although ours was nearly ten years older than Dulecki. He was just hitting retirement age."

"Not really. As it turns out, his wife admitted he lied about his age by ten years so he could keep working."

Donovan scribbled in his notebook.

"Well, there's also the cut-off hair. The naked thing. But, the real puzzle is the brands. Any idea what they mean?" asked O'Neil.

"Wish we did. So far we've come up with everything under the sun," said Scully, pulling several stapled printouts from the file. "For example, it's a specimen number for something called Cantharus auritulus from the Malacology Collection at the Academy of Natural Sciences in Philadelphia. It's also a filing I.D. number for the Canadian Energy Board. Then there's an ARKive Wildlife Photo Image Number for a video of a Bittern – that's some kind of bird. Want me to go on?"

"That won't be necessary," said O'Neil.

O'Neil drove them over to the Cook County Morgue on Chicago's west side. They parked along side an uninspired, modern building dominated by a tapered, bright blue roof that seemed to start at the foundation and climb high into the trees where it was lopped off flat. The sign on the iron fence surrounding the lawn proclaimed the building: *Office of the Medical Examiner*. A cadaverous little man wearing a white lab coat and thick glasses met them at the reception desk. His identification badge read; *Stanley LeBarge - Assistant Medical Examiner.*

They followed LeBarge down a corridor to a large autopsy room where he opened one of the many refrigerated compartments and rolled out the stainless steel shelf containing the remains of Milos Dulecki.

"We do over 5,000 autopsies every year, but I don't remember anything like this," said LeBarge, pushing up his glasses. "He's really busted up."

He reached for the zipper on the body bag, pausing to evaluate the uneasiness of his visitors. "Ready?"

Donovan and Scully nodded and the LeBarge slowly pulled down the zipper to reveal the white, lifeless face of Milos Dulecki first and then his grotesquely misshapen body.

"Geez," said Scully, accelerating his gum-chewing speed. "He's busted up all right."

"Blunt force trauma," said LeBarge, looking over his glasses. "We had to straighten his arms and legs to get him on the tray – they were arranged in such odd angles."

LeBarge lifted one of the arms. Bone shards puncturing the skin were everywhere. "It's fairly obvious he was struck repeatedly with a club of some sort," he said. "But, what's really quite fascinating are the bruises on the opposite side of each broken limb."

Donovan moved closer.

"See these impressions about a foot apart on the back of the arm? Apparently the killer elevated each limb with something, you know, to get the same effect as a sawhorse, so that the bones would snap in two more cleanly when he brought the weapon down on them. Let me show you."

The detectives followed the LeBarge across the room to a huge glowing, light box on the wall. Arranged there were several x-rays of the victim's arms and legs revealing dozens of fractures.

"Just like snapping a stick over your knee," said Scully.

Donovan returned to the body and studied it. "Do you have everything collected at the crime scene?"

"Of course. Everything was bagged and tagged."

"Could I see it, please?"

LeBarge left and returned a few minutes later carrying a carton labeled, Dulecki, Milos.

Donovan found Dulecki's clothing and a work shoe in one plastic bag. Another contained his personal belongings: watch, wallet, keys, half a pack of Marlboro Lights, a small amount of cash, some change and a book of matches imprinted with Polaski's Bar in fat, red letters. Several lengths of polyethylene rope were individually bagged. Each was neatly knotted.

"Bowlines," said Scully.

CHAPTER 16

Scully pulled off I-94 at an exit several miles past Baraboo, Wisconsin on their drive back to Eau Claire. Donovan had dozed off while studying his notes and woke with a start just as the Crown Vic pulled into a roadside cafe that advertised itself as the Wigwam Diner.

"I could use some coffee and something to eat." Scully said. "You hungry?"

"I could eat," Donovan replied. "I'll drive the rest of the way. You must be bushed."

The Wigwam was brightly lit and smelled of fried foods and cleaning agents. Country western music whispered in the background as customers ate and chatted or sat alone reading newspapers. The detectives took a booth near a table of regulars nursing cups of coffee and arguing good-naturedly. They studied the placemat menus until they were greeted by a world-weary waitress identified as Betty by the nametag on in her pink uniform.

"Welcome to The Wigwam, boys." She set glasses of water in front of them and took an order pad from her matching apron. "Know what'cha want?"

"Coffee for starters and a cheeseburger," Scully replied.

"Chicken sandwich on whole wheat and a small salad," said Donovan.

"You both look like high test, right," she said, seeing their haggard appearance.

They nodded and Betty disappeared.

"Bet you're glad to take a break. What dya think? Another couple hours?" asked Donovan, already knowing the answer but trying to make conversation.

"'Bout that."

Betty reappeared, filled two coffee cups and left the pot. They soon found themselves listening to the rapidly changing, free-for-all conversation at the nearby table.

"Saw on the news some nut job murdered a guy and branded him with some kind of serial number," proclaimed a pudgy, grizzled man wearing a Green Bay Packer stocking cap.

"Branded him? Where," asked a man munching on a donut.

"On his butt?" asked another.

"No, I mean where did it happen?" asked donut.

"Chicago. An old guy. Found his body in an empty factory. Somebody tied 'em up, lopped off his hair and beat the living shit out of him. Broke every bone in his body," the Packer fan replied.

"Doesn't take long for the word to get out, does it," said Scully.

"They know what the number means?" asked another, spitting tobacco juice into a paper cup.

"Not a clue," replied the Packer fan.

"Do you suppose it's some kind of coded message?" suggested another picking his teeth with the corner of a match book cover.

"Damned if I know," the fan replied.

"You know where each number stands for a different letter. One for A. Two for B and so on," said matchbook.

Donovan and Scully locked eyes and sat a little more erect in the booth.

"What's the number?" asked matchbook, removing a fresh napkin from the dispenser and clicking open a ballpoint.

"Hell. I can't remember what I had for breakfast," said tobacco juice with a yellowish brown grin.

Betty brought the men a fresh pot of coffee. "There's a morning newspaper in the back. Might be in there," she said.

Donovan turned in the booth to face the group. "A18733," he called.

The coffee group looked up as if they were puppets with their heads all on the same string.

"I'm sure," said Donovan.

Matchbook wrote the number on the napkin while the Packer fan listed the entire alphabet from A to Z on the back of an envelope and numbered each letter sequentially from 1 to 26. Soon they were all doodling. Donovan and Scully did the same on their menus until their meals came.

"These guys might be on to something," Scully said, biting into his cheeseburger. "Know anything about coding messages?"

"I know it can get pretty sophisticated," Donovan replied. "Did you read Bletchley Park?"

Scully shook his head.

"True story. A bunch of British mathematical geniuses cracked the Nazi's secret code. Everyone thought it was impossible, but they did it."

Donovan stabbed his salad and continued talking. "The German's had this thing called an enigma machine. Don't know how it worked, but it mixed up messages into a code that supposedly could only be unmixed and decoded by another enigma machine. But those Brits did it and helped win the war."

They finished eating, left the waitress a nice tip and nodded to the table regulars who by now had abandoned their code breaking efforts and moved onto arguing about the size of the white tail population for the hunting season.

Scully doodled number and letter combinations in his notebook all the while Donovan drove the remaining two hours back to Eau Claire. Neither of them could let go of the idea that the Wigwam regulars might have been onto something.

The early morning streets were empty when they crossed the Chippewa River to Barstow Street and continued through downtown Eau Claire. By the time they arrived at Police Headquarters, the mysterious number and circumstances that linked the murders had been sent to every police department in North America by the FBI's National Crime Information Center.

Both men were exhausted. "Let's get some shut eye and meet back here around noon," said Donovan. "Maybe the NCIC bulletin will have scared something up by then."

Scully drove to the furnished studio apartment he had rented after splitting with his wife when their marriage counseling didn't work. He had planned to buy a home with the very hefty inheritance he had received when his mother passed away, but never seemed to get around to it. Expensive clothes and cars were more interesting.

Donovan kept the cruiser and drove across town to his two-story colonial. He parked in the driveway so the noisy garage door wouldn't wake Tess.

"What time is it?" she mumbled when he crawled into bed.

"After three. Sorry, I didn't mean to wake you," he said.

"Did you catch the bad guy?" she whispered, half asleep.

"No. But, we know a little more about him than we did 24-hours ago. He's one sick puppy."

Donovan told her about Milos Dulecki.

"Poor guy. Did he leave a family?"

"A wife and two married daughters. He was just about to retire."

"I think you got the investigation you always wanted, Copper," she whispered. "Forget Dillinger. This guy is scary."

Donovan put his hands behind him and buried his head in the pillow. "Scary and very, very sick," he said, staring into the darkness.

"What's next?" asked Tess.

"Well, with three victims, he qualifies as a full fledged serial killer so now I suppose the FBI will want in on it."

"You don't sound thrilled."

"I'm not. I know they can help, but I don't want to be pushed into a background role."

"Is that what they do? Take over?"

"Not if I can help it. I want to get this guy myself."

"Any new ideas on the number?" she asked, steering him away from the FBI.

"Scully's checked it seven ways from Sunday. All we come up with are numbers for stuff like scientific reports, a wildlife video and other meaningless crap."

"Well, it must mean something, Copper. You'll figure it out," she said, patting his shoulder.

Donovan closed his eyes and tried to sleep. Time was running out. He was in a race to stop the killer before his life as a cop was over. Even if the killings went on, Donovan knew his own finish line was getting closer.

CHAPTER 17

"Good morning, Eau Claire! It's six o'clock." Donovan opened one eye and listened to the weather, a far-too-upbeat jingle for Folger's coffee and the national headlines.

"Locally, WBIZ has breaking news that the slaying of a Chicago tire worker reported yesterday may be related to the gruesome murder of Greta Bauer in Eau Claire several weeks ago and one other murder." Michael Donovan sat bolt upright in bed. "Ah, shit," he said.

"The mutilated body of the victim, identified by Chicago law enforcement authorities as Milos Dulecki, was discovered in an abandoned factory building on that city's north side.

"Dulecki was branded with a serial-like number, A18733, with a type of branding iron normally used to identify livestock. WBIZ has now learned that an identical brand was also burned into the body of Greta Bauer as well as an unidentified man murdered earlier in Oklahoma. In each case, the victims were bound and gagged, their hair was cut off, and they were left for discovery."

Donovan threw off the covers and headed for the shower. "Word's leaked about the branding. I better get in there. Make some coffee will ya, Tess?"

When he called-in halfway to the station, the dispatcher redirected him to the Greta Bauer cottage. He discovered why when he turned onto the alley and saw the news crews and their satellite trucks already setting up.

Donovan pulled the cruiser to a stop next to Scully's red Porsche by the garden.

"It's already getting crazy," said Scully, jumping into the front seat. "The chief is even getting calls at home. Everyone wants to know why we withheld information about the vegetable lady's death. He wants you to explain things. Set everyone's mind at ease."

"This could be unpleasant," Donovan replied, scanning the growing crowd. A knot grew in his stomach.

"I'm going to finish my coffee," said Donovan.

"You mean stall," jabbed Scully.

"That works too," said Donovan. "I need to think it through for a minute. Don't want to say anything stupid."

"Just tell 'em what you told O'Neil in Chicago," said Scully. "Tell 'em we kept it quiet so that only the police and killer knew about the branding. That way if someone claimed to be the killer, we would know if they were legit."

Donovan finished his coffee and wrote in his notebook while Scully got out of the cruiser to tell the growing group of newsies that a statement would be made in a couple of minutes.

"They'd like you to stand in front of the cottage," Scully said when Donovan finally emerged.

Donovan walked slowly to the chosen spot surrounded by cameras, lights, hand-held boom mikes and, of course, reporters. He was suddenly nervous.

"I'll make a brief statement then open it up for any questions," he said, trying to sound calm and authoritative. "As many of you have already reported, the murder of Greta Bauer here earlier this month appears to be linked to two other murders. The first was an unidentified man in Oklahoma in early July."

Donovan checked his notes. "Yesterday, upon learning of yet another murder victim in Chicago that exhibited similar crime scene characteristics, Eau Claire Police detectives met with the Chicago police and determined that each of the murders were likely perpetrated by the same killer or killers."

"In each case, the victims, one female, two male, were advanced in age and murdered in different but very brutal manners and probably tortured. I would prefer not go into more detail on specifics of this aspect of the investigation at this time."

"What about the branding?" clamored some of the reporters.

"I'll get to that."

"How would you characterize the murders?"

"I can't say. However, I can tell you that each victim was found naked, bound, their hair had been roughly cut off and their mouths were taped shut. It's as if they were prepared for execution."

The group of reporters quieted noticeably for a few seconds as they wrote frantically into the note pads.

"What about the branding?" a reporter demanded again.

"All three had been deceased for several days before their bodies were discovered," Donovan continued purposefully, determined to maintain control. "The most distinctive similarity was an identical serial-like number that had been branded on their persons–in half-inch figures; the letter "A" followed by the numbers 18733. At this time we have no idea of the significance of this but continue to investigate possibilities."

Donovan sighed and looked at Scully standing nearby who nodded approvingly.

"Questions?" he asked. Suddenly the air exploded in a cacophony of voices–each trying to out shout the others.

Scully stepped forward with his arms held high. "C'mon people. One at a time. Give Detective Donovan a chance to answer."

Donovan nodded gratefully to his partner. "You," he said, pointing to a reporter barely old enough to shave who he recognized from the local television station, WEAU.

"Many residents are upset that the Eau Claire Police intentionally withheld knowledge of the number found branded on Greta Bauer," the young man said. "Some believe that it might have been recognized by a local who could have provided critical information about the identity of the killer. Would you comment on that?"

"It was a tough call but we thought it best to keep it quiet initially to aid in our investigation. Often in sensational murders such as these, people with absolutely no involvement come forward and falsely claim responsibility causing us to waste valuable time. Anticipating this possibility, we believed it would be helpful to withhold a key piece of evidence that only the killer would have knowledge of. That way we could invest our time in finding the real perpetrator rather than chasing dead ends."

The second Donovan paused, the group of reporters erupted in a din of more questions.

"You," he said motioning to a stunning blond who looked more movie star than reporter.

"But, isn't it true that the number could have had significance to someone in the community? Something that could lead to the identification of the executioner?" she challenged.

Donovan paused and made little effort to hide his irritation "As I said, we agonized over that and believed that if the killer was local, someone would step forward with information based on the other known facts. Perhaps an acquaintance of the victim would share information with us, or a neighbor."

"Did they?"

"No."

"So if the executioner struck again and left the same brand on another victim in Eau Claire and it turned out that someone here could have recognized the number, that would have been acceptable?"called another voice.

Donovan's irritation grew visibly. "Of course not. It was a judgment call and I'd like to point out that the subsequent murder took place in Chicago. In view of that, I am satisfied that the perpetrator is very unlikely to be a resident of Eau Claire."

"What do you believe is the significance of the number?"

"We're still trying to determine that," Donovan replied. "We're exploring every possibility."

"What have you found so far?"

"It could be almost anything," said Donovan, flipping through his notebook. "Among other things for example, it's a specimen number for something called Cantharus Auritulus from the Malacology Collection at the Academy of Natural Sciences in Philadelphia."

Immediately several reporters shouted questions simultaneously. Donovan held up his hands.

"Please, let me continue. It's also a filing I.D. number for the Canadian Energy Board. And it's an ARKive Wildlife Photo Image Number for a video of a Bittern – that's some kind of bird. There are many others, as well."

"Are there any areas you're considering that you haven't yet looked into?"

Wishing instantly he had avoided a direct answer, but worn

down by the incessant questions, Donovan blurted out, "A code of some sort?"

"What kind of code?"

"Wish I knew. It's possible it's some kind of alpha-numeric code is all I can say. I don't know. Code breaking is not my area of expertise," he said, now sensing again that he was beginning to lose control.

Donovan continued answering questions for several more minutes about the significance of the cropped hair, the age, the background of the victims and other probes requiring speculation. He vaguely responded to each until it was clear that the reporters no longer had any questions of significance to throw at him.

"Have you begun to develop the executioner's profile?" called one reporter.

"We'll be working on that. That ought to do it for now. Thank you," he said, stepping away to join Scully near the Crown Vic.

"You did good, partner," said Scully.

"I feel like a weenie at a weenie roast. I shouldn't have used the term 'execution' or brought up the code thing. Now we're going to be sorting through crackpot theories until the cows come home."

CHAPTER 18

Chief Krumenauer was waiting in his office when Donovan and Scully dragged into the station after the crime scene briefing.

"I've lost count of how many phone calls we've had from locals who watched you on the news," he said. "Most of them were pissed off that we withheld information. One was from a toy collector."

"A toy collector?" asked Scully.

The chief pursed his lips and smiled sardonically. "Yeah. He offered to loan us his Captain Midnight Secret Decoder Ring."

"When can he have it here?" asked Donovan, collapsing into a worn, leather chair.

"Do you really think it could be a code?" asked Krumenauer.

"I don't know. Could be anything. But, we better pull out all the stops to check it out."

"Is Belchy Park still operating?" asked Scully, popping a stick of gum.

"That's Bletchley Park and no it isn't," said the chief.

"It was shutdown when World War II ended," added Donovan.

"Jesus. Am I the only one who doesn't know about this stuff?" asked Scully.

"Yes, but you dress nice," jabbed Donovan.

"The CIA may have resources we can tap into," the chief offered. "Make some calls, will you guys? Maybe they'll give us a hand."

The detectives returned to their office where Scully faxed a photo of the boot prints found in the factory to forensics at the Wisconsin State Crime Lab in Madison for identification and to have it compared to the boot print found in the woods behind Greta Bauer's garden. Donovan got the number for the CIA in Washington and began the arduous task of finding someone there who was knowledgeable about code breaking. After several transfers and callbacks, it was nearly 6:00 in the evening when he finally connected with an agent named Brady Collins.

Collins was familiar with the murders and anxious to help, but not optimistic. "Not much to go on. If it's a string code, the sample isn't long enough to establish a pattern. We could run it through known codes but it's a real long shot. There are thousands."

"I'd appreciate any help you can offer. I figured it was a long shot." He left his contact information and set the phone back in its' cradle.

"Maybe we should work at the more obvious," he said to Scully. "See what you can dig up on branding iron manufacturers. Send out close-up pictures of the brand. Maybe one of them will recognize it and have a record of a customer who bought one."

"I'm on it," Scully replied, turning to his computer and signing on to the Internet.

The desk Sergeant appeared at Donovan's desk with a stack of pink message slips. "You're famous," he said. "These are just since you've been on the last call. Apparently every major news program in the country picked up the story. You've got offers to help break the code, suggestions of what it could be–even theories about the identity of the killer."

Donovan's bushy, red eyebrows climbed up his forehead in surprise. He handed a stack to Scully. After reading for several minutes, they decided to divide the messages into two categories; serious offers of help and crackpots.

The crackpot stack grew fastest. Several suggested the murders were part of a Satanic ritual. Another was equally certain that aliens were responsible and that the number provides the coordinates to their galaxy.

Throughout the day, the pile of messages grew faster than they could be read so, when Tess called to tell Donovan to come home, he happily obliged and even offered to stop at Jimmy Woo's Pagoda Restaurant for takeout.

Donovan trudged into the house with a brown paper bag filled with more food than they would ever eat. Tess was waiting with a Bushmill's.

"Hi babe," he said, kissing her forehead.

She handed him the drink and told him to relax in his "cave" while she warmed up the dinner. Donovan kicked off his shoes, took off his coat and tie and dropped into the green club chair in his den. It was heaven–every hump and dent perfectly fit the contours of his slowly widening body. The Bushmills felt wonderful on his tongue and sliding down his throat. At $65 a bottle, it was one of his few indulgences.

"Pour one for yourself and join me," he called to Tess.

Minutes later she was curled up in her wingback by the fireplace across from him. "Big day, Copper. Bet you're tired," she said soothingly.

"Looks like we have a serial killer," he said somberly.

"You think there'll be more murders?"

"The killer is so methodical. So dedicated. It makes me think he's just getting started."

She could see the stress in his face as he sipped his drink and waited for him to continue. She learned long ago that sometimes it was best to just listen.

"He's certainly isn't shy about advertising that he's the same guy. The branding iron thing is like spittin' in my eye and saying 'catch me if you can'."

"Any new theories on what the numbers mean?"

"Not really. But, we're getting plenty of suggestions ever since the media tied the murders together and I suggested the possibility of some kind of secret code."

"Yes. I saw," Tess replied, the corners of her mouth raised slightly.

Donovan read her expression and raised his eyebrows with an equally subtle rebuff. "Hey, it could be a code Tess. Trouble is, now everyone from Satan worshipers to aliens from outer space are being thrown out there."

"I'm sorry, Copper. It's just that I could see it coming," Tess said, suitably chastised but still grinning.

Donovan ignored her. "I talked to the code experts at the CIA and they're going to run it through their computers, but they're not expecting anything. Sample's too short to develop a pattern or something like that.

"Some guy in New Jersey called to offer the use of his Captain Midnight Secret Decoder Ring," chuckled Donovan, taking a sip of whiskey. I may take him up on it."

The Bushmills worked its' magic and he began to relax. "I could sleep for a week."

Tess topped off his drink and went to the kitchen to see to dinner while Donovan turned on the news.

"Tess. I'm on CNN," he called.

"You have been all day."

"Oh my God! They've given him a name," he bellowed. "The Executioner."

"Appropriately grim. But, I think you get the credit for that," said Tess, carrying two loaded dinner plates into the den.

Donovan turned up the sound just in time to hear himself answer the last question at the chaotic crime scene before the picture switched to a talking head in the CNN studio.

"I sound like a dork–detective trying to impress them with my mastery of cop-speak," he said, digging into his chow mein.

"I don't agree," Tess protested. "I thought you sounded very erudite. Very professional."

"I was nervous," he said, turning his attention back to the television.

"In both cases, the naked victims were bound with rope and duct tape and their hair was crudely chopped away as if, according to Detective Donovan, they were being prepared for 'execution'. Most distinctively, the executioner left his tell-tale alpha-numeric signature branded into the victims – A18733."

Donovan ate without tasting the food. The gravity of what was happening began to really sink in for the first time – this serial killer was about to redefine a banal, unmemorable career and change his life forever.

"Be careful what you wish for," Tess had said. He was learning how right she was.

CHAPTER 19

The Athena was busy as usual on Monday morning. "Ready to hit it?" asked Donovan, sliding into the booth where Scully was waiting.

"Been hittin' it. Or trying to," Scully replied.

Stavros brought coffee and took their orders.

"Whacha got?" asked Donovan.

"What would you like to know about branding irons?"

"Everything."

"Well, there are branding irons for livestock. Some brand meat. Furniture makers and woodworkers even brand their furniture and stuff. There are electric branding irons, branding irons you heat in a fire. Propane branding irons. They even have 'em for livestock that freeze the brand onto the poor critters."

Donovan sipped his coffee, listening intently.

"You can get a custom branding iron. Just send 'em a drawing. There's even NFL logos."

"For die-hard fans," grinned Donovan.

"But, what you really want to know is that I found several outfits that sell branding irons with half-inch letters."

"Like how many?"

"Not certain, but we can narrow it down. For starters, I doubt that our guy used an electric branding iron, so we can eliminate a few of them right there."

"Yeah. He'd probably go propane."

"Right. And we can eliminate the outfits that only make custom brands. Ya know, like the rocking R, or the double T. More than likely then, I figure we can narrow our search to non-electric branding iron manufacturers that offer half-inch letters.

"They'd have a record of making a brand for A18733?"

"It's possible," Scully replied. "But, if I was the killer and I wanted to buy a branding iron, I'd get one with interchangeable letters so I didn't leave such an obvious trail."

"Can you buy them retail?" asked Scully.

"Looks that way, partner. Still, it's worth checking around to see if the number is on file somewhere for a custom made."

"I suppose, but I wouldn't be optimistic. I'm thinking our boy is up there on the intelligence scale," offered Donovan.

Stavros brought their orders and freshened their coffees.

"So you have some thoughts about our guy?" asked Scully, salting his eggs.

"The murders took no small amount of planning," Donovan replied. "The victims were methodically subdued and executed. And he was careful not to get caught. That should indicate a high level of intelligence. Don't you think?"

"Makes sense."

"That much planning means he must have done his homework. He selected his victims and scouted them out. They weren't random."

"Do you think he knew them?" asked Scully.

"Unlikely. The vics were hundreds of miles away from each other and at least two of them had been long-time residents where they lived. They didn't seem to know each other. Had no reason to."

"The two we know about were European immigrants and elderly," said Scully. "Hate crime, maybe?"

"Must be something like that to do the things to them that he did. Making sure they died slow, painful deaths."

"Why the branding? And the hair?"

"My guess is he wanted to send a message. Wanted the world to know that the murders were related."

"Or maybe he wanted to make certain he got credit for them," added Scully.

"Could be. He wouldn't be the first."

"It worked," said Scully, popping the last bite of toast into his mouth. "The hair?"

"Trophies," Donovan replied. "Lots of serial killers have kept mementos of their victims. Photographs. Jewelry. Body parts. Whole bodies for that matter. Sometimes they take clothing that they can get off on later."

"Tufts of bloody, gray hair, though?"

"I've read about worse," said Donovan, throwing a few dollars on the table. "My treat. Let's get to work."

They briefed Chief Krumenauer and returned to their small office. Scully concentrated on contacting the most likely branding iron manufacturers and faxed photos of the victim's brands to see if they could be identified.

Donovan called Brady Collins at the CIA to see if he had made any progress making anything out of A18733. He hadn't, so Donovan began going through the pile of pink message slips. He worked his way through the stack one at a time and called the most likely. Most were genuine attempts to help, like the guy from North Carolina who told him that A18733 matched an after market part number for a 54 Chevy. More than a few of the suggestions were utter nonsense. None led anywhere until he came to a message that had gone unnoticed for two days from a man named Abe Stein. It read simply; 'may know origin of tattoo number'. The return phone number had a New Jersey area code.

Donovan called.

"Hello," answered the soft, gentle voice of an elderly man.

"Is this Abraham Stein?"

"Yes."

"Mr. Stein, this is Detective Michael Donovan of the Eau Claire Police Department in Wisconsin. You left a message indicating you may have information about a murder investigation we're conducting."

"Yes. About the number."

"A18733."

"I can give you one possibility you may not have considered."

"Go on, sir," said Donovan.

"It may be a number from Auschwitz. Used by the Nazis to identify prisoners."

CHAPTER 20

Donovan's heart raced.

"Just one minute, Mr. Stein," he said, frantically waving at Scully as he switched to speakerphone.

"You say a prisoner number from Auschwitz, Mr. Stein? Are you certain?" asked Donovan, writing 'Auschwitz' on a legal pad.

"Yes. I was there in 1944 and 1945," the old man replied matter-of-factly.

Donovan and Scully locked eyes.

"And you remember the numbers?" Donovan said more than asked.

"The Nazis tattooed on my arm number A18734. Only one number away from the one left on your victims. I suppose that is why I noticed it."

Scully wrote 'A18734' in large block letters on the yellow pad and jotted 'Abraham Stein' next to it.

"I don't know what to say, Mr. Stein. It was before my time, but I've seen the documentaries on television and read accounts –heard the stories. It must have been horrible," said Donovan, taking pains to be respectful.

"It was a horrible time for many people. A nightmare," Stein replied without elaborating.

"I'm sure this is painful for you, sir. I am very grateful that you called."

"I thought you should know. I don't know if it means anything, but this I thought you should know."

"It could be important. I don't know. We've had so little to go on. Do you know more about the numbers? Is there a list somewhere?"

"Perhaps. I don't know."

"Do you happen to remember the man who was in line ahead of you that day when they, the Nazis, tattooed you?"

"That I have wondered since the newspaper I read. About the

number and the murders," It was a long time ago. I am an old man, now."

"So you don't recall who the man was? The one ahead of you?"

"The boy. Little more than boys we were then. The Nazis took us. Came to the ghetto and put us in trucks. Took our families. One hour only we had a single suitcase to pack. They took us to the trains and pushed us into cattle cars. So crowded, there was only room to stand. No water. No toilets. Barely enough air to breathe. For days we traveled like that – in our own filth. Many died. When we arrived, my mother and sisters were taken away. I never saw them again. It was chaos. Only the men and older boys remained. Anyone that boy could have been."

"When did they put the number, the tattoo, on you?"

"Shortly after we got off the train. We were forced to strip naked and they inspected us. I only remember that the boy ahead of me had a large birthmark on his back because the guards made a spectacle of him. My father and others who were sick they took away. I was selected for labor. They shaved our heads. Later some of us were taken for medical experiments."

"Your father?" asked Donovan.

"My father I never saw again. I learned that he and my mother were both gassed. My little sisters were identical twins. Others said the doctors did things to them before they were killed."

"I'm sorry to ask you to remember this," apologized Donovan.

"I never forget," Stein said solemnly.

"Was there anyone who remained in your group that you can recall? Someone who might remember who A18733 was?"

"Someone still living?"

"Yes. Who we could talk to?"

"I don't know. So few of us survived," said Stein. "Some starved or died from disease. Others were killed. I doubt that any survived the medical experiments."

Donovan looked up a Scully and saw that a subtle change had come over him. His face wore a somber mask he'd never seen before.

"We were liberated on May 5th, 1945," Stein continued. We

stayed in camps for several months while what to do with us the Allies decided. No families we had left, no homes to go to – nothing. In time we went in many directions. A few ended up in the United States. I came to New Jersey. The Red Cross located a relative here who gave me a home and a job. Only a few survivors I have met over the years, but I could ask around."

"And there aren't any records anywhere that you know of? A record of who the numbers were given?"

"I don't know. The Nazis took our names. I remember they wrote them in a ledger, but it may have been destroyed. When they learned how close the allies were getting, they destroyed what evidence they could. Including many prisoners."

There was a moment of silence. "I'm sorry I am not more help," lamented Stein.

"You've given us a lot of help, Mr. Stein," said Donovan. "Just one more question. The birthmark you saw on the boy ahead of you, can you describe it?

"I don't recall that it looked like anything. It was quite large and I think it was on the upper right half of his back."

"If you can recall anything later, you'll let me know, right? Sometimes people remember things after a while."

"Of course. I will call again if I do."

Donovan hung up and turned to Scully who was staring out the window. "What'ya think, Brian?"

"Feels like it could be something," he replied without looking away.

"All of the victims would have been alive during the war and they were all European. It's possible they could have been in Auschwitz," Donovan said.

"They were all found naked with their hair cut off like the Jewish prisoners," said Scully. "But, they weren't Jews, were they?"

"Not everyone sent to concentration camps were Jews. Something like 6 million of them were–that's how many died anyway," said Donovan. "But there were gypsies, political prisoners, and captured soldiers. Even the mentally ill."

Scully pulled a stick of Juicy Fruit from a pack but turned it in his hand instead of unwrapping it. "But, wouldn't they all have had numbers tattooed on their arms if they had been prisoners in Auschwitz?"

"I don't know, but at least we have something to go on now. Let's see what we can get on the Nazi numbering system and look closer at the victim's backgrounds. Contact the Immigration and Naturalization Service. See what we can find."

CHAPTER 21

The United States Immigration and Naturalization Service has 18,000 employees. After wading through several layers of them with phone calls and callbacks, Donovan found himself talking with Francis Brubaker, the Deputy Director of Field Operations. Brubaker spoke in a clipped, edgy voice and exuded a sense of her own importance.

Donovan introduced himself and provided a lengthy explanation of the background of the murders. Brubaker was intrigued. Her manner softened.

"So you want to know if we have documentation on any of the murder victims?" she asked when he finished.

"Exactly. We know they were European immigrants, but we're trying to find another connection beyond the identical number left branded on them. We have reason to believe that it may have something to do with Auschwitz."

"They were in the concentration camp?" she asked.

"We don't know. But, we researched it and what we do know is that the number is consistent with the identification numbering convention used by the Nazis there."

"Fax what you have to us here, Detective Donovan. I'll see what we have, if anything."

Twenty minutes later, Scully ran the last of the police reports through the fax machine. One from Oklahoma. One from Chicago and the report made out by the detectives themselves.

When Donovan arrived at his desk the next morning, there was a message on his answering machine in the now familiar voice of Francis Brubaker.

"Detective Donovan, this is Deputy Director Brubaker. We have some information that may help you with your investigation. Call me back when you receive this."

Donovan punched in the number and waited for Brubaker to pick up.

"We found immigration records on Greta Bauer and Milos Dulecki," she said.

"Great."

"Greta Bauer legally immigrated to the U.S. from Poland. She came through the Port of New York on March 3, 1951 on the French ship, the Flandre. Both Bauer and Dulecki qualified for entry under The Displaced Persons Act of 1948."

"Slow down. I want to make sure I get this right," pleaded Donovan, writing furiously in his notebook.

"Look, Detective Donovan. I'll fax you what I have on both of these individuals. There isn't much, but I'll send what I have."

Minutes later, Donovan was standing at the fax machine reading the documents as they came in. He was still reading the visa application on Greta Bauer when the machine spit out the final page. He returned to his desk and organized the documents in two neat folders on which he wrote Greta Bauer and Milos Dulecki in careful block lettering,

He was lost in reading from the open file in front of him when a grease-stained, brown sack plopped onto his desk. He looked up to see Scully. "Bacon and egg on toast. No butter. No salt."

"Thanks."

Scully looked haggard. "Late night with the ladies?" asked Donovan.

"Nah. Didn't sleep so hot."

"I have some reading for you." Donovan handed Scully the file on Milos Dulecki from the INS. "This just came in. I'm boning up on Greta Bauer. You can start with Dulecki, okay? When we're finished, we'll swap."

"What am I looking for?" asked Scully opening his own brown bag and retrieving a bagel with cream cheese.

"Your guess is as good as mine, partner," Donovan replied, biting a corner off half a sandwich.

Except for the ruffling of paper, the office was silent as the detectives read, munched on their breakfasts and jotted down notes. Most of the documents contained hand-written annotations and bore the smudged, uneven imprints of various official rubber stamps. Finally, Donovan closed his file and looked up just as Scully cried out, "Bingo".

"Got something?"

"Dulecki was a dairy farmer in Poland before the war," said Scully. "The Germans recruited him as a policeman and put him in Krakow to help guard the Jewish ghetto they set up there. Later he was sent to Auschwitz, but as a guard, not a prisoner. That's why he wasn't Jewish. He was once looked at by the OSI for possible war crimes as a Nazi but was cleared. Not enough evidence."

"What about you? You turn up anything on Greta Bauer?" asked Scully.

"Nothing we didn't know," Donovan replied just as his phone rang.

"Detective Donovan."

"This is Abraham Stein, Detective Donovan. We talked several days ago about a murder investigation. Remember?"

"Yes. Of course, Mr. Stein," said Donovan as he hurriedly reached for his notebook and flipped through the densely inked, wrinkled pages.

"I made some inquiries of several synagogues who may have yet members who were sent from Krakow to Auschwitz at the time I was there," said Stein. "I thought perhaps one may have the number you are looking for."

Donovan felt his heart speed. "Any luck"

"No. I am sorry. None of them were A18733. But, one of them remembered a boy who was with us from his town who had a large birthmark on his back."

Donovan's heart was in his throat now. "Did he remember the boy's name?"

"Solomon Geller. He remembers that Geller was taken from Auschwitz near the end. Loaded on a train with hundreds of others. He never heard his name again. All of them were probably killed."

"Can you spell Geller for me, Mr. Stein?"

"It is either G-E-L-L-E-R or A-R. The spelling of names is often corrupted over time."

"Do you have the name of the individual who told you about Geller? His phone number and address? The synagogue he goes to?"

"His name is Herman Roth. He lives here in New Brunswick. I don't have his address, but I know he is a member of Emanu-El Synagogue. I can give you his telephone number."

Donovan wrote the number below the name in his notebook. "Thank you, Mr. Stein. You've been a big help."

Herman Roth answered the phone after several rings. His voice was thin and weak and he sounded out of breath. Donovan introduced himself and confirmed everything Abraham Stein had told him.

"Did you know anyone else who was put on the train with Geller?" asked Donovan.

"No. Only Geller."

Donovan prodded and probed, but learned nothing more from Roth and thanked him for his time.

Francis Brubaker returned from her usual lunch of salad and ice tea in the INS cafeteria and saw the call message on her desk. A minute later she was on the phone with Donovan.

"Thank you for the information you sent, Miss Brubaker. You've been very helpful," he said.

"Glad I could be of help."

"I have another name for you," said Donovan.

"Another murder victim?"

"No. It might be a long shot, but this could be the man whose serial number was burned into them."

Brubaker was silent for a moment. "What do you have?" she finally asked.

"One Solomon Geller." Donovan provided the different

spellings. "We have reason to believe he might have been the prisoner at Auschwitz who was tattooed with the number that keeps turning up."

"How did you dig that up?" she asked, her tone suddenly cool.

"We got a call from a man in New Jersey who identified himself as Abraham Stein. He had been in Auschwitz during the war. He read about the murders and recognized that the number was the last one before his own in the sequence."

"Mr. Stein knew this... Solomon Geller?" she asked indifferently.

"He didn't remember the name. But, he remembered the man. Or, more accurately, the boy with a distinctive birthmark. They were both in their early teens."

"How did he come up with the name?" asked Brubaker.

"There are still a fair number of Auschwitz survivors living in the east," Donovan replied. "Mr. Stein queried several synagogues and another survivor stepped forward with the name of a man who matched the description; Solomon Geller."

"Do you know where Geller is today?" Brubaker probed.

"Don't know. So far we've turned up 16 in the U.S. And we're checking them out. I was hoping you could look into it on your end. Can you see what you can dig up?"

"I'll have to get back to you, detective."

"When?" he asked, sensing a reluctance.

"I can't say, right now. I'll have to talk with the Director.'"

"You didn't have to talk to the Director before," said Donovan after a thoughtful pause.

"It's policy, Detective Donovan."

"We have a serial killer on the loose, Ms. Brubaker."

"I'm well aware. I'll get back to you when I can, Detective," she said and hung up.

By noon of the following day, they learned that of the sixteen Solomon Gellers found, only three were the right age. Of those, two had never been outside the United States. A third had immigrated to the United States and New York after the war. A check with the Social Security database indicated he was recently deceased. Shortly after one o'clock, Donovan had his widow on the phone. Hannah Geller listened politely as he introduced himself.

"I see. You say a policeman you are," she replied cautiously in a heavy Brooklyn accent.

"Are you the widow of Solomon Geller who was imprisoned at Auschwitz?"

"Yes," she reluctantly acknowledged.

"It's very important that I speak with you about him," pressed Donovan.

"Why in Solomon are you so interested?" she replied.

"It's complicated," Donovan replied. "It would be best if I talked with you in person."

CHAPTER 22

Their plane touched down at JFK on schedule. Donovan and Scully picked up a rental car and found their way to New York 27 for the short drive to Brooklyn. To their surprise, they were parking on Carol Street in front of the Solomon Geller residence in Crown Heights within minutes of the appointed 11:00 a.m. meeting time.

Turn-of-the-century brownstones stood shoulder-to-shoulder on the broad, tree-lined street. Each with masonry steps that led to massive wooden doors poised regally under carved stone entries.

Hannah Geller had been watching the street from an iron-barred bay window and opened the door before they could knock. Donovan could tell the tiny, red-haired woman had once been pretty.

"I'm Detective Donovan and this is Detective Scully of the Eau Claire Police Department in Wisconsin. Thank you for seeing us."

She examined their shields. "Please come in. Such a long way to come. From Wisconsin I know nothing. How I can help you I can't imagine."

Donovan smiled. "Is there someplace we can talk?"

"Of course. Come." They followed her to a small kitchen in the rear through a living room filled wall-to-wall with family photos and too much furniture.

"The sun is more brighter here," she said, directing them to chairs at the table already set with coffee cups and a plate of cookies.

"We're conducting an investigation and have reason to believe that information about your late husband might help us."

Her penciled eyebrows lifted.

"A few days ago we talked with a man in New Jersey. His name is Abraham Stein. He lived in Krakow during the war and may have known your husband. They were taken to Auschwitz and imprisoned there at the same time."

Mrs. Geller shifted in her chair.

"I hope this isn't too difficult to talk about," said Donovan.

"Go on," she replied stoically.

"Mr. Stein recalled that Mr. Geller was the first man ahead of him in line when they were given–when they were tattooed with serial numbers. If that's true, the number on your husband's forearm would have been...."

"A18733," finished Mrs. Geller.

"So that *was* your husband's number?"

Her eyebrows lifted again. "My Solomon this man knew?"

"They were assigned the same type of work in the camp."

Her eyes glazed. "My Solomon he knew?"

"Apparently he did," said Donovan, sipping his coffee.

"My Solomon was forced to work in the crematorium."

"That's what Mr. Stein told us," said Donovan, checking his notebook.

"Here's the thing, Mrs. Geller," said Scully. "There have been three murders recently and the victims had your husband's Auschwitz number branded into their bodies. We're trying to figure out why. We are hoping you could help us."

Mrs. Geller suddenly stiffened. Donovan saw a look of surprise come over her.

"We believe the killer put the number there," said Scully.

"Why Solomon's number would they do this?"

"Think hard, ma'am. Did he belong to any organizations? That sort of thing?"

"The synagogue," she replied. "Solomon kept mostly to himself."

"No societies or brotherhoods or lodges. No organizations like B'nai B'rith?" asked Donovan. "Anything like that?"

The old lady shook her head.

"Is there anyone who knew your late husband that might help us? Anyone at all who knew him?"

Mrs. Geller quieted and stared out at the tiny yard separating her home from the row of brownstones across the way.

"Who there could be I have no idea."

She talked about Solomon's applicance business and Poland without revealing any more information of value. Finally, they thanked her for her time, left their cards and began the drive back to the airport. There were three hours before their return flight to Minneapolis, so when they saw a parking spot open up in front of a delicatessen on Flatbush Avenue, they took it. Large letters under a brightly painted sign read; Rosen's Kosher Deli. They both ordered pastrami on rye and took them to a table in the rear.

"So what'ya think?" asked Donovan, gesturing with a pickle wedge as he watched Scully take a huge bite of his sandwich.

"It's goob."

"No. I mean about Solomon Geller and the number. Maybe it's just a coincidence. I was hoping we finally had something to go on but we sure came up empty."

"Maybe we didn't push her hard enough."

"Can't get blood out of a turnip."

"Maybe we need to talk to more turnips."

"I'm listening."

She said there was no one else we could talk to who might know something, right?"

"Yeah."

"Then who are the people in all those pictures in her living room? Someone with about a hundred family photos must know someone who might know something. We have time to kill and precious little else to go on, I think we should chase this lead to the bitter end."

Donovan smiled. "You're right. He took out his notebook and cell phone, punched in Hannah Geller's phone number and waited. It was busy. He worked on his sandwich for a few minutes and called again. This time she answered on the third ring.

"Mrs. Geller, this is Detective Donovan again. I am sorry to bother you, but I wanted to ask you one more time to try to think of anyone else we might talk to. We were wondering about the people in your family photos..."

She cut him off. "Of anybody I don't know. If someone I think of, I will telephone." The phone went dead.

"Bring your sandwich," said Donovan.

Traffic was heavier on the way back. When they turned onto Carol Street, they found themselves stuck behind a double-parked delivery truck only a couple hundred feet from Mrs. Geller's brownstone.

"Mike. There! A white van parked in front. Some guy just got in," Scully screamed.

Donovan honked frantically to get the truck driver to move. Scully shoved the last of his sandwich in his mouth, threw open the car door and raced up the street. He was fifty feet away when the van shot away from the curb and pulled out into traffic.

By the time Donovan maneuvered around the delivery truck, the van had turned the corner and disappeared. Scully stood there breathing hard. He tossed the remains of the sandwich and jumped in when Donovan screeched to a stop. "Son of a bitch," he said. "We'll never catch up with him. Couldn't see the plate."

"Gotta try," said Donovan, slamming down the accelerator. Out of the corner of his eye, Scully saw Hannah Geller watching from a window as they pulled away.

They drove aimlessly for an hour before returning to the brownstone. There was no answer at the door so they separated and canvassed the neighborhood hoping to find anyone who knew the owner of a white Ford Econoline van. Most simply replied 'no' and closed the door. A man who lived across the street remembered seeing one now and then but didn't know who owned it and never noticed the driver.

Donovan was about to give up when he heard Scully's shrill whistle and looked up to see Mrs. Geller walking slowly toward home. He trotted across the street. "We were still in the neighborhood and have some time before we have to be at the airport. I thought we'd stop in again just to see if we can help you remember."

Hannah Geller's narrowed eyes glared from below pinched eyebrows. "I will phone if to my mind someone comes."

"Mrs. Geller, we saw a man get into a white van in front of your home and drive away. Can you tell us who it was?" asked Donovan as they climbed up the steps of the brownstone behind her.

"Anyone it could be," she replied, dismissing him with a wave of her hand and turning to unlock the door.

"You're certain you don't know anyone who drives a white van?" asked Donovan.

When she didn't answer, Donovan said, "May we come in?" She sighed heavily and motioned them to follow.

"If you don't mind," said Scully once they were inside, "we'd like to stay here in the living room. Maybe you could tell us who some of these people are in the photographs."

"Family," she replied. "Gone now are most of them. Some live in Poland. Some in Israel."

"Maybe one of them might talk to us. Might remember something you forgot," said Scully, now noticing that a handful of photos were missing from the picture arrangements on the wall. He moved closer and saw that hangers and nails still remained.

"Where are the pictures that used to be here and here?"

"They fell. The glass broke and ruined them. I had to throw them out."

"So the other pictures. You say that all of these people have either passed on or live in another part of the world?"

"A Ouija board I would need to talk again to most them."

She continued to stonewall them picture after picture. Each had passed away, moved away or she could no longer remember. They finally gave up. "Thank you for your time Mrs. Geller. Please remember to call if anything occurs to you that you think might help."

The second the door closed behind them, Donovan said, "Let's run a background on Solomon and Hannah Geller. See what we can dig up."

"Yeah. Something isn't right."

CHAPTER 23

Just minutes after their flight touched down at Minneapolis International Airport, an exhausted Donovan and Scully were back in the Crown Vic driving east on I-94. Donovan called Tess to tell her he'd be home in a couple of hours. Although it was later than Chief Krumenauer usually worked, Donovan also punched in his direct office number on the outside chance he was still around. Krumenauer picked up just as they crossed over the St. Croix River south of Stillwater on the bridge that connected Minnesota and Wisconsin.

"How did it go?" he asked.

"We met with Mrs. Geller. The number belonged to her husband all right. The Nazis tattooed it on his arm while he was a prisoner at Auschwitz. He died several months ago."

"Incredible what the Nazis did," said Krumenauer.

"The thing is chief, we think there's something she isn't telling us. Tomorrow we're going to dig up anything and everything we can."

"The INS should have a file on him," said the chief. "He was an immigrant."

"I already called them. When I mentioned Solomon Geller, the Deputy Director suddenly clammed up. We'll have to see what we can find on our own."

"Why would he do that?"

"She–Francis Brubaker. The Deputy Director of something in Field Operations. I have no idea why they don't want to play nice, but there are other resources."

"Do what you have to."

"Yes, sir." Donovan could hear the irritation in Krumenauer's voice.

"I'll make some calls myself. In the morning. Let's all go home."

Scully was into his second cup of coffee at his desk when Donovan arrived the next morning.

"Got an obit on Geller," he said. "From the Jewish Voice in Brooklyn."

Donovan took the document and read.

SOLOMON GELLER
Death Camp Survivor

March 17, 1997 – Solomon Geller died unexpectedly in Brooklyn, New York, on March 9. The deceased survived the horrors of two years of forced labor in the notorious Auschwitz concentration camp. At the age of 20 in April 1945, he and 700 other prisoners were loaded on a train headed toward the mountains where they were to be slaughtered and their bodies hidden. Rumors circulated about why and where they were being taken and Mr. Geller feared he was living his last day when the train was stopped near Tutzing, Germany by the U.S. Army and the "starving, barely human cargo" was liberated.

Mr. Geller, 73, was born in 1926 in Warsaw, Poland where he lived with his family until they were forced into the Warsaw Ghetto in the 1940s after Adolf Hitler's rise to power in Germany. After more than a year there, he was taken to Auschwitz, the "death camp" where he was separated from his family whom he was never to see again and forced to work in the crematorium where tens of thousands of people were incinerated. Although he owned a successful Brooklyn appliance business, he would never forget the experience and struggled with severe depression the remainder of his life.

Mr. Geller devoted much of his time to chronicling the experiences of other Holocaust survivors and was instrumental in identifying suspected Nazi war criminals living in the United States. He was publicly critical of the United States Departments of Justice, the Central Intelligence Agency, the Immigration and Naturalization Service and the Office of Special Investigation for their inaction to seek justice.

Mr. Geller is survived by his wife of 48 years, Hannah Geller and a son, David, a former member of Mahal Israel Defense Force. Services were held at King David Chapel, Brooklyn.

Donovan highlighted the part about Solomon Geller having a son with a bright, yellow marker. "Why wouldn't Hannah Geller tell us they had a son?"

Scully wadded up the wrapper from a fresh stick of Juicy Fruit and tossed it in a wastebasket. "What say we find out."

CHAPTER 24

Scully searched the Internet for David Geller. There were hundreds. He narrowed the search to New York. He found nine in Brooklyn. One in his mid-twenties showed a relationship to Hannah Geller.

Next, he read up on the Israeli Defense Forces online and fired off an email to them requesting instructions on how to get access to Geller's records. Then he e-mailed Interpol on their secure web site, explained the reason for the request and asked for assistance in cutting through any red tape with Israeli law enforcement.

Within twenty-minutes he received a phone call from the Israel Ministry of Foreign affairs. After a brief discussion, he was given the name and telephone number for the head of the IDF Personnel Office who had access to the records on former Mahal soldiers.

It was after 5:00 p.m. in Israel when Scully called. He was told that records personnel were gone for the day, but they would make it a priority first thing in the morning. It would take some time to retrieve David Geller's records from the inactive archive, but they would be faxed as soon as they were found.

Donovan was first in the next morning and saw the slim file folder marked, GELLER, DAVID – MILITARY RECORDS, sitting on his desk. The cover sheet indicated it was received at 2:20 a.m.

"Mornin' partner. Whatcha got there?"

"Geller's military records," a startled Donovan replied, holding up a grainy photo of a soldier staring stoically into the camera.

"Looks like the mug shot of a hardened lifer," said Scully, pouring a cup of coffee.

Donovan gave him the pages he had already read. "He's hardened all right. Read all about it."

When Scully finished reading, he sipped the now cold coffee and grimaced. "Interesting guy."

"That would be one choice of words. Let's brief the chief."

They dropped into the chairs in front of Chief Krumenauer's desk. "I think we're onto something. Scully found Solomon Geller's obit and learned he left a son named David. Apparently, a very troubled young man," Donovan said, nodding to his partner.

"David Geller. Mid twenties," read Scully. "An American-Jewish wonder boy who joined the Israeli Defense Forces. He was bright, tough. Fluent in Hebrew and Yiddish. That opened the door for him to join the Duvdevan–an elite Special Forces unit that works undercover.

"His records show he was an outstanding, even heroic, soldier for nearly two years. Chest full of medals and all that. Then things fell apart. Geller apparently began to withdraw into his own world. Crippling headaches. Acted strange. Began taking unnecessary risks during missions. Absolutely fearless. No regard for his own life whatsoever."

"Stress got to him," said Krumenauer.

"It gets worse," said Donovan. "After a while, Geller was going on his own missions. Unauthorized. When he was caught, he admitted sneaking into opposition camps at night and killing enemy soldiers. Couldn't remember how many he took out. Nice and quiet. Just used a knife."

"Jesus," said Krumenauer. "Talk about a self starter."

"His unit commander tried to get him help. The docs said his headaches and weird behavior were linked to his psychological problems. He spent a few weeks in a hospital and returned to his unit. Within days he started up again.

"It's like he had a death wish, chief," said Donovan. "The IDF had no choice but discharge him and boot him out of Israel."

"Have you talked with Mrs. Geller again?"

"We wanted to bring you up to speed first," said Donovan.

"She's next."

"Go back there or anywhere you have to. Don't worry about the expenses. We can do without one new cruiser."

CHAPTER 25

"Mrs. Geller?"
"Yes."
"This is Detective Donovan calling from Wisconsin."
No response.
"Do you remember me, Mrs. Geller? I'm calling about your son, David."
The phone went dead. "She hung up on me!"
"Dip into some of that Irish charm," said Scully.
Donovan pushed redial and let the phone ring until Hannah Geller answered again.
"Don't hang up, Mrs. Geller. We have to talk about David. Why didn't you tell us you had a son?"
Silence.
"She hung up again!" cursed Donovan.
There was no answer on next attempt.
"How do you feel about another pastrami on rye?" he asked Scully.
"I'll check on flights."

※

The flight to New York was not as smooth this time. They arrived late, had trouble getting a rental and fought traffic all the way to Crown Heights. No one answered the door when they arrived at the Geller residence. There was no movement inside. They waited in the rental car for nearly an hour until they saw the little, redheaded woman pulling a two-wheeled grocery cart up the street. She was accompanied by a bearded old man dressed in black and wearing a black homburg hat. They said their goodbyes in front of the brownstone and he continued slowly on his way. The detectives waited to make their move until she had pulled the cart half way up her steps. When she saw them coming, she quickened her pace, spilling groceries from the wildly hopping cart.

"Mrs. Geller. We have to talk about David," said Donovan as he and Scully gathered up the strewn items.

"David isn't here!"

The old man in the black homburg hurried back when he heard the commotion. "Hannah! What is this?"

"It's about David, Rabbi. These are the policemen I told you about."

"I am Rabbi Hershel Tannenbaum. I am Mrs. Geller's friend and counsel," he said indignantly.

Mrs. Geller nodded and they showed their shields. "David may be in trouble, Rabbi. We can get a court order to talk to her but, we didn't think she'd want to be arrested."

The old woman looked for an answer in the sky and sighed. Her small shoulders collapsed in surrender. She led them inside. Rabbi Tannenbaum followed.

"Sit," said Mrs. Geller, impatiently gesturing to the couch. A moment I need with the rabbi. They disappeared into the kitchen while the detectives sat and waited. They could hear a muffled conversation lasting for several minutes then Rabbi Tannenbaum returned. "This is very difficult for her, gentlemen. She has lost so much. But, she will talk with you now."

"I'll show myself to the door, Hannah. I'll see you at Temple tomorrow," he called out and was gone.

A composed Hannah Geller returned to the living room, walked directly to a neatly arranged desk and returned with a wooden box. From it she removed a photograph of a powerfully built, young soldier with intense, yellow-green eyes. His hair was closely cropped–almost shaved. His raw-boned features emphasized a strong, square jaw.

"This is my David. He was in the Israeli Defense Forces then. A hero he was. With medals." She held up a bright, red ribbon with a silver medal showing an olive branch with crossed swords that formed a menorah.

"Do you know where David is now?" asked Donovan.

Hannah Geller looked away and closed her eyes. Lips tightened across her teeth. "No. David has been gone since my Solomon committed suicide."

The detectives exchange glances.

"He has had no contact with you? No phone calls? No letters? Nothing?" asked Scully.

"No."

"That wasn't David we saw earlier getting into the white van out front?"

"No," she said stiffly, refusing to look Scully in the eyes.

"Is this the most recent picture of him?" asked Scully.

She nodded.

"May we borrow it?"

"Why?"

"It might help us find him."

"You will give it back?"

"Yes, ma'am."

She handed Donovan the photograph.

"Please don't hurt him. He's sick."

"We just want to help him. Can you tell us why Solomon took his own life? How it affected David?" asked Donovan.

"Take your time," said Scully.

She gathered herself. "It's time I talked about it," she said wistfully "I don't want my head any longer to hide in the sand."

Donovan and Scully both shifted forward on the couch.

"From Auschwitz, Solomon never recovered. Scars remained. He suffered depression. He couldn't sleep from the nightmares. He heard the screams–remembered the terror–even the heat of the ovens and the smell of burning flesh. Sometimes, sometimes, even the ashes he could taste. His mother. His father. His sisters he lost. His past he lost."

"Can you tell us about David, Mrs. Geller?" Scully gently prodded.

Hannah glowered. "About David I can't tell you without about his father telling you."

"I'm sorry," Scully said, looking sheepishly at a disapproving

Donovan. He waited for her to calm.

"Solomon's suffering became David's suffering. We could see it. We tried to get him help. A psychiatrist said he had the same scars without the wound.

"David couldn't understand why his father and the others didn't resist. Didn't fight back. Meir zayn sheps' Solomon would say."

"Ma'am?"

"'Yiddish–'we were sheep'," she clarified. "The shame never left him. He spent the rest of his life atoning. David tried to help. He learned to read Yiddish. Together they read the Yiddish newspapers for stories about the monsters who did these things. Together the others they found."

"The others?" asked Scully.

"Other Jews who survived the concentration camps. Who remembered the Nazi animals by name."

"What then?" asked Scully.

"Solomon tracked them down and found many of them. But, when he gave the information to the government immigration people, nothing happened. No deportations. No legal actions. They didn't even investigate."

"Why not?" asked Scully.

"Umph! Better things they had to do. Communists they chased in those days–not Nazi war criminals. Solomon even wrote to senators and congressman, but a deaf ear they turned," she said, tears welling in her eyes.

"Solomon grew frustrated. David grew angry. He wanted to fight back. That's why he joined the Israeli Defense Forces. His father was so proud. His son the warrior! No one would push him around. He was hero. The medal they gave him."

"We know," said Scully. "We have his records. What concerns us is his discharge for, well, his mental problems."

"David was very troubled. Solomon blamed himself for filling him with so much hate. That's why he took his own life."

"Did David live here until that happened?"

"Yes. I've kept his room. He was going to go back to school.

He was always such a good student. Very bright."

"Could we see his room?" asked Scully.

They followed her up the stairs to the end of the hall. "This is David's room, just as he left it."

"Mind if we look around?" asked Scully.

Mrs. Geller pushed open the door and stepped aside. "I'll wait downstairs."

Except for a bookcase, the room reminded Donovan of a barracks. A military cot with an olive drab blanket stretched taut over the mattress sat along one wall. Next to it, a single dresser with a reading lamp. To the right was a small closet.

Donovan studied the contents of the large bookcase. Shelf upon shelf bent under the weight of dozens of books–nearly all of them on a single subject.

CHAPTER 26

"So, anything did you find?" asked Mrs. Geller when the detectives came back downstairs.

"Nothing that would lead us to David's whereabouts, but I think we understand him much better now," said Donovan.

"I noticed he had several books on the Holocaust," Scully added.

"Yes. David often read books from his father's library."

"Are there more?" asked Scully.

"Oh, my, yes," Mrs. Geller replied, seemingly more willing to cooperate now. "In Solomon's office."

"Can you show us?" asked Scully.

"I haven't been in since my Solomon died. It is too full of him."

"I understand. Do you mind if we take a look?" asked Donovan.

"Suit yourselves. It's next to David's."

The room was crowded. Crammed bookshelves were everywhere. A brass lamp with twin black shades sat on a huge library table stacked with files and folders. Along one wall stood a row of mismatched, four-drawer files. One, larger and more substantial, was clearly fireproof.

"Did you bring a change of underwear and a toothbrush?" asked Donvovan. "This could take a while."

Scully searched the room and the closet. Donovan began with the bookcase. Every volume was neatly organized by subject matter; Death Camps, Nazi War Crimes and Criminals, U.S. and Foreign Government Agencies, Post World War II Policies, The Displaced Persons Act, U.S. Immigration policy, the Nazi War Crimes Disclosure Act and more. There was even a section of well-known best sellers that included *The Odessa File, The Boys from Brazil, Judgment at Nuremberg*, and dozens more.

The Nazi death camp section alone was several feet long: Auschwitz-Birkenau, Bergen-Belsen, Buchenwald, Dachau and so on. He took the final volume from the shelf and paged through it. It was the record of Treblinka, a Nazi extermination camp in Poland where nearly a million people were killed. He read slowly, pausing at the neatly written annotations by each of the dozens of bookmarks. Several pages contained photographs of prisoners; living skeletons crowded together in tiers of wooden bunks, corpses stacked like firewood, terrified, naked women trying pathetically to cover themselves as they ran a gauntlet of Nazi guards and snarling dogs.

Although Donovan had seen photos like them before, they seemed more real now. Even more sickening. Scully finished going through the dresser and the closet and was about to open the first drawer of the fireproof file when Mrs. Geller appeared in the doorway.

"You'll need this to open the master file," she said, handing a key to Scully.

"I'm not sure it's locked," he replied, tugging tentatively on the handle.

The drawer labeled "A - L" opened with ease to reveal dozens of neatly labeled, color-coded file folders.

Hannah Geller looked perplexed. "But, always locked Solomon kept it."

Scully closed it and opened the "M - Z" drawer beneath to find more files. Each was neatly labeled with German or Polish-sounding names.

"Who are these people? asked Donovan.

"Nazi criminals who came to the U.S. who Solomon identified before he died. Most of them never even bothered to change their names."

"There are fifty-nine," said Mrs. Geller.

Scully looked through both drawers. There were noticeable gaps where files were missing. He ran his fingers over the alphabetized blue, yellow and green folders and counted. "I count fifty-one," said Scully.

Her thin eyebrows rose. She moved closer. "Where are the red ones? Missing are the red files! Solomon's most wanted," she gasped.

"Your husband had a most wanted list?" asked Scully.

"'Shlekht Farzeenish', he called them; 'The Evil Monsters'. They were the worst of the worst."

The detectives flashed knowing looks at each other. "Do you think David could have taken the files?" asked Donovan.

Mrs. Geller grew weak, felt her knees buckle and sat on the bed in a sudden rush of realization.

"Are there copies of the files anywhere else? Or a list of the names?" pressed Scully.

"A list I don't know. But, to the Immigration and Naturalization Service he gave copies of everything. To the government he sent letters. Some of the files were huge. New information turned up all the time–especially from Russia. Names and dates and records. Solomon was so confident. But, nothing they did."

It was late when Donovan and Scully checked into a Comfort Inn near Brooklyn's Botanical Gardens after arranging with Mrs. Geller to return the next morning. On their way, they purchased toothbrushes and toiletries and even found socks and underwear in a sprawling drug store that was open all night. Dinner was a bag of White Castle burgers they brought to the room. Scully canceled their flight for the following day. Donovan called Tess, then Chief Krumenauer and filled him in.

"It's sure looking like David Geller could be our Executioner."

"Solomon's Executioner," the chief offered, giving the name more gravity.

"Apparently he took the files with him and we're going to have to lean on INS for copies. It's our best chance of finding him. But there's still a ton of other material to go through here. We're bound to turn up something."

"His mother doesn't know where he could be?"

"Says she doesn't. He disappeared after his father committed suicide. She says hasn't heard from him since."

"You believe her?"

"I don't really know, chief. But she seems to understand that he's pretty fucked up. I want to put a tap on her phone."

The wakeup call came at 6:30 the next morning. Both men were still tired but anxious to get back to Solomon Geller's office to pick up where they left off. They arrived with a sack of bagels and coffee. Scully began by going through the files that were still there.

"Geller was nothing if not thorough," said Scully. "Our records should look so good. There are complete biographies of each criminal. Affidavits from victims. Nazi documents. Foreign government documents. Immigration forms. Photos. Employment records. The yellow ones seem to have death certificates."

By noon Donovan was well into the shelves of books. When he came to Satan's Handmaidens: Female Nazi War Criminals, he found a bookmark with a red "X" drawn over the name Else Klaff. He turned to the page to find a photograph of a strangely familiar young woman wearing a Nazi uniform and heavy jackboots. Her expression was at once arrogant and disdainful. In her fist was a riding crop.

The caption read: *Else Klaff, known as the Bitch of Buchenwald, before her escape from an allied detention center where she awaited trial for war crimes in 1945.*

"Brian, take a look at this. Does this woman look familiar to you?"

Scully glanced at the photograph. "Before my time, partner."

"Must be a reason she's bookmarked like this."

Donovan studied the black and white photograph more closely before reluctantly moving on. Suddenly it came to him: "The box! I think this is the same woman whose picture was in the box we found in Greta Bauer's cellar."

He flipped back to the page, covered everything below her face with his hand and held the photo for Scully to see again. "Forget the uniform. Remember the young blond woman with braids? She had on a pleated skirt with knee high stockings."

"My God," said Scully. "That's her!"

Donovan moved into the light of the window and read out loud: "Else Klaff was born March 1924 into the large family of a postal official, Ernst Klaff and his wife Beata in Krakow, Poland. She left school at 16 to work in a hospital to help provide for the family. During this period, Klaff became a member of the Hitler youth. She moved to the all-female Ravensbrück concentration camp in June 1942, the year in which she joined the SS. In April 1943, Klaff transferred to Auschwitz-Birkenau where she was in charge of the 30,000 female prisoners held there. With Nazi Germany's withdrawal from Poland, Klaff moved back to Ravensbrück in January 1945 and then on to Belsen in March 1945.

"In all the death/concentration camps in which she worked, Klaff developed a reputation for brutality. Many survivors testified that they witnessed Senior SS-Supervisor (Oberraufseherin) Klaff at Auschwitz-Birkenau shoot prisoners in cold blood, beat some women to death and whipped others mercilessly using a plaited cellophane whip. Others testified that she turned loose her trained and half starved dogs on them and selected prisoners for the gas chambers with what appeared to be sexual pleasure at these acts of cruelty."

Donovan turned the page and came to a sentence that had been neatly underlined in red ink. The hair on the back of his head went up.

"Jesus, listen to this. It has been claimed that in her hut were found the skins of three inmates that she had made into lampshades. Each had been selected by Klaff personally for the tattoos that decorated their skin."

Scully listened spellbound.

"Some at her post-war trial believed that she was personally responsible for 30 deaths a day. In June 1945, the British indicted Klaff under a Royal Warrant. Captured at Belsen in the last days of the war, Klaff was charged with crimes against humanity in the Belsen Trials held between September 17th 1945 and November 17th 1945. Klaff, aged just 21, was found guilty of her crimes and sentenced to death. She escaped just days before her execution was to be carried out and is believed to have been assisted by an organization sympathetic to the Nazis to enter Brazil or possibly North America under an assumed identity."

Donovan set the book down. "I don't suppose there's a file still here for Else Klaff," he asked.

Scully's fingers walked the files. "No. No Klaffs."

"Somehow we have to pressure the INS or some other agency to produce copies of the Geller files. I'll bet you a butter burger that eight of them include Milos Dulecki, some son-of-a-bitch without a name who was cremated in Choctaw County and Greta Bauer. And I'll bet there's evidence from Solomon Geller that Bauer's real identity is Else Klaff."

CHAPTER 27

Scully set the box of books on a table in the Dugout Sports Bar at JFK. They ordered beers while they waited for their return flight to Minneapolis. Donovan took out his phone and punched in a speed dial number.

"Krumenauer."

"Chief. I think we have enough to go after David Geller as the Executioner. Can you get a warrant issued and put him out there with his military photo on the NCIS and give it out to the media? I'm certain he has more victims on his list. We need to figure out who or where he might hit next."

"Keep talking."

Donovan explained what they found in Geller's office. "He sent requests for documents on the Nazi war criminals he found to the OSI, CIA, INS and God only knows who else And his widow said that he sent copies of his own files to the INS. If they still have them, and I'll bet they do, we might be able to find out who Geller's next targets could be. It's our best chance at stopping him before he can kill again. It's essential for them to cooperate. Somewhere they have copies of every file."

"Sounds like we have enough for the FBI guys to get their teeth into," said Krumenauer.

There was a brief, cold silence before Donovan responded. "This is my investigation, chief."

"We've got three victims in three states, Mike. We have to bring them in. They have people and resources we don't have. Like profilers."

"What the hell do we need with a profiler? We know who he is," Donovan protested. He knew all about The FBI's National Center for the Analysis of Violent Crime. They advertise that they "partner" with other agencies and police in investigations involving terrorism, gang violence, and serial murder, but Donovan could imagine being steamrolled out of the picture.

"C'mon, Mike. They can do things we can't. You know that."

"I know I sound like a prima donna, Chief, but I'm really invested in this thing. I hate to turn it over."

"You don't have to. I expect you to remain the lead investigator. You make the contact, put together your own team. You run the show. Not them. No one is more on top of this than you. You have the best chance of busting this guy. If I didn't believe that, I'd pull the plug on you or anyone else to put him away. But, the FBI can be a big help and you know it."

"You're right," said a contrite Donovan.

"So we're straight?"

"Straight."

"OK. Let's move on. Is Mrs. Geller cooperating?"

"She is to a point. I don't think she knew what David has been up to until we talked with her. Her Rabbi gave her a talking to and she's cooperating now, but you can bet she's not going to set him up for a shootout. Maybe she knows where he is and maybe she doesn't. I'd like to get a record of her phone calls since the killings began."

"We can do that," Krumenauer replied.

Donovan took two books from the box and shoved it into the overhead compartment of the 747. He settled in and opened the one titled *Nazi Death Camp Atrocities*. By the time the plane was over Detroit, he stopped reading a chapter about Nazi medical experiments on death camp prisoners in mid-sentence. By changing a word here and there, it could have been lifted from the Choctaw County Coroner's report on John Doe.

In the 21 months that SS Medical Doctor, Joseph Mengele spent at Auschwitz-Birkenau, witnesses testified that he performed unspeakably painful experiments on thirty-six children in which he attempted to alter the color of their eyes by injecting them with blue dye.

"My God," he said, turning to a dozing Scully, "I think he's killing his victims using the same methods the Nazi's used on prisoners."

CHAPTER 28

Tess was sitting in the dark when Donovan got home. "Why aren't you in bed?" he asked, setting the box on the kitchen counter. "It's nearly two in the morning."

"Couldn't sleep," she said, greeting him with a peck on the lips. "It's weird when you're not there next to me."

"Missed you, too."

"How'd it go? You didn't call," she said. "What's in the box?"

"Books. I wanted to talk to you about it, but not on the phone."

"What is it?"

"It's turning out to be not so simple, Tess. It isn't just the good guys against the bad guys anymore. It's gotten complicated."

"What do you mean?"

"It looks like the bad guy could be sort of a good guy who is killing people who are turning out to be bad guys."

Tess turned on a light. "Sounds like a long story. Why don't you take a quick shower and come back down. Have you eaten?"

"Not hungry."

"I'll pour you a drink and we'll talk. Tomorrow's Sunday. We can skip mass and sleep in."

She was curled up in the den by a fire when Donovan returned in his robe and slippers. A tumbler of whiskey was on the table next to his chair. He sat gratefully.

"Okay. It turns out the victims were probably Nazi war criminals. Some real bad actors," he said, taking a sip and feeling the delicious burn work its' way down his throat to his stomach.

A surprised look fell over Tess Donovan's face.

"Solomon Geller was a prisoner in Auschwitz during the war when he was just in his teens. His entire family was killed. Mother, father, his little sisters; probably all gassed and cremated," said Donovan pausing to sip his drink. "That's the way they worked it."

"Jesus, Copper. This is really scary."

"Geller survived by a near miracle. Never got over it though. Had severe depression. Eventually he came to New York, married and raised a son who became as screwed up as he was."

"Together they read Yiddish newspapers for first hand accounts of other survivors. They did interviews, documented the crimes and identified the war criminals believed to have immigrated here."

Tess's mouth fell open as she listened.

"For years Geller pleaded with government agencies to look into the accusations and take legal action toward deporting them to be tried for war crimes. When tons of new documentation was made available from the U.S. as well as Russia after the Soviet Union fell apart, he even sent the INS complete sets of files that documented everything."

"And they turned him away," finished Tess.

"Every time. Finally, it all got to be too much for him. When his only child, David, developed secondhand mental problems and was forced to leave the Israeli Defense forces, Geller killed himself. Combined with his depression, it was more than he could handle. David snapped and disappeared with the files on eight of the war criminals that he and his father had located," Donovan said, staring into the fire. "And an emotionally disturbed, highly trained killer was on the loose."

"Why eight? You said there were 59 files," asked Tess.

"Most of them hadn't been located yet or had already died from natural causes. David Geller left those behind."

"And he's killing the rest," said Tess.

"It all fits," Donovan said softly. "Just like the Nazis did, he stripped his victims naked and chopped off their hair. But instead of tattooing them, he branded them with his father's Auschwitz serial number before killing them in the same gruesome ways."

"He made the brand his calling card," said Tess.

"Take Greta Bauer. We think Solomon Geller figured out that she was actually Elsa Klaff. You may not have heard of her, but she was a high-ranking, sadistic prison matron known as the 'Bitch of Buchenwald'. David Geller killed her and skinned her just like she had prisoners skinned–at least the few she found with interesting tattoos. They say she had the skins tanned and made stuff out of them. Lampshades. Purses. Like is was leather."

Tess shivered.

"The John Doe in Oklahoma," he continued. "He was injected with all sorts of stuff. Including dyes into his eye balls just like Joseph Mengeles did to prisoners at Auschwitz under the pretense of medical experiments."

"And the victim in Chicago. I'm sure you wouldn't have to look very hard to find stories of Nazi's who beat prisoners to death," Tess added.

"So all of David Geller's victims are war criminals?"

"Well, Solomon Geller thought so and he apparently made some pretty convincing cases that he was right," said Donovan, grimacing with another swallow of Bushmills.

"It's a game changer, Tess. If the victims are the monsters written about in these books, your noble crime fighter here is thinking maybe they got just what they deserved."

"Oh, Copper. You don't really feel that way," said Tess.

"I don't know how I feel, honey. When this started, I wanted nothing more than to catch this sicko and make him pay for what he did to that old lady and the others."

"And now?" asked Tess.

"There are five more people Geller is probably going to try to kill and I'm not sure I still care."

CHAPTER 29

The quiet, young man known as David Abraham to his apartment building neighbors, stopped packing his duffle bag when he heard his name and looked up to see his picture on television.

"Eau Claire, Wisconsin Police Chief Clarence Krumenauer has identified a twenty-six year old New York man as the prime suspect in a series of recent killings in Oklahoma, Chicago and in his own community in Northern Wisconsin. A nationwide manhunt is underway to apprehend David Geller, shown here in a photo taken while he served in the Israeli Army. Known as 'The Executioner', Geller is a white male with green eyes and short, dark hair. He stands six feet two inches tall and weighs 185 lbs. He may be driving a late model White Ford Econoline van. Anyone who knows Geller's whereabouts or has seen him should contact local law enforcement immediately. Do not approach Geller. He is armed and extremely dangerous."

Geller smiled. Since the photo was taken, he had grown his hair out and sprouted a thick black mustache. He doubted anyone would recognize him. Coupled with the fact that he always wore a baseball cap and sunglasses when going out, he felt relatively safe.

"Authorities have reason to believe that Geller may be driving a white late 1980's Ford Econoline van with New York plates AKI-344."

Geller knew he would soon have to get rid of the van or paint it even though he had replaced the New York plates with plates from the truck belonging to the man he had killed in a barn in Oklahoma a month earlier. But, there was no time now. He had another long drive to make and now that they knew who he was, time might be running out.

CHAPTER 30

The atmosphere in Eau Claire Police Department was already electric when Donovan arrived on Monday morning.

The now familiar media trucks crowded the street out front. Several messages waited on his desk. He replied first to a request from the FBI for more details. Now that there was a suspect, the FBI serial killer task force was ready to go into high gear. Donovan gave them the background highlights and promised he would fax copies of everything. He also requested around the around clock surveillance on Hannah Geller's home and Federal authorization to tap her telephone.

"We'll find him faster if we can get the INS to cough up the files that Geller sent them," he told the agent in charge. "We need to know who he's looking for."

"How many are there?" the agent asked.

"There were eight files missing from Geller's office. With three victims so far that we know, that leaves five still out there."

"Five old Nazi's without a clue that their days might be numbered," the agent sighed. "If we can't track him down, at least he'll run out of victims sooner or later."

"Maybe he'll run out of ways to murder them first," Donovan replied.

"What do you mean?" the agent asked.

"You know–ways to kill them. It looks like he's duplicated some of the more horrific ways the Nazi's carried out their killings."

Donovan flipped the notebook and read the neatly written list penned in watery blue ink.

"Beginning with our first victim, Greta Bauer, there is flaying alive. The next victim died from injections of various chemicals including kerosene, bleach and so on. Geller even injected dyes into the victim's eyeballs just like Joseph Mengeles was known to do. The third victim, Milos Dulecki was literally beaten to death. One bone broken at a time until he either died from shock or loss of blood."

"That leaves several other options for the remaining five victims unless he repeats himself. There were shootings, usually execution style in the back of the head," he said flipping the page.

"I know they gassed millions," offered the agent.

"Right," said Donovan. "They started with carbon monoxide but that took too long, so they tried other things and finally settled on Zyklon B. That's how most of the six million victims went. They were given a little bar of soap to mislead them, crowded into a room with gas valves disguised as fake showerheads and didn't come out alive. Most of them were found still standing because there wasn't enough room to fall.

"Also on the list is hanging, burning alive, various medical experiments involving hypothermia to see how long a prisoner could survive in ice water, hypoxia resulting from high altitude exposure, starvation, the introduction of various diseases, exhaustion from forced labor, death marches. Believe it or not, there are stories that they even fed Jews alive to the bears the Nazi kept at a small zoo at Auschwitz. There was also castration, amputations... apparently they even buried some people alive."

"It's hard to imagine, isn't it," said the agent.

After finishing up with the FBI, Donovan called his team together in the squad room. He and Scully described their meeting with Hannah Geller in detail. In return the team brought them up-to-date with their own investigation. Donovan began planning what he would say to the reporters outside in the freezing December air.

CHAPTER 31

Dec 21, 1997 - Ontario, Canada

Karl Aachenbach was the first fisherman on the frozen Canadian lake that morning when he drove his aging Ford pickup across the rock-hard mud ruts of the boat landing onto the ice. It was warm inside the cab as the old truck rattled and shook along the frozen, rough tire tracks he had left on previous days when it was warmer. The radio blasted the Polka Hour on Radio Herz out of Waterloo, Ontario. Aachenbach hadn't touched the dial since he discovered the only Deutsch language station years before.

The old man tucked a generous pinch of Copenhagen snuff into his cheek and "oompahed" along with the tuba as the radio blared the "She's Too Fat for Me" polka. He was halfway across the lake when the music ended with a final tuba fart and the weatherman came on the air to report that with the temperature at −32F and dropping, it could become the coldest day of the winter. So far it appeared the weatherman would be right.

Nearly incessant winds had chased most of the snow from the lake leaving only vaporous wisps of white powder to whirl across the ice through the bitter cold. He passed the clusters of fishing shacks on the main part of the huge lake and continued on to his shanty sitting by itself in a distant bay. He liked fishing alone and had learned over the years to enjoy a solitary life. Besides, he still struggled with English and meaningless conversations did not interest him.

He left the truck running with the heater on full blast when he parked and stepped out onto the ice. After the warmth of the inside, the sting of the frigid air took his breath away. Aachenbach pulled off his thickly-lined buckskin mittens to unlock the heavy steel paddle lock and in less than a minute his hands were red and raw from the dry, arctic air. The 12-foot by 8-foot shanty was eerily quiet and cheerless inside. The morning light filtered through the single, frosted window at one end. His fingers cold and stiff, it took him two tries to strike a wooden kitchen match and light the kerosene lamp on a small table. Instantly a welcoming, warm yellow glow filled the space.

The old man put his mittens back on to warm his fingers and looked around before lighting the stove. He was usually content to find that everything was undisturbed, but this time something seemed wrong–out of place.

He looked around. The cot was still neatly made. The few food supplies and cooking utensils were still arranged on the single shelf. Nothing seemed disturbed on the little table where he carved blocks of wood into rabbits, squirrels and other animals while he waited for fish to bite. The old blue-black kerosene stove waited to be lighted as usual and the dilapitated kitchen chair with it's worn cushion was exactly where he had left it next to a large rectangular opening in the plank floor where he augured holes in the ice.

Finally, Aachenbach inspected the fishing equipment and gear hanging on the far wall. His new 3HP ice auger, the skimmer for keeping the fishing holes free of slush, ice fishing jig rods, tip-ups that he sometimes set up outside, his tackle box; everything seemed accounted for, yet it didn't feel right.

"Ach. Ich bin alt." He grunted blaming it on his age.

He slipped out of his mittens again, topped off the kerosene tank on the back of the stove and got the flame going. For all his love of ice fishing, he disliked being cold and would wait in the truck until the temperature inside the shanty was at least above freezing. He had insulated it well and knew it wouldn't take long. In the mean time he would stay warm, listen to the radio and nod off for a few minutes.

David Geller was all but invisible as he waited in the cold

watching the shack from a thicket near the shore. All that could be seen of his face inside the dark hollow of the deep, fur-lined hood was the suggestion of long, straight nose, a mustache white with frost and two penetrating green eyes. He dismissed the growing numbness in his fingers and toes and remained so still that a chickadee landed on his shoulder.

Geller straightened when he saw Aachenbach leave the shack and climb back into the truck. He knew the old man's routine after watching him for two days. He had picked the lock and been inside the fishing shanty the night before to familiarize himself with the Spartan interior. He removed the only weapon he found; a large knife that hung from a peg on the wall. But, mostly he wanted a mental picture of the place where he would watch Aachenbach slowly die. Everything was ready.

He took a thermos from the backpack on his snowmobile, poured a cup of strong, black coffee and watched the truck as he waited for the old man to fall asleep. If no one else came onto the lake, he would begin.

The familiar knot of pain began at the base of Geller's skull by the time he finished the coffee and tossed the last drops. Soon his head was throbbing and he felt himself begin to drift up and hover outside himself.

By the time the old man's head fell back in a loud snore with his mouth agape, Geller's other self had taken control. He eyed his victim one last time to make certain he was asleep, then grabbed his backpack and walked across the ice toward the idling truck. He didn't have the same element of surprise he had with his other victims and it made him anxious–he had to expose himself.

Geller made it to the shanty unnoticed and opened the door without taking his eye off the truck. The warmth from the kerosene stove was a welcome relief. He quickly pushed back the hood of his parka, removed the taser from the backpack and put the pistol in his pocket. Then he waited and listened.

It seemed forever until he heard the idling truck shudder and go quiet. His heart began to race. By the time he heard the tinny sound of the truck door squeak open and slam closed, he was crowded against the wall behind the door, waiting with the taser in his hand. But, the old man didn't come.

Geller felt for the pistol and was about to abort his original plan when Aachenbach opened the door. He had stopped to piss and was still zipping his fly as he entered.

Once again something seemed wrong to the old man, but this time his senses went on high alert. Uneasy, he stopped and turned to go back outside when he felt an arm grasp him around his neck and saw the taser from the corner of his eye.

He pulled at the arm to get away and kicked back into his attacker's shin with a booted foot. Hearing his assailant grunt in pain and feeling his grip weaken, the old man pushed up and away, collapsed his knees and dropped to the floor under his substantial weight.

"You fuckin' putz!" screamed Geller, frantically trying to get the old man in a chokehold once again and reapply the taser.

But, Aachenbach was surprisingly strong and fast. In a split second burst of energy, he catapulted himself to the opposite end of the shack where he kept his filleting knife and the rest of his fishing gear. He realized in horror it was gone. The knife was the something that was missing. In an instant, he remembered the fork-like, ice fishing spear he kept in the low rafters overhead and reached for it.

Heart pounding, the old man jabbed the razor sharp, ten-inch tines forward. Geller backed off, his expressionless face studying Aachenbach as the old man crept slowly forward—waiting for just the right moment to lunge. He set his feet, drew the spear back to thrust and stopped. Aimed at his forehead was a large black, pistol.

"Put down the spear," Geller ordered.

"What do you want?" Aachenbach demanded breathlessly. "I haf nothing."

"You, Sergeant Fiedler," whispered Geller coolly. "I want you."

Aachenbach's eye's widened. His heart raced faster. His breathing grew shallow. He was found at last.

"Drop the spear now and turn around or I will shoot you in the back of your skull."

"I am not Fielder," pleaded Aachenbach desperately as he dropped the spear and turned. "You have me mistaken for someone else. I am Karl Aachenbach. Not Fiedler. Don't you see?"

Suddenly the arm was around his neck again and he felt the taser shoot through his body with excruciating, paralyzing pain. The words he heard next seemed like a vague echo.

"I know who you are. In fact, I might know more about you than anyone else in the world," said Geller.

Several minutes passed before Aachenbach could move again. By then he was naked and tied face down on his cot. He gagged on something stuffed in his mouth and tried frantically to breathe. He could feel the duct tape wrapped around his head. The shanty was warm by now, but he was cold. He was very cold and very afraid.

Suddenly he heard the brief sputter of the ice auger engine and turned to see Geller pulling the starter rope. Then again. Finally on the third pull, the engine roared to life with a deafening din and he watched wide-eyed as Geller drilled hole after hole in the ice, clearing out the slush as he went until there was large rectangle riddled with 8-inch holes cut clear through to the water. An almost eerie quiet enveloped the shack when he killed the auger engine but was soon replaced by the steady rhythm of an ice saw. Its huge teeth made fast work of the remaining ice and soon there was a coffin-size opening. Geller forced the huge, bored-out block under one end of the hole and pushed the whole thing away under the ice with a pole.

"That's more work than I thought it would be," Geller said, stopping to rest. "Getting warm in here. You're not too warm are you, Sergeant Fielder?"

The old man stopped shivering as the heat from the stove warmed the air. Still, his flesh was turning the color of a fresh bruise. He tried to talk, but could only mumble. His jaw ached from being held open so far for so long.

Geller leaned menacingly close to the old man's ear. "My father told me that during the war you were quite an expert on how long humans could endure cold," he whispered. "Of course, you were only an observer then. Let's say I help you find out what it's like first hand. But, first we have some work to do. We have to prepare. It'll give you time to look back and remember."

Geller took the branding iron from the backpack, opened the propane valve, struck a match and sent blue flames whooshing onto the row of brass numbers. He set it down in view of Aachenbach so he could see them slowly begin to glow.

"While we're waiting for this to get good and hot, we'll see to your haircut, Sergeant Fielder," he said, removing a long knife from the pack and sliding it from its' sheath to test the keenness of the edge with his thumb. "Hair has to come off, you know. We don't want any lice infesting your shack. Besides, you want to look your best for your funeral."

Karl Aachenbach thrashed frantically as Geller moved closer.

"Don't struggle so, Sergeant. You might get a little nick."

Aachenbach let go a muffled scream as Geller grabbed a handful of gray hair and slid the razor-sharp knife through it. When he held up the prize tuft, a thin slice of meaty flesh still attached.

"See what you made me do?"

The branding iron glow grew brighter as he continued to slice off the old man's hair. Soon all that remained were clumps of stubble and shallow, neatly sliced wounds oozing blood that ran down his face.

Numb with fear and cold, the old man began to cry, his naked body shaking convulsively. He could no longer feel his bleeding scalp. He only saw the red-hot branding iron.

"That should do it," said Geller indifferently, stuffing the clumps of hair into a plastic bag and wiping the blood from the knife with the flannel shirt that lay in the heap among Aachenbach's other clothes. He placed the knife and hair in the backpack and examined the glowing red branding iron.

"Now for the all important identification number. You don't have one of your own, so I'm going to loan you my father's. I don't know if you ever met him, but he was just like all the other Jews at Auschwitz you murdered. The children you took from their mothers and burned alive in your ovens. The women you humiliated before you gassed them. The men...." His voice trailed off and for the first time Geller showed emotion. Then all went quiet except for the sound of Aachenbach's labored breathing and the hiss of the flame.

"Now it's your turn," Geller whispered as he moved closer and held the old man's head as he tried in vain to twist away. Then Aachenbach felt the searing heat press into his forehead and smelled his own burning flesh and fainted. An unearthly animal growl issued from his nose and mouth as piss dripped from the thin mattress turning the bluish-gray ice to yellow under the cot.

Sergeant Fiedler was shocked back into consciousness when his naked body was lowered into the hole cut into the ice. Soon all but his flaring nostrils were immersed in the stinging, freezing water. Geller studied the old man's face and wondered if the sounds and images of long ago came back to the old man as his life slipped away.

CHAPTER 32

Dec 25, 1997

"Good morning, Eau Claire. Merry Christmas!" blared the radio. "It's 6:00 a.m. Monday and a fresh new holiday week to celebrate. Time to rise and shine. Sawdust City is a deep freeze today so dress warmly if you're going out. Even better; stay home, build a fire and enjoy those gifts under the tree."

Donovan groped in the dark for the lamp, turned it on and lowered the radio's volume. Throwing off the covers, he stood to put on his robe and peered out the frosted bedroom window. Snow swirled in the predawn light and blew off the neighborhood roofs. Smoke poured from the furnace chimneys.

"What's it doing out there, Copper?" Tess asked sleepily.

"The weatherman called it. Looks seriously cold," he replied. "Lousy weather."

Donovan showered and was drying off when Tess called to him through the bedroom door. "Brian's on the phone. Says it's important."

"Doesn't he know it's Christmas? Tell him I'll call him back, I'm in the shower," Donovan replied.

After a few seconds he heard her voice again. "He says he'll wait on the phone."

Donovan toweled off and threw on his robe. "What's up?"

"Got a call from the Ontario Provincial Police in Kenora. They have an old man frozen in the ice on Lake Vermillion in Canada. He's inside his fishing shack. The only thing showing is the top part of his head.

"There's a number burned into his forehead. They checked it with Interpol and came across Greta and Dulecki."

"A18733?" asked Donovan, catching his breath.

"You got it."

"Jesus," said Donovan, knowing there was more to come.

"The vic is an elderly German immigrant named Karl Aachenbach who has lived there for years. Apparently he was tied up naked and thrown in a hole in the ice. His clothes were strewn around the shack."

"Jesus. Froze to death?"

"Hard as a rock."

"Get out your long underwear partner, we're going to spend Christmas in Canada."

There were no flights available so they drove to Ontario from Eau Claire. The trip took nine hours with stops for gas and one stop to eat at the only place they found open, a Chinese restaurant in Thunder Bay.

Detective Drew McAdam met them when they arrived at the Ontario Provincial Police in Kenora. Mountains of plowed snow were piled around the perimeter of the building.

"He's still in the ice. We thought we'd wait until you got here. This is a new one for us so we're going slow," said McAdam. He filled them in on what little he knew and the detectives brought McAdam up to the minute on their investigation. A short time later they drove through the area known as the Lake of the Woods and found themselves cruising across a vast, frozen sheet of ice to Aachenbach's fishing shack.

They stopped on their way to talk with the man who discovered the body, Orville Bonham. His fishing shanty sat among several others in a small cluster half way across the lake.

"That old German was deader than a doornail, eh?" said Bonham.

"What made you think to check on him? Did you see anyone or anything unusual?" asked Donovan.

"Not a soul. Checked when his truck was in the exact same spot for a couple of days and there wasn't any smoke coming from the chimney. Found him in his shack. Deader than a doornail."

"What did you do then, Mr. Bonham?" asked Donovan.

"I skedaddled over to Henry's. That's the Indian Lake Bait Shop. 'Gotta use the phone, Henry', says I. Call the police. That old German's a goner, says I."

"'Old Aachenbach? says Henry."

"'He's as old as he's ever gonna get, says I. So I call the police, eh, and tell 'em that old Aachenbach is frozen in the lake. Deader than a doornail. 'Tell whoever you send to bring an ice pick', says I," Bonham chortled.

"Did you return to Mr. Aachenbach's fishing shanty after calling the police?" asked Donovan.

"No. He tells me wait at Henry's and keep warm," Bonham replied. "I don't argue cause it's colder than a dead witches tit. A while later this officer on a snow machine comes along. So I goes outside to meet him and offer to take him to Aachenbach's, but he tells me no."

"So you stayed at the bait shop?" asked Donovan.

"No. He followed me back to my shanty and I pointed out Aachenbach's place. That's it way out there," said Bonham pointing across to the far side of the lake where the small fishing shanty sat alone in a bay. Next to it was a pickup truck.

Night came fast in the Canadian wilderness so the detectives opted to wait until the following day to continue. "The old boy will be there in the morning," said Donovan. McAdam posted an officer at the shanty for the night and the detectives found rooms at a local lodge.

By nine o'clock the next morning they were back in McAdam's cruiser returning to the crime scene. Orville Bonham flagged them down as they drove by his shanty. Once again his services as an escort were declined and the small group continued across the ice.

They drove through bright yellow police "crime scene" tape strung across the narrow opening of the bay and parked the squad car short of the shanty. Both Donovan and Scully soon wished they had dressed warmer as the wind cut into their faces, reddening their cheeks and stinging their ears.

The temperature inside the shanty was as frigid as it was outside but, bathed in the ethereal blue glow of the ice showing through the rectangle opening in the plank floor, it seemed even colder. At least they were out of the blast of the arctic wind.

They moved cautiously in silence, giving their eyes a chance to adjust to the dim light. One by one they turned on their flashlights, scanned the shack's interior until the beams came to rest at a rectangle on the floor.

Donovan swallowed hard. There, held in the vice-like grip of the ice, emerged the partially exposed head of an old man—nose up as if to breathe.

"Never seen anything like it," McAdam said, dropping to one knee. "I've seen eyes like this before but only in fish that were trapped in the ice."

Donovan and Scully knelt beside McAdam and studied the amorphous shape suspended in the cloudy, blue ice. They could just make out the top part of the man's torso and see that his hands were together and lifted as if in prayer—only these hands were tied. The gray, dead eyes were wide with terror. Donovan moved closer and saw, below a stiff thatch of rigid white hair, the familiar number burned in the victim's frozen forehead – A18733.

A generator was brought to the shack to power lights and heaters and several hours were spent examining, dusting for prints and photographing the crime scene and the truck. Possible evidence was tagged and bagged including a few dark hairs that were collected from the blanket on the cot. Donovan was reasonably certain they could provide possible DNA evidence linking Geller to the murder.

Later that morning, one of the police officers assigned to inspect an area beyond the shoreline around the bay returned to report finding snow machine tracks and footprints nearby. There were indications that someone had waited there for some time.

The scene was photographed and the snow machine tracks were followed to where they disappeared on a remote logging road perhaps a mile away.

Meanwhile, the shanty was skidded away from the site by a tow truck and a team of loggers armed with chainsaws were recruited to a cut away a large block of ice with the corpse inside. The huge saws whined and rumbled for nearly twenty minutes before the three foot thick block was freed and enough room cut-away to allow several lengths of rope to be wrapped around it with pike poles. Finally, the tow truck lifted the massive ice coffin onto a flatbed truck where it was covered in a tarp and taken into Kenora to thaw in the morgue. It would take several days.

Chief McAdams agreed to send all information to Eau Claire as the investigation progressed and by early afternoon the following day, the tired and cold Donovan and Scully passed through Thunder Bay and crossed back into the United States.

Donovan put in a call to Francis Brubaker telling her about Karl Aachenbach and hoping the news of another murder would open her eyes and induce her to cooperate. It didn't.

"In view of a fourth victim turning up, Ms. Brubaker, I thought you might revisit your policies and ask the director to allow the INS to help us."

"Look, Detective Donovan, if Karl Aachenbach entered Canada through the United States, we have no record of it. I suggest you contact Canadian Immigration to see if they have anything on him," she told him curtly.

"We've learned more about Solomon Geller," said Donovan. "I thought you'd like to know we're not moving our investigation in another direction as you suggested."

"I'd like to chat, Detective, but I have another call. Best of luck with your investigation." The phone went dead.

Donovan called Tess. "Hey, good lookin'. I heard your husband is gone and I thought I'd stop in for a little lovin," he said.

"Is this Tom or Harry?" she quipped.

Donovan chuckled. "Well, I am pretty hairy, but aren't we all?"

"Where are you, Copper?"

"Just crossed into the US from Thunder Bay. Be at least another six or seven hours."

"How did it go?" she asked.

Donovan gave her the highlights and promised he'd fill in the gaps when he got home.

Finally he called Chief Krumenauer and filled him in.

"How are you doing shaking things loose from the INS, chief?," he asked. "We're gonna be up to our necks in branded bodies if they don't help us."

"Francis Brubaker has to be the biggest tight ass I've ever come across. She couldn't shit a pin," the chief replied.

"I'm beginning to wonder if Brubaker isn't the problem–that it's someone higher up who doesn't want the INS scrutinized. From what I've read, the government let hundreds if not thousands of Nazi war criminals in after the war and they're not eager to have the world know about it."

"I'll call Senator Leffler. Maybe he can build a fire under someone," Krumenauer replied.

CHAPTER 33

"Good news," said Chief Krumenauer when Donovan walked into the station the next morning with a load of books. "Apparently it takes at least four murders, but Senator Leffler's office has agreed to look into the INS thing."

"Great! Did he say when?"

"His people said it would be a priority."

"His office? His people? Did you talk to him?" asked Donovan, making no effort to hide his aggravation.

"Look, Mike. He's a fucking Senator for Christ's sake. Those guys are busier than one-armed paperhangers. They have to rely on their 'people' to keep up," countered an equally irritated Krumenauer. "Is this thing becoming too much for you?"

"No," Donovan replied contritely. "I appreciate your support, chief. I'm just tired."

"Well, I'm giving you extra help just the same. I'm assigning Nolan to work with you."

Luther "Lute" Nolan was a skeleton-thin, 42-year old man who looked to Donovan as if he might tip over at any minute. The only color in his face were the bluish-red acne scars in his hollow cheeks and the combed over wisps of thin brown hair that lay like wet grass across the crown of his head like they were blown flat by a strong wind. Despite his run-down appearance, Nolan worked long hours and never called in sick. More than likely, it had something to do with having the seven school age children at home and an angry, overworked wife who called several times a day to vent about this or that. Donovan wasn't a fan because the years had made Dolan so cynical, but he knew he was a good cop and was glad to have him on board.

Donovan was unpacking the books when he heard Scully's voice. "Morning, partner," Scully said, taking off his heavy winter coat and dropping into his desk chair. "Where do we begin?"

"The chief is giving us Nolan. We'll brief him when he gets in and give him copies of everything we have."

Ten minutes later Donovan looked up from his notes to see Nolan standing in the doorway wearing a cheap gray suit that hung on him like a shower curtain.

"Morning, Mike," said Nolan. "The chief asked me to give you a hand."

"Morning, Lute. We can use your help all right. It looks like we have a serial killer on our hands," he said, pausing for affect. "Let me grab Scully and we'll brief you. Get yourself a cup."

Nolan returned with a Coke and a Little Debbie Snack Cake. Chief Krumenauer followed close behind dragging a chair from the next office.

"Thought I'd join you," said the chief.

They all sat around Donovan's desk. Scully handed Nolan a file folder.

"That's everything we have, Lute. We think we know who the perp is and what's motivating him. He's one sick puppy and very dangerous."

Donovan held up the two photographs of David Geller.

"His name is David Geller. He's the only child of Hannah Geller and the recently deceased Solomon Geller, an appliance dealer in a Jewish enclave in Brooklyn, New York called Crown Heights."

Scully handed out copies of the two photographs of David Geller along with a third one of Solomon Geller that Donovan held up.

"It is important that you know about Solomon Geller because his life had a profound impact on his son." Donovan reviewed what they knew and noticed that Lute hadn't touched his Coke or snack cake.

"The Nazi's were eager to hide evidence of the atrocities when the allies moved into Germany at the end of the war. Thousands of records were destroyed and a last ditch attempt to eliminate prisoners was undertaken. As a result, Solomon Geller and hundreds of other death camp prisoners were loaded on a train bound for the mountains where they were to be killed and their remains buried."

As he listened to Donovan, Scully thought about how important being a policeman was to his partner and how good he really was.

Donovan sipped his coffee. "Any questions so far?"

Silence.

"Like other Jews who survived the Holocaust, Geller tried to rebuild his life. He married. Had a son. Started a business. He also began a crusade to find Nazi war criminals that had come to the United States by reading other survivor's accounts in the Yiddish language newspapers. But, he never recovered emotionally from his experience. He suffered from PTSS or Post Traumatic Stress Syndrome with severe depression and reoccurring nightmares. Eventually it led to his suicide."

Donovan picked up a marker. "That brings us to his son," he said, writing the name David Geller on the white board.

"Solomon Geller had a huge impact on his son. His wife said he relived his death camp experience in flashbacks every day of his life and in nightmares every night.

"David Geller saw all this and more. Let me read you something I found that might give us all a better understanding," said Donovan opening a book to a page marked with a yellow post-it note and read outloud. "A psychologist who treats Holocaust survivors and their children, suggests there is a second generation 'complex' characterized by processes that affect identity, self-esteem, interpersonal interactions and worldview."

"It all fits together, doesn't it?" said Scully.

"Yeah. David Geller is smart. Straight A's. Chess champion. That sort of thing. So when his father asked him to learn Yiddish and to help him find Nazis war criminals, he picked it up fast. The more he learned, the more obsessive his hatred grew of the Nazi's and anything that smacked of anti-Semitism. He volunteered to join the Israel Defense Forces and was accepted into an elite special forces unit. He was decorated for heroism and highly regarded for his bravery. Then he came unglued and started going on unauthorized missions by himself. We're told that he single handedly killed several of the enemy force using only a knife."

Donovan returned to the white board and made a list under the name David Geller.

- Emotionally disturbed/possibly psychotic
- Angry
- Fearless
- Intelligent
- Highly trained
- Struggle with self-esteem
- Loner
- On a mission

"I ended the list with 'on a mission' because I believe that Solomon Geller's suicide triggered a response in David that has led to four murders as a way of avenging his father's suffering and death. If the government was going to turn a blind eye to evidence the Gellers presented, David was going to take matters into his own hands."

"Now let's move on to the victims," said Donovan, moving to the board again and writing.

When he finished the briefing, Donovan handed out assignments. "Scully I'd like you to continue to update and monitor the national law enforcement web site and see if you can find any of Geller's friends in Brooklyn. Guys he went to school with or played chess with. See if there is anyone he might still be in contact with."

"Lute, I want you to make a visit back to Canada and show Geller's photo around at hotels, motels, lodges and restaurants in the Vermillion Bay area to see if you can find anyone who remembers seeing him or anyone resembling him. Maybe we'll get lucky."

Lute opened the crisp new file folder, extracted the photos of David Geller and studied them. "How recent are these?" he asked.

"The Official Israeli Military ID photo was taken maybe four years ago. The other one maybe a year or two."

"I'd like to scan the latest and Photoshop some other versions of it with longer hair and maybe a beard and mustache," Lute replied. "And glasses. Glasses can really change an appearance."

"You know how?" asked the chief.

"My seventeen year old recluse son does. You can't believe the things he can do on a computer," Lute replied. "He's the wondrous result of a misspent youth. But, we can't get him to leave his room to take out the garbage."

"Can you be ready to roll first thing in the morning?" asked Donovan. Lute nodded.

"I'll contact Geller's military unit again to see if he had any close friends he might still have stayed in contact with. I'll also check with Oklahoma authorities on the outside chance that a missing person was reported around the time of the John Doe murder. I wouldn't be surprised if an elderly immigrant was a no show somewhere.

"Our best hope is to learn who is left on Geller's hit list and get a step ahead of him. That isn't going to happen until the INS agrees to open their files. The chief has gotten the ball rolling on that through political channels."

"Any word, chief?" asked Scully.

"Not yet. I have a call in to speak directly with the Senator. His people are dropping the ball".

CHAPTER 34

Three days passed since Chief Krumenauer had made his request to Senator Leffler's office for access to the Geller files. When he called again, an officious-sounding staffer answered the phone who acted as though it was an enormous interruption.

"Your request has been passed along to the Justice Department," said the staffer. "It's out of our hands now."

Krumenauer imagined his request slowly filtering through the layers of bureaucrats. "Where is it now?" he asked.

"Just a minute." Krumenauer could hear the clunk of the phone being set down and waited. "It was routed to the Attorney General's office. You'll have to check with them."

"So do I call the Attorney General?" asked Krumenauer in frustration.

"Well, I suppose you could start there."

Krumenauer took the staffer's name, wrote down the number he was given and punched it into the phone. He drummed his fingers until it was answered by a recorded message.

"You have reached the office of the United States Department of Justice. If you know your party's four-digit extension, please enter it now. For a directory of department personnel, press one. For a directory of Justice Department Branches, press two. To speak to an operator, press 0 or stay on the line."

Krumenauer pressed 0. "Justice Department Information. How may I direct your call?" oozed a woman in a syrupy, southern drawl.

He explained the situation and asked to speak with someone in the Attorney General's office who might know the status of his request.

"Yes, sir. I'll connect you."

A few seconds later the phone rang again.

"This is the office the United States Attorney General. If you know your party's four-digit extension, please enter it now. For a directory of personnel, press one. For a directory of Office Branches, press two. To speak to an operator, press 0 or stay on the line."

Krumenauer's scalp began to itch. A sure sign that his temper was getting the best of him. He took a deep breath and pressed 0 again.

"Attorney General Boykin's Office. May I help you?" A man's voice this time.

"My name is Krumenauer. I am the Chief of Police in Eau Claire, Wisconsin. We're investigating several serial murders and have an urgent need for you folks to open your records. Two weeks ago, a request for information was sent to the Attorney General on my behalf by Senator Leffl48er. I have not received a reply and the urgency of the request is growing."

"Do you have the file number, Chief Krumenauer?"

"No. I wasn't given one."

"I see," said the man, making no attempt to hide the dismay in his voice. "And you say the request was made by Senator Lefler two weeks ago?"

"Yes."

"I'll have to track it down. Can you give me a number where I can call you back?

"Sure," Krumenauer rattled off his phone number. "Now can you give me your name and number? This really is a matter of life and death."

"Potts. Arlen Potts. I'm an assistant administrator. Extension 5943."

Krumenauer hung up and called Donovan into his office to report his unsuccessful attempts to track down the request. "Potts said he'd look into it and call back," he said. "I'll let you know when I hear from him."

Donovan returned to his office and dropped into his desk chair. The murder book on his desk was open to the photograph of David Geller. "Where are you?" he said out loud to no one just as the phone rang.

"Donovan," he said picking up.

"Mike, this is Lute calling from the frozen north."

"Lute. Whacha got?"

"I checked in with Ontario Provincial Police when I arrived

and updated Drew McAdam. He had already phoned a few of the lodges near the murder scene on Vermillion Bay without success and agreed to help me cover a larger area to show Geller's photograph around.

"This place is enormous. Vermillion Bay is located on Eagle Lake and Eagle Lake is interconnected with too many others to count. There are dozens of hotels, motels and lodges here and in the area. We focused on the lodges on Eagle Lake that rented snowmobiles and got lucky this morning. The Sunset Lodge is about six miles from Aachenbach's fishing shanty. The owner recognized the photograph of David Geller–only with longer hair and a mustache. He was staying there at the time of the murder. He registered as David Abraham, but the owner's certain that it's our man."

"Good work, Nolan."

"He took his meals in his room and didn't mix with any of the other guests. Said he was a bird watcher when he made his telephone reservation and wanted to rent a snowmobile. Left every morning early and didn't return until late. McAdam is checking with the Ontario telephone company for a log of inbound calls for that period. I also checked the tracks that were found in the woods near the crime scene and they match the tracks on the snowmobile he rented."

"What kind of vehicle did he drive?" asked Donovan hopefully.

"A white Ford Econoline. Oklahoma plates. BNC-098."

CHAPTER 35

By Saturday, the Air Policeman on duty at the back gate to McDonald Air Force Base recognized the black Ford van with the cheap paint job. Still, when it pulled to a stop, he studied the photo of the bearded man with the shaved head on the photo ID and compared it to the driver in the Cubs cap. Once again he found the name David Abraham on the authorized list and waved him through. Abraham was one of the civilians regularly enrolled in a two-week high altitude training class at the hypobaric chamber of the 831st Flight Training Squadron. The chamber was capable of simulating altitudes up to 85,000 feet, It was used to train pilots to recognize a dangerous drop in pressure at high altitudes by understanding the early symptoms of hypoxia; nausea, vomiting, weakness, dizziness and headache. If gone uncorrected, the pilot's coordination would deteriorate, they would become disoriented, experience loss of memory, hallucinations, irrational behavior, and coma. Eventually it would result in a manner of death that never failed to grab the attention of even the most blasé pilot.

Even though the FAA-sponsored classes were held during the day, the guard had become accustomed to Abraham's odd hours and assumed he was getting in extra training time or just liked to watch the fighters take off at the end of the flightline. Many visitors did–especially at night. At any rate, there was no time restriction on his pass. He was free to come and go for the duration of the two-week operating course.

David Geller was relieved when he could no longer see the gate in the rear view mirror. This would be his last day as David Abraham. He smiled to himself as he drove along Runway Avenue through the unpopulated north end of the base where the primary take-off runway ended. When he came to a long dark stretch, he pulled over and took a flashlight from the glove box. Turning, he aimed the light at a large tote bin tied down securely to the van floor in the back. He crawled between the seats, lifted the lid and shown the light inside. A pair of frightened eyes peered back at him from the deeply wrinkled face of an old man. The eyes blinked blindly before closing against the glare. After making certain the old man was still securely bound and gagged, Geller returned to the driver's seat.

Now the familiar ache began to climb up his neck to his head. He drew a deep breath. His mind began to drift. Slowly the soft separation from reality grew and he felt his body ascending above himself while his mind went deep inside where the other self waited, eager to begin.

Gradually the world around him became dreamlike. Even the powerful roar of the F4 Phantoms taking off barely registered as the afterburners disappeared into the night sky.

It's time, he thought. He turned off the van's headlights, pulled away from the side of the road and drove the now familiar route to the remote concrete block structure that was home to the 831st Flight Training Squadron. A single lamp illuminated the rear parking lot as he backed up to the loading dock. Geller grabbed his backpack from the passenger seat floor, got out and fished in his pocket for the key stamped REAR ENTRANCE that he had taken from the trainer's desk. He opened the loading dock door and muscled the tote bin from the back of the van into the building where the hypobaric chamber waited.

The old man crammed inside the stifling bin was finding it increasingly difficult to breathe. His nose had been broken when he collapsed from being tasered and the swelling made every breath a struggle. The rubber ball jammed into his mouth and the duct tape made it worse. So when the lid was opened he was at once grateful for the fresh air and terrified at what would happen to him next. As his eyes adjusted to the dim light, he could see his abductor's shaved head then, gradually, his bearded, angular face and strange yellowish, green eyes.

"We are here, Herr Mandel."

The old man was stunned to hear his real name as Geller grabbed him under the arms and lifted his frail body with surprising ease from the sweltering tote bin into the coolness of the air-conditioned room. His panic grew as he realized that he was being lowered into a wheel chair. He struggled helplessly with the nylon rope that tied his feet and hands. Pathetic begging sounds came from his swollen mouth. He looked for some sign of humanity in his assailant's cold eyes. There was none.

Suddenly the light from a small lamp revealed a large room dominated by a long, white metal cylinder the size of a tanker trailer. Thick steel casings bolted along the cylinder held small round portals and a maze of pipes and cables from tanks and assorted machines fed into it from every direction. The old man fixed his gaze on the large steel hatch. The massive hinges and wheeled locking mechanism signaled it was the main access to the cylinder. A workstation next to it glowed with an ominous array of monitors, switches, and blinking lights.

Mandel's breathing grew more shallow and quicker. He saw that the bald man was watching him take it all in. He seemed to enjoy the old man's fear.

"You may not recognize this. It's a hypobaric chamber," Geller said, reaching into the backpack and withdrawing a small device of some sort. Instantly the bright flame from a tiny propane cylinder bathed the area in a warm glow. He set the device carefully on a table with the flames shooting upward at a row of brass numbers.

Mandel saw his assailant suddenly grimace as if in excruciating pain and bend forward at the waist with his hands flattened on the table. The bald man didn't move for two or three minutes then slowly straightened and turned to face him. When he did, Mandel saw that something about him was somehow more evil. His eyes more menacing.

The old man's eyes fluttered wildly. Even more urgent mumbling issued from his taped mouth. His assailant paid no attention.

"The chamber is bigger than you're used to," Geller said,

removing a sheath from his backpack and sliding out a long knife with an ominously curved blade. "It can hold a dozen people all at once. Imagine that. You could get a dozen Jews in here."

In that instant the old man understood. A rush of images came back to him of the men he watched die horrible deaths so many years ago. His breathing grew even more labored. He felt his heart pounding. He closed his eyes tight as his assailant moved toward him, knife poised for the first cut. He braced himself for the pain, but instead felt his body lift violently and his clothing being roughly pulled and torn. He looked down to see the shining blade slice through his shirt. Buttons flew. Shreds of cloth ripped away. He felt his thick leather belt slashed and stripped, and the odd freedom of the too-tight shoelaces on his swollen feet being cut away. He was completely naked in less than two minutes.

A sickening feeling of overwhelming vulnerability overcame him and he began to shake uncontrollably as the chill of the air conditioning cooled his fear-sweat skin. When urine puddled under the wheel chair on the shiny, grey painted floor, the old man saw the corners of his capture's mouth lift in an almost imperceptible grin. He struggled not to vomit.

Geller checked the branding iron. The brass was just beginning to change color. Plenty of time, he thought, turning back to his naked, shivering captive. He approached the cowering figure, grabbed and pulled-tight fistfuls of gray hair, slicing off clumps again and again until the old man's head was a mass of bleeding wounds. Geller stuffed the handfuls of hair in a plastic bag, wiped the knife on a scrap of torn shirt and returned to the now red-hot branding iron. He turned off the flame and held it so close to the whimpering old man that he could feel the heat on his face.

When it came, the shock of the blistering hot metal pressing into his forehead and the smell of his own burning flesh was more than he could endure. Everything went black.

He awoke to the pungent odor of ammonia from a small bottle being held under his nose and discovered that he had been rolled into the hungry mouth of the chamber.

He felt his assailant's warm breath in his ear and heard him whisper, "It is time, Herr Mandel."

The old man wrestled frantically to free himself until he heard the heavy steel door slam shut. The last thing he heard was his own heavy breathing above the sound of compressors pumping the air from the chamber.

CHAPTER 36

Before Luther Nolan returned from Canada, a search by the Oklahoma DMV revealed that the plates on the white Econoline belonged on a 1962 Chevy pickup registered to one Sigrid Bender whose last known address was a rural route in Pokesa, Oklahoma. Bender was more or less a hermit who lived alone in a tiny trailer a short distance from where John Doe had been killed in the remote area of Choctaw County. Authorities determined from moldy food in the trailer that it had been vacant for some time. Broken furnishings found in disarray indicated a struggle.

When Bender's driver's license photo was identified by the Choctaw coroner, the trailer was sealed and treated as a crime scene. Latent fingerprints found inside were matched to those taken from the body of John Doe.

Sigrid Bender was officially listed as a murder victim.

A search of the trailer uncovered a lock box containing a birth certificate from Hamburg, Germany dated January 12, 1917, a Swiss passport, a visa and naturalization papers. There were no family photos or personal correspondence—no clue to a next of kin. The only mail was the standard utility bills, a stack of social security checks and a pile of junk mail. Apparently Bender had no telephone.

The morning following Lute's return, Donovan assembled his team to bring the chief up to date on the investigation.

"The John Doe in Oklahoma has been positively identified as Sigrid Bender. Eighty years old. Born in Germany. Came here legally 1956. He lived alone in a small trailer and has no next of kin we are aware of," said Donovan, nodding to Lute.

Lute read from his notes. "Bender's license plates were on a white Ford Econoline van driven by a white male, registered at the Sunset Lodge on Vermillion Bay in Canada as David Abraham. The manager identified a photograph of David Geller retouched with a mustache and longer hair. He was a guest for two days prior to and on the day Karl Aachenbach was murdered. Around Christmas. He rented a snowmobile from the lodge reportedly to get around the lake bird watching."

"Did he give a home address when he checked in?" Scully asked.

"A fictitious address in Tulsa."

"So now we have an alias to work with and a stolen Oklahoma plate—either of which could already be changed. Still, let's see if they lead anywhere. Put the license number out there with the Crime Information Bureau. Scully will work his magic on the internet to see if the name David Abraham turns up anywhere."

"I also tracked down a couple of Geller's old school acquaintances in Brooklyn," said Scully. "Couple of guys remember him, but he mostly kept to himself. Kind of sad character. Smart. Very focused. But, no one has seen him in years."

"Anything new at your end, chief?" asked Donovan.

"Not much to report except red tape," he said. "I contacted Senator Leffler's office. I was told that the Attorney General had been asked to look into our request to release the Geller files. A Justice Department assistant administrator I spoke with told me that since I didn't have a file number to track it, he would look into it and call me back. I called back this morning but could only leave a message. I'll try again this afternoon."

"Scully," said Donovan. "Anything on the branding iron?"

Brian Scully cleared his throat. "The branding iron used by Geller is either custom-made or has interchangeable brass characters that slide onto a hand-held device and heated by propane. An electric branding iron is unlikely because of the remote locations in which at least three of the victims were murdered. There were two manufacturers in China that offered interchangeable half-inch letters and numerals. Just one in the United States; a small company located in El Paso, Texas. The Lone Star Brass Works. I sent a close-up photograph of the brand on one of the vics to the owner said it was possible that they produced it. He was compiling a list of dealers. They were also sold directly to consumers by the hundreds."

"Check to see if the name David Abraham is in his records, will ya?" asked Donovan.

"Way ahead of you," he replied.

Scully's briefing continued for several more minutes. "The rope was determined to be a 16 strand, quarter inch polyethylene. It's lightweight, strong, melts at a relatively low 200 degrees Fahrenheit and remains flexible even in cold temperatures."

"Perfect if you're going to torture someone in a frozen lake," said Donovan.

Scully nodded and continued, "You can buy it by the foot in damn near any store that sells hardware, sporting goods, boating supplies–you know. The duct tape is made by 3M in Minnesota – probably by the mile. The rubber balls could have come from anywhere."

"Not much to go on," said Krumenauer. "We're running out of time before he does another one."

CHAPTER 37

An hour before sunrise as he cruised down Runway Avenue on a clear Monday morning, Staff Sergeant Daniel Garber's sweat-stained uniform already looked like a khaki Rorschach test. He leaned his Harley gracefully into the empty parking lot of the 831st Training Squadron Flight Center and rumbled to a stop.

Garber was surprised to see a light on in the big room that held the hypobaric pressure chamber they called Big Bertha. He had shut down the facility for the weekend on Friday night and was certain he had turned it out. He unlocked the door, threw on the lights and looked around the office. "Anyone here?"

He paused a few seconds to listen, tossed his keys on his desk and walked to the door leading to the chamber. "Hello?" he called, peering in to see a lone lamp glowing on the counsel desk–a warning light was flashing on the control panel. Garber flipped on the bank switches for the overhead lights and the presence of the enormous steel, hypobaric chamber filled the room. He rushed to the control panel, pushing an out-of-place bin away and saw that the flashing red light was a warning indicator that an emergency override of the system had taken place.

"How could that be?" he thought. He booted up the computer and accessed the activity log expecting to see that the last recorded event was the final shutdown procedure on Friday night. It wasn't. There was activity on Saturday night beginning at 2223 hours that indicated a sustained atmospheric episode peaking at an astonishing 83,000 feet before Bertha automatically shut down.

Gerber picked up the phone and called Lt. Eleanor Bishop, his immediate supervisor. "Something's wrong here, Lieutenant. Somehow Bertha hit 83,000 feet over the weekend before the override shut her down."

"Holy shit! Thank God no one was inside." There was a long

silence. "There isn't anyone in there, is there Sergeant?"

"Just a minute, Lieutenant."

Ten-seconds later she could hear Sgt. Garber retching in the background.

Donovan paused on his way out the door to wait for Tess to answer the kitchen phone.

"Hi Brian. Sure," she said. "Copper, it's for you."

Donovan took the phone from her. "What's up, Brian?"

"We've got another one."

CHAPTER 38

Senator Malcolm Leffler tucked a white linen napkin into his collar and smoothed it over his silk tie. He was about to dip a spoon into a bowl of bean soup when he heard his name mentioned in reference to an upcoming story on CNN. He looked up just in time to see the television go to a commercial.

Reaching across his desk for the remote, he nudged the volume up and returned to his soup until the talking head of the newscaster reappeared.

"The latest victim in a series of bizarre murders attributed to a serial killer known as 'The Executioner' has been reported in Florida. The naked body of an elderly man identified by authorities as Josef Mandel, was found tied in a wheelchair and locked in a high altitude training chamber at McDonald AFB several miles from his home in Panama City. Like the Executioner's other victims, his hair had been cut off, he was bound with duct tape, gagged and the number A18733 was burned into his forehead with what authorities believe to be a branding iron..

"Mandel, a former soldier in Nazi Germany, immigrated to the United States at the end of WW II. The cause of death has not been determined, but it appears likely that he succumbed to high altitude cerebral edema, also known as HACE, from exposure to the high altitude conditions up to 80,000 feet created in the hyperbolic chamber used by the Air Force to train pilots to recognize it's symptoms."

Senator Leffler listened intently and tried to imagine how his name could be associated with this heinous crime.

"With us by from the Houston Aerospace Institute is Professor Carmine Updahl." The image of a middle aged, overweight man with thick glasses appeared on the screen.

"Professor. Precisely what happens to a body in an environment of such low pressure?"

Updahl blinked nervously and cleared his throat.

"Yes. First the gases in the lungs and digestive tract would expand and rupture. Fluids in the victim's mouth and eyes would quickly boil away. As the water in the muscles and soft tissues evaporate, some parts of the body swell to twice their normal size. The reduced pressure would also cause the nitrogen contained in the blood to form gaseous bubbles–an extremely painful condition known to scuba divers as the bends. In time the blood itself would begin to boil."

"Thank you, professor," said the visibly upset reporter abruptly ending the interview. "We apologize for not warning viewers in advance of the graphic nature of that report."

"The latest victim is the fifth in a rash of gruesome serial killings. The first is believed to be an elderly woman in Eau Claire, Wisconsin in July of last year followed by others in Oklahoma, Ontario Canada, Chicago and now Florida."

"Eau Claire, Wisconsin Police Detective Michael Donovan who has led this investigation since July, made this statement to reporters just minutes ago."

The Senator set down his spoon and punched up the volume even more as Michael Donovan, surrounded by microphones in front of Eau Claire Police Headquarters, appeared on the screen.

"We have released the name and photograph of a 26 year old New York man as the prime suspect, whereabouts unknown." David Geller's photo appeared in the corner of the screen.

"His name is David Geller, but has also used the alias David Abraham. Geller is six foot two, 185 pounds and has green eyes. Although he appears clean-shaven and has short hair in this photograph, he is known to alter his appearance and was last seen wearing a mustache. Geller was last seen driving a white Ford Econoline van with stolen Oklahoma plates BNC-098.

The shot of Donovan was replaced by a title slide that read *The Executioner* in bold letters superimposed over a swastika and an image of Adolf Hitler.

"CNN has learned that Geller, now known as The Executioner, is targeting individuals he believes to be Nazi war criminals who were identified by his father, the late Solomon Geller, a former prisoner of the Auschwitz concentration camp during the final years of the WWII. The senior Geller spent years researching war crimes reported by other death camp survivors and eventually provided various government agencies with documentation that identified 59 war alleged criminals believed to have immigrated to the United States. Despite this documentation and eyewitness accounts, he claimed his attempts to convince any of these agencies to investigate and possibly deport these individuals to stand trial went ignored. When the senior Geller took his own life nearly a year ago, his son, David Geller, disappeared from his home in Brooklyn, New York taking with him the files of last eight of these war criminals still known to be alive.

"According to our sources, the United States Immigration and Naturalization service does have knowledge of these files as well as additional information that could help identify the three remaining potential victims–unfortunately they continue to withhold it for political reasons. When Eau Claire Police Chief Clarence Krumenauer contacted Wisconsin Senator Leffler two weeks ago regarding the lack of cooperation, Leffler expressed his outrage of the INS's refusal to release these documents and offered to intervene. However, no information has yet to be forthcoming and his office has been unresponsive to further efforts to move forward."

Donovan reappeared on the screen. "We hope that this horrific new murder will induce the INS to give the request the attention it deserves," he said. "There is a mentally ill serial killer on the loose who must be apprehended before he can kill again."

Leffler marched red faced out of his office into the office of the deputy director, Thomas Finney, with the napkin still tucked into his collar. "Tom. I want you to find out what happened to my request to have the INS make information available to Police Chief in Eau Claire. We have egg on our collective faces."

Five minutes after the press conference was over, Donovan and

Scully were summoned into Chief Krumenauer's office to watch the CNN report.

"Well, I think our cage rattling went well, didn't you?" he said.

Donovan nodded. "How long do you think it will take before we hear?"

Krumenauer looked at his watch. "Any minute," he said just as the phone rang on cue.

The three of them shared a look of victory as Krumenauer pressed the button for the speakerphone.

"This is Chief Krumenauer," he said calmly.

"Please hold for Senator Leffler."

The chief mouthed the words, "I'm going to enjoy this."

"Chief Krumenauer. Thank you for taking my call," said the Senator. "I see on the news that you made a breakthrough in this 'Executioner' thing. Excellent work. Excellent."

"Thank you sir. We have our very best people on it," he replied, looking a Donovan and Scully.

"Look I want you to know that you can expect full cooperation from the INS on this from now on. Sometimes things fall through the cracks in Washington," Leffler said. "It shouldn't happen, but it does."

"You will be getting a call within the hour from them. In the mean time, feel free to call me directly. In addition, I have assigned one of my best people to stay on top of this and see personally to any request you may have."

"Who would that be?" asked Krumenauer.

"His name is Potts. Arlen Potts."

"I'll look forward to working with him, sir. Thank you."

Donovan and Scully were back in their office when they got a call from INS twenty-two minutes later.

"Donovan."

"Detective Donovan. This is Francis Brubaker at the INS. I have all 59 Geller files in front of me."

CHAPTER 39

Donovan asked Brubaker to hold while he faxed her a neatly typed, two-column list.

"I have it," she said when the transmission was complete.

"These are the names we found on the fifty-one files in Geller's home–suspected war criminals that he identified and located. They came here, lived the American dream and died natural deaths while the NIS and other government agencies looked the other way," said Donovan.

"Look, Detective Donovan...."

"No, you look," he barked, cutting her off. "I'm not saying they were all guilty. Who the hell knows? Some were probably victims themselves. But, for years that old man spoon-fed your agency information about them that you should have investigated. Some of these people were monsters and you looked the other way. You say you have all fifty-nine files he sent you?"

"Yes. We have them all," she replied nervously.

"If you eliminate the ones on the list I just faxed, there should be eight files remaining. I'm betting I know who five of them are," he told Brubaker. "They're all Geller's victims. If we don't find the three remaining before he does, I don't want to think about how they are going to die. It won't be pleasant."

"I'll sort out the deceased files and send you everything we have on what's left. There should be eight. Right?"

"Eight. Right."

"I'm on it," said Brubaker. "And Donovan. I want you to know it wasn't my idea to block your investigation. I was just following orders."

"Where have I heard that before?" Donovan replied, hanging up.

Minutes later, the fax machine was churning out copies of passport photos, immigration documents, visas, foreign identity papers, military records, birth certificates, social security documents and other official documents from the INS files. They came in eight separate batches. Each finished with the additional documents that had been presented to the INS by Solomon Geller. Included was page after page of correspondence imploring the INS to help.

"Geller certainly did his homework," said Donovan, admiring the printouts piling up in the receiving tray. "Very impressive."

There were depositions from victims, eye witness reports, census data, employment records, newspaper articles, records taken from the Nuremberg Trials held in 1945, copies of declassified records released under the Nazi War Crimes Disclosure Act of 1998, archives opened by the Russians after the fall of the Soviet Union and dozens of others. Donovan and Scully carefully assembled them into eight files. Five belonged to the Executioner's first victims; Greta Bauer, Milos Dulecki, Sigrid Bender, Karl Aachenbach and Josef Mandel–Donovan set them aside.

Scully and Nolan pulled their chairs close as Donovan placed the three remaining files in front of him on his desk in a neat row.

"We're coming down to the wire. Where do you suppose we'll find these old Nazis?" he asked.

"Could be next door for all I know," Scully replied.

Donovan gave him a quizzical look and raised a bushy eyebrow.

"Well, Greta Bauer was," said Scully.

"No doubt a lot of the information in these files is dated and these people may have moved on from the addresses," said Donovan. "But, there's good reason to believe they're still alive and we have plenty to start searching with."

"They could have changed their identities," said Lute.

"It's unlikely," Donovan replied. "After all this time without any threat of deportation, there's no reason to. They misrepresented their pasts to the United States Government when they applied for citizenship and no one ever checked. Except for Solomon Geller."

Donovan opened the first file and read out loud. "Dieter Eichel. Austrian. Born in Vienna August 1, 1918. Date of entry into the United States; September 8, 1951. Naturalized 1953. Became a member of the Hitler Youth as a boy. Claims to have been only a low level prison guard at Majdanek death camp in Poland where 200,000 people were killed."

Donovan opened the envelope sandwiched in the file and removed the Solomon Geller documents. "Geller tells a different story. We have affidavits from three eye witnesses who testified that Eichel was one of the SS soldiers who operated the machine guns on November 3, 1943, when 17,000 Jews were machine-gunned to death as part of the 'Erntefest Aktion'."

Geller found two Dieter Eichels. One, a retired accountant living in Victorville, California, the other in a Sarasota, Florida retirement community since 1995 living on social security and a pension from Connecticut Light and Power where he was employed for 37 years.

Donovan handed the file to Nolan. "See if you can figure out which Dieter Eichel he's going after, will you, Lute?"

Lute took the file and leafed through it.

"Am I the only one who feels conflicted about this?" asked Nolan, holding up the Eichel file. "If this old asshole helped machine gun 17,000 people in a single day, doesn't he deserve whatever Geller can do to him?"

Donovan and Scully exchanged uncomfortable looks. "We don't know for certain that he did it, Lute. He was never tried," said Donovan unconvincingly.

"He was never even investigated," Lute replied sarcastically.

"Well, it doesn't matter. It isn't your job to prove him guilty or innocent. It's your job to catch the bad guy–that's David Geller," Donovan replied.

"That brings us to Kurt Mueller," said Donovan, opening the next file. "Born in Dusseldorf, Germany in 1920. According to his military record, he enlisted voluntarily in the German Army in 1939. First deployment was as a guard in the Jewish Ghetto of Krakow, Poland of that same year then went on to serve as a truck driver in North Africa in the "Afrika Korps," under German General Erwin Rommel. Mueller was captured in May 1943 in Tunisia and presumably sat out the rest as a prisoner of war.

"According to the INS documents, he applied for a visa to

the United States after the war under the Displaced Persons Act stating on his application that he was merely a foot soldier in the Wehrmacht. After establishing that he had a relative here who would employ him and provide a home, he was approved and immigrated to the United States in 1955."

Donovan removed the envelope containing the additional documents submitted to the INS by Solomon Geller. "During the time when Mueller was a guard in Krakow," he said, "Geller asserts that he shot and killed three children as punishment for stealing bread. He included affidavits to that effect from two eyewitnesses. He made several unsuccessful attempts to persuade the INS to confirm this and his identity. Geller discontinued correspondence after indicating in his final letter to the INS two years ago that he had reason to believe that Mueller was living in Iowa should they ever decide to pursue investigating his background and consider deportation."

Donovan replaced the envelope in the file and handed it to Scully. "He's all yours, Brian. If Geller was right, Mueller is still in Iowa."

The final file was that of Adolf Reinhardt. "Born in Munich, Germany in 1919. Stated on his citizenship request that he was a German foot soldier stationed in France and was captured toward the end of the war. Date of entry into the United States: September 22, 1949. Naturalized 1952. Last known address; Fiddler's Gap, North Carolina. Former prisoners of Buchenwald made statements to Geller that Reinhardt was a murderous psychopath who tortured and killed dozens of Jews in all manner of ways."

"I'll see if I can find Mr. Reinhardt," said Donovan, closing the file.

CHAPTER 40

Nolan walked down the hall and disappeared into his office with the Deiter Eichel file in one hand and a Coke in the other. Scully followed Donovan back to their office, dropped into his desk chair, popped a fresh stick of Juicy Fruit into his mouth and opened the Kurt Mueller file. In it he found a thick stack of two-hole punched papers held together by metal fasters; a US Visa and a Visa application stating Mueller's occupation as a farmer, Approval Notice, green card and other documents issued by the US Citizenship and Immigration Service. He also found Mueller's military records from his service in the German Wehrmacht including an old photograph of him as a handsome young man with closely cropped hair and rimless glasses.

A copy of a letter from the Social Security Administration indicated Kurt Mueller's mailing address as 603 Galloway St., Storm Lake, Iowa; a good day's drive from Eau Claire. A separate manila envelope addressed to the INS from Solomon Geller was inserted in the file lose. Scully set it aside to read last.

The documents painted a portrait of an unremarkable man caught up in the circumstances of war who survived and ultimately built a good life in the United States. Scully read carefully, filling in the gaps left by Donovan. Slowly, Kurt Mueller was coming to life in his mind.

By the time he finished reading the official documents, his Juicy Fruit was reduced to a gray wad of tasteless rubber. He spit it into the trashcan and opened the envelope containing Geller's file on Mueller. Gradually the image of a very different man began to emerge that was both disturbing and wildly inconsistent with a German farm boy.

Two eyewitness accounts provided by Solomon Geller identified Mueller as a Nazi guard in the overcrowded, disease-ridden Jewish ghetto in Krakow, Poland. Both accused him of the cold-blooded execution of three starving children who had done nothing more than to go outside the ghetto walls to find bread to eat. When they were caught returning through a small opening in a wall, an arrogant young soldier they knew to be Kurt Mueller, they said, lined the children up against the wall and shot them on the spot.

Scully leaned back in his chair and conjured up a stark, black and white newsreel of the scene and shuttered. The private thought that had been lurking in his mind since he returned from New York crept into his mind; perhaps Geller's victims deserved to die.

Scully popped a fresh stick of Juicy Fruit and turned to his computer–he quickly found five Muellers listed in the online Storm Lake telephone directory. To his surprise, the only one listed with the first name Kurt came with the prefix of Reverend. He jotted down the Galloway Street address and phone number on a note pad and punched it in on his desk phone.

"Reverand Kurt Mueller?" asked Scully when the voice of an elderly man answered after several rings.

"Ya, this is he," came the reply.

Scully sat erect in his desk chair.

"Do you reside at 603 Galloway, Mr. Mueller?" he asked.

"Yes. That is the parsonage. Who is calling please?" asked Mueller politely.

Somewhat off balance now, Scully introduced himself then asked, "My records indicate that you're a farmer."

"I was a farmer at one time. That was a long time ago. I'm a Lutheran Minister now. Semi-retired. Is there something wrong?"

"Were you a member of the German army stationed in Krakow, Poland during World War II?" asked Scully.

"That's not something I brag about," Mueller replied calmly after an uncomfortably long pause. "I've put that behind me."

"But, you were a Nazi?"

"No. I never joined the party. I was simply a soldier in the German army."

"Are you familiar with the recent serial murders of former German World War II soldiers?" asked Scully.

Scully waited through another pause then finally said, "Reverend Mueller?"

"Yes. It's all over the news," Mueller replied.

"We have reason to believe you may be on the killer's list," said Scully. "I'm calling to warn you that your life may be in danger."

"Oh, my goodness. Why me?"

"I'm driving down tomorrow. I'll explain when I get there. Is there somewhere you can go until then? Somewhere you can wait until adequate security can be put in place?"

"I think I'll just stay here at home," Mueller replied. "I'll keep the door locked."

"At a minimum, I want to call the Storm Lake police and ask them to keep an eye on you. We'll figure the rest out tomorrow."

The sun was shining and the six-hour drive from Eau Claire across the flat plains of Southern Minnesota to Storm Lake would have been pleasant if Brian Scully didn't have Kurt Mueller on his mind. He thought of little else as he sped through the vast expanse of newly plowed fields that dwarfed the neat red barns and white clapboard houses they surrounded.

Who was Kurt Mueller? Even though Mueller acknowledged that he had served in the German Army and was stationed in Poland, Scully could scarcely believe the soft-spoken Lutheran Minister he talked with on the phone could be the same man.

He crossed into Iowa and leisurely drove south for nearly two hours on Highway 71 into the town of Storm Lake, past a quiet street lined with small businesses and followed the signs to the Storm Lake Police Department on Milwaukee Avenue. The building appeared to be empty, so Scully poked around down a hallway and found the office of the Police Chief Conrad Sorenson. He had called ahead to tell Sorenson he was coming and that it regarded protecting a former Nazi who lived in Storm Lake.

Scully poked his head inside and said to the balding, overweight officer with thin blond hair; "You must be Chief Sorenson."

Sorenson lifted his tiny, dark, wide-set eyes from a newspaper and wrinkled an acutely turned-up nose that made him look as if he smelled something bad.

"You detectives don't miss a beat do you?" he said, twirling a toothpick from lips so thin that his mouth appeared to be little more than a horizontal slash across the pink skin of his face.

Scully narrowed his eyes and returned the look.

"Brian Scully," he said, extending his hand.

"Conrad Sorenson," the chief replied, returning a half-hearted handshake.

"You surprised me when you called, detective. I had no idea that our own Reverend Mueller was a Nazi."

"That was a long time ago. And he says he never joined the party."

"Not so long," Sorenson replied, gesturing to a black and white photograph on the wall of a group of young soldiers holding up a captured German flag in front of a bombed out building. Next to it was a framed collection of medals that included a purple heart and Silver Star.

"The war is over, chief."

"Well, it sure is for those fellas. I'm the only one in that picture that came home. Now what is it you want again?" asked Sorenson.

Scully took the hint, skipped the chitchat and went directly into an explanation of the investigation and Reverend Mueller's involvement. Sorenson listened attentively as he twirled the toothpick and said little more than "Uh huh" now and then.

"I've read about Geller. Guess he doesn't care much for Nazi's," said the chief. "He's not alone on that score."

"Does that include you?" asked Scully.

"You might say that–especially Nazis living in Storm Lake. Why? Are you big fan of Hitler?"

"No. But, not everyone who dislikes Nazis is going around torturing and killing people," Scully replied. "We could use some help to put him away before he kills again."

"What kind of help would that be?" asked Sorenson suspiciously.

"Keeping an eye on Reverend Mueller," Scully replied. "Like

I explained on the phone, he might be next on Geller's list."

"We got Geller's picture. We'll keep an eye out," said Sorenson indifferently as he returned his attention to the newspaper.

"I'd like you to do more than that, chief," Scully replied. "Mueller needs protection."

The toothpick stopped moving. "Look, detective. We don't have the money to guard an old Nazi twenty-four hours a day."

"Can you at least have a unit check on Reverend Mueller from time to time until we can get FBI agents in place?"

"The FBI won't be necessary. We keep an eye on all our neighborhoods, detective, and see to it that Storm Lake is a nice, law abiding town."

"I'm sure you do, but this is a federal investigation now," Scully replied, barely hiding his growing anger. "Agents will be here. Count on it."

"Just make sure they check in with us so we don't mistake them."

"In the mean time, I'd appreciate it if you would to keep an eye out for David Geller or anyone driving a white Econoline van."

"We'll do that very thing, detective. Wouldn't want anything to happen to our nice Nazi minister."

Scully used the towering spire of St. John's Lutheran Church as a landmark to guide him to the perfectly maintained Victorian style parsonage that stood next door. On the huge front porch surrounded by rose bushes, a slender, elderly man in a clerical collar pushed out of a white wicker rocker as Scully pulled up to the curb.

"Gonna rain," he said to Scully as the detective approached.

Scully paused and looked up at the sky then back at the old man. "Think so. Are you Reverend Mueller?" he asked.

"We need it," he replied. "Yes. I'm Kurt Mueller. You must be Detective Scully."

Scully plodded up the steps to the porch and was greeted with a surprisingly strong handshake he would expect from a much younger man.

"How was your drive?" asked Mueller, gesturing for Scully to sit in an adjacent chair.

"Fine. About six hours," Scully replied, settling in.

"I'm still not sure why you made the trip," said Mueller. "I've tried to think why my life could be in danger."

"Well, I wasn't exactly honest with you on the phone, Reverend," said Scully, leaning forward to place his elbows on his knees to get closer.

Mueller knit his eyebrows and squinted.

"I told you that I read your immigration and military records. But what I didn't tell you is that there are sworn statements from two eye witnesses that claim they saw you shoot and kill three children for leaving the Krakow ghetto to find bread."

Mueller looked at Scully in astonishment. "It is not true," he said. "Who are these people?"

"Their names are on the documents," Scully replied, removing two folded sheets of paper from his jacket pocket and handing them to Mueller.

Reverend Mueller put on his glasses and spent several minutes carefully reading the statements. When he finished, his hands dropped to his lap and his eyes began to glisten.

"It wasn't me. Yes, I was there but I never did such a thing," he protested. "I was assigned to patrol the Podgorze section of Krakow where the Jewish Quarter was established early in the war. It was a horrible time. The Jews who remained after most had been expelled from Krakow we crammed together with little food or water. Everything they had was taken from them. So much hate. So much sadness. And the hunger...." Mueller's voice trailed off.

"I cannot say that I was unaware that such things happened and things even more horrible," he said. "But, I could not have stopped them. I was there for only a short time."

Scully saw the genuine pain and anguish on the old man's face.

"I carry the memory of that time like a millstone. Each day I ask God to forgive me for being a part of it and I know he has. But, I do not ask forgiveness for what these people say I did. I never killed anyone."

"Look, Reverend, what you did or didn't do during the war is between you and your Maker," said Scully. "I am here to warn you that there is a very dangerous man on the loose who wants to kill you. He has already killed five other former German soldiers and there are only three remaining on his hit list. You are one of them."

"But, these people are wrong," said Mueller, almost pleading now. "I tried to save them!"

"And I'm trying to save you, Reverend," Scully replied. "This man believes you are a war criminal and there is no way I or anyone else can convince him otherwise. If we don't stop him first, he's going to come for you. We know who he is but we don't know where he is."

Scully told him everything he knew from the murder of Greta Bauer forward to Solomon Geller and the other murders committed by David Geller. It took twenty minutes. The Reverend was pale when it was over.

"So much hate in the world," Reverend Mueller sighed. "Can he find me?"

"I did," Scully replied.

CHAPTER 41

"Welcome back, partner," said Donovan when Scully dragged in the next morning. "How did it go with Reverend Mueller?"

"He's scared shitless. He doesn't deny being in Krakow, but swears he was reassigned before the killings took place, Says he never killed anyone. Hated what the Nazis were doing."

"Can he prove it?"

Scully shrugged. "I don't know. He's very convincing. But at the end of the day it doesn't matter as long as Geller thinks he's guilty. How did you do with Reinhardt?"

"I found seventeen Adolf Reinhardts in the United States and several more A. Reinhardts," said Donovan. "I eliminated the ones too young to have been in the war and I'm down to three. All of them German immigrants. One in Possum Holler or some damn place in Tennessee. One in New Ulm, Minnesota and one in Helena, Montana."

"Can I give you a hand?" asked Scully.

"Sure," Donovan replied. "Is everything under control in Iowa with the Reverend?"

"He refuses to leave. Thinks God will protect him, but he's keeping his doors locked and one of his children will move in with him until this is all over. I expect the FBI will make agents available to watch him–which is good because the Storm Lake police chief isn't being cooperative. He's still fighting the war. Until I told him, he didn't know that Reverend Mueller had fought for the Germans. Now I think the chief would probably give Geller a hand if he could."

"Well, how about you check on our Reinhardt in Helena and I'll do New Ulm," Donovan said, giving Scully the file along with his hand-written notes containing an address and a telephone number. After reading through the file, Scully picked up the phone and dialed Reinhardt's last known number.

CHAPTER 42

Nolan caught a connecting flight from Los Angeles to San Bernardino and rented a car for the drive through the pass of the mountain range of the same name. He watched the outside temperature on the dashboard display climb to 112 degrees. Heat waves from the asphalt distorted the landscape. Two hours later, he pulled off the long, barren stretch of highway and parked in front of the roadside store that advertised itself as *The Mojave Curiosity Museum – D. Eichle, Proprietor.*

Dieter Eichel didn't have a phone and lived alone in the back. He got along on social security and the few dollars he could make selling sodas, snacks and a variety of hand-crafted rattlesnake belts, wallets and purses. The museum collection consisted of a mineral display in a dusty glass case, dried skulls and a moth-eaten menagerie of stuffed indigenous animals including a two-headed jackrabbit.

Eichel was dozing in a rocker next to a grizzled, three-legged German Shepherd in the shade of the store's covered porch when Nolan's slamming car door startled him awake. The dog rose, hobbled to him, sniffed lazily then returned to the shade.

"Dieter Eichel?" Nolan called.

"Who wants to know?" responded the old man.

Nolan climbed onto the porch and displayed his badge.

"You wanna talk to me, ya gotta buy somethin'," said Rhinehardt cagily.

"Cold Coke sounds good," Nolan replied.

"How many?"

"Let's start with one."

They went inside and the old man pulled a barely cool can of Coke from a flickering refrigerator case.

After a long drink, Nolan explained the reason for his visit. "Are you the Dieter Eichel who was a prison guard at Majdanek," he asked.

"No. I was in a Wehrmacht Panzer Division freezin' my ass off in Russia. Prison guard duty would have been a holiday."

Not exactly, thought Nolan. "Can you prove it?" he asked.

"I have my discharge papers and I have this," Rhinehardt replied, pulling off his unlaced boots and his socks. "Frostbite," he said.

Nolan counted the empty spaces where toes should have been. Three on one foot. Two on the other.

"Not our guy," Nolan told Donovan on a telephone call from LA International as he waited for his return flight. "He was in a tank at the Russian front for years before he was captured at Stalingrad. Got the documents to prove it. Still, I asked the local guys to keep an eye on him and to watch for Geller just in case."

"I guess that just leaves the Sarasota Eichel," said Donovan.

"There's a flight to Miami in a couple of hours and I still have a change of clothes. Should I go?" as Nolan.

"Yes. I feel like we're running out of time," Donovan replied.

CHAPTER 43

Donovan was at his desk going through the list of Adolf Reinhardts he was given by the INS. Since Senator Leffler turned up the heat, they seemed very eager to help, he mused. He was pouring his third cup of coffee and hurried to his desk when the phone rang. It was Nolan calling from Florida.

"I just left Dieter Eichel in his nursing home in Sarasota. He's already gone you might say. Last stages of Alzheimer's. The old guy doesn't even know who he is so he isn't any help. Just sits in a recliner and stares at nothing," said Nolan.

"I alerted the staff and the local police that there may be an attempt on his life, but no one here seems too excited about it. I guess they figure he's already a goner. But, the nursing home will move him to the most secure wing they have. You know, where they keep an eye on the old folks who tend to become violent or wander away."

"And the police?" asked Donovan.

"They're working with the nursing home security guys. I've given them Geller's picture and they're tightening up the security at all entrances and monitoring the parking lot. They don't have the money to have someone stay with Eichel twenty four-seven, but they'll keep a close eye on him."

"I'll see if the FBI can put a couple agents on it. Good work, Lute. When are you coming...." Donovan stopped in mid sentence when he was handed a note that read, "FBI on line 3. Urgent.'"

"Gotta run, Lute. Come on home," he hurriedly finished.

"Donovan," he said after punching the flashing button on the phone.

"Detective Donovan. This is agent Palmer," he said. "We just intercepted a phone call on Hannah Geller's tap. The caller was David Geller."

"What did he say?" asked Donovan, feeling his heart pump in

his chest.

"I'll play it for you. It's very brief."

Donovan listened intently.

Caller: *"Momma?*

Hannah Geller: *"David. Are you all right?"*

Donovan thought she sounded suitably surprised.

David: *"I'm fine, momma. How are you?"*

Hannah Geller: *"David, the police, they know about you."*

David: *"I know. That's why I called while I still can."*

Hannah Geller: *"You have to stop. This isn't right. Your father wouldn't have wanted...."*

David: *"I think it's exactly what he wanted. He just never knew how or didn't have the stomach himself."*

Hannah Geller: *"Justice. Justice he wanted, David. Justice this isn't. Murder this is."*

David: *"It's almost over, momma. Almost done. That's why I'm calling to say good-bye."*

Hannah Geller: *"David, you must stop. To the police turn yourself in. Or run away. A little money I have left. Enough for you to run away."*

David: *"No, momma. It will be over soon."*

Hannah Geller: *"These horrible things how can you do? One of them you have become."*

David: *"He's doing them, momma. I only help."*

Hannah Geller: *"He isn't real, David. He's make believe. He's all in your head. You know that."*

David: *"Oh, he's real, momma. He's the one in control and he's one scary guy."*

Hannah Geller: *"Come home to me."*

David: *"It will be over soon enough, momma. I love you."*

The phone went dead.

Hearing David Geller's voice made him more real to Donovan than he ever imagined. "Was there time to trace the call?" he asked hopefully.

"Yes. It was made at a pay phone outside a gas station near Chattanooga, Tennessee."

"Jesus. One of our possible victims is in Tennessee," said Donovan.

"I know. Adolf Rhinehardt," said Palmer. "We just don't know where. Do you have anything yet?"

"We're working on it. A check of Social Security records came up empty. We've gone through the Tennessee DMV. Apparently, Reinhardt surrendered his license several years ago and the address they have is years old, but we're checking it. Can't find anything on the web. Looks like Rhinehardt has been out of circulation for some time," said Donovan.

"So concentrating on Geller might be our best bet for now," said Palmer.

"I'll get his photo out to every law enforcement agency in the area. Can you have your agents show it to the gas station employees and other people in the area? Maybe someone can identify him. He could be going by David Abraham or something else, who knows."

"Media? Would you like us to contact the media there?" asked Palmer.

"Absolutely. Let's get Geller's face out there any way we can. Scully and I will be on the first flight down there from Minneapolis. I'll call you with an arrival time and contact the Chattanooga Police and let them know we're coming. I'll tell them you guys are in this with us. Geller probably isn't still there by now, but it's a place to begin."

The flight to Chattanooga took a little over five hours with one stop in Atlanta. The plane touched down late in the afternoon at Lovell Field where they were met by a towering hulk of a man standing several inches over six feet and weighing, Donovan guessed, nearly 300 pounds. A hand as big as a baseball mitt reached out to Donovan and Scully. He introduced himself as Police Chief Delbert Plant in deep baritone with a Tennessee drawl.

Plant reminded Donovan of famed former Cleveland Browns running back, Jim Brown, only friendly.

"We appreciate your help, chief," said Donovan as his fingers disappeared into Plant's like a tiny bundle of pink sausages.

"I'm putting my best guys on the team. Along with the FBI guys, if your boy is still around here, we'll find him," said Plant, ushering them to the unmarked police car double-parked at the main entrance passenger drop off.

Donovan brought Chief Plant up to date on the investigation as they sped down Tennessee-153 to the Amnicola Highway exit and was surprised to learn that he was already very familiar with the case. In a matter of minutes they were pulling into the chief's reserved parking spot at the rear of the newly completed stone trimmed, red brick police station.

Plant's office was spacious with thick carpeting, an enormous desk that matched the raised walnut panels on all four walls and a comfortable seating area with a couch and two club chairs.

"Nice digs," said Scully.

"The people here are very big on law enforcement," he smiled, gesturing to the two side chairs in front of his desk. "Have a seat."

Instead of sitting, Donovan moved to an enormous glass-encased map of Chattanooga and the surrounding area. "Can you show me where the pay phone is located?" he asked.

Plant took a box of brightly colored stickers from his desk and eyed the map. "Right there," he said, placing a small round dot on Williams Street between 21st and 22nd. "BP Station. High traffic area. Business district.

"We interviewed the employees working at the time of the call and showed them the perp's photo. Nothing," said Plant. "They have a couple of security cameras outside. The FBI is already part of the investigation team. They have the recordings. They're going through them now."

"With any luck we'll get an idea what he looks like now. With a lot of luck we'll see what he's driving and maybe get the plates," said Donovan.

"That's a lot of luck, Detective," said Plant.

Donovan studied the map more closely. "What else is around there?" asked Donovan.

"It's a light industrial area. Body shops, supply companies, like that. There's a La Qunita Inn next door."

"We're showing the photo everywhere for several blocks around, but so far we haven't turned up a thing."

"I doubt he works or lives close to there and it looks like there's plenty of access to major thoroughfares," said Scully.

"He might know the area, but chances are it was just random," said Plant. "He could be in Tennessee, Alabama, North or South Carolina, Georgia, Mississippi – near anywhere on a tank of gas."

"We better hope someone recognizes him from the news programs or the papers," said Donovan.

"Oh, they love this kind of stuff," said Plant. "By tonight everyone will be talking about 'The Executioner'. You come up with that?"

"Sorta," Donovan replied. "I used the term 'execution-style killings' in a press briefing, CNN picked up on it and started referring to him as 'The Executioner'. The newsies were on it like white on rice."

"It's right up there with Jack the Ripper," Plant said somberly.

"With five victims so far," Donovan replied, "he's closing in on him."

CHAPTER 44

It was late when Donovan and Scully arranged for a rental car to be delivered to the police station and, armed with a map of the area courtesy of the Chattanooga PD, drove to a nearby motel. The next morning, while Scully was busy primping in the bathroom, Donovan brewed two cups of complimentary coffee and was studying the map when the phone rang.

"Donovan," he answered.

"Chief Plant," came the response.

"Morning," said Donovan.

Plant explained that a number of calls had come in since Geller's picture appeared on the evening news and in the morning paper. Most were tips from the nearby area but a few were out-of-state from people who thought they had seen him. None recalled a white Econoline van.

"Can you give our FBI guys the out-of-state leads and start checking the local stuff? Scully and I will work the Rhinehardt angle beginning at his last address. Let's stay in touch."

Donovan and Scully drove north on I-75 to Sweetwater then turned east and navigated an endless number of back roads that wound through the hills. Finding Adolf Rhinehardt's last known place of residence took longer than expected and the sense of urgency grew with each wrong turn. The densely forested slopes were dotted with dilapidated cabins and trailers that sat atop concrete blocks. After stopping at several to ask the locals for directions, they finally arrived at the rough, old house where Adolf Rhinehardt had lived.

A very pregnant, very young woman carrying a baby came out onto the porch when she heard the car door close.

"Kin I hep you?" she called, squinting into the sun with narrow set, blue eyes.

Donovan made the introductions and explained they were trying to locate the previous owner, Adolf Rhinehardt.

"He been gone from these parts near two years, now," she said in a thick-as-honey drawl.

"Do you know where we can find him?" asked Scully.

"They say he in a home somewhere. Got ol' an din haf nobody ta tik care a him. He was a foreign feller. Din haf no kin in these parts," she replied. "Don' know whar he is naw."

"You think any of the neighbors might know where he is?" asked Donovan.

"Don' know. Mebee. Folks mostly keep to themself round har. But, mebee," she replied.

"Well, thanks for your time," said Donovan, pulling a business card from his wallet and handing it to her. "If anything comes to you, give me a call, will you?"

The young woman accepted the card with a look of embarrassment. "Aint got no phone, but I can get to the store sometime," she said. "They's got one thar."

Donovan and Scully continued cruising the area and made inquiries with several nearby locals also without success before stopping in Sweetwater to grab a sandwich on the way back. While they ate, they went through the local yellow pages for area nursing homes. One by one they called each of them to inquire if they had a resident by the name of Adolf Reinhardt. None did.

Donovan called Chief Plant and asked him to check with the nursing homes around Chattanooga then he called Agent Palmer at headquarters to update him on Rhinehardt.

"I'll put a list together of nursing homes and assisted living residences within driving distance of Chattanooga. That takes in several states, so it's going to take a while," said Palmer.

"We'll help with the phones," said Donovan. "We have to move fast now."

An hour later they were back in Chattanooga in Delbert Plant's office.

"We've called two dozen nursing homes around here so far and none have an Adolf Rhinehardt. But, we've just scratched the surface," said Plant.

"Excuse me chief," said an efficient looking middle-aged woman in civilian clothes. "This just came in from the FBI. I thought you'd want to see it."

Plant read silently for a few seconds then out loud. "There are 321 nursing homes listed in Tennessee. Alabama 228. Georgia 360. Mississippi 203. North Carolina 422. South Carolina 286."

"Instead of one state at a time, let's make a circle around Chattanooga with a 50 mile radius and keep working out from there in increments. We have to assume that Geller is more likely to be closer to here than farther away," said Donovan. "Scully you take the homes starting with A through D within this radius, I'll take E through H. Chief, can your guys handle I through L and M through P? I'll give the Bureau guys the rest,'

"We're on it. We'll let you know the second we get a hit," said Plant.

CHAPTER 45

Adolf Rhinehardt disliked everything about the Mason's Forge Rest Home. To him, the low, flat-roofed structure looked like one more, cheap tourist motel in the remote Great Smoky Mountain foothills where he had lived alone for nearly fifty years. The dimly lit rooms were all painted the same nicotine yellow. The furnishings were cheap. Paths were worn into the linoleum floors.

The window unit air conditioner in Rhinehardt's small room rarely worked, and rattled noisily when it did. And he swore he could pee faster than the water came out in the tiny shower.

Fastidious in his dress and grooming, the old German found the ever-present smell of bedpans, sour old people and death offensive. There was no relief from it even in sleep when the moans and coughs and cries filtered through the paper thin walls keeping him awake throughout the long, hot Tennessee nights.

Since failing health and a diminished income forced him to take up residence in the home, the old German had become increasingly angry and isolated. He called the staff 'Minimum wage mutterfickers' to their faces. They in turn referred to him as "The Kaiser" for his heavy accent, imperious attitude, and the huge brush of a mustache that underlined his long, aquiline nose.

And so, his delight with the new attendant who brought him his evening pills one Saturday night was not surprising. The large, powerfully built young man had a pleasant, respectful demeanor that the old German found reassuring.

"Good evening, Mr. Rhinehardt. My name is David," said the square jawed man in a crisp, neatly pressed white uniform. David had the look of a military man, thought Rhinehardt. His hair was neatly cut and brushed with a crisp part, his black mustache was carefully trimmed and he stood erect as a soldier in black boots that were polished to a mirror shine.

"You're new," said Rhinehardt, accepting the little paper pill cup.

"Yes, sir," he said.

"I suppose they warned you about me," Rhinehardt grumbled, tossing the pills into his mouth and accepting a glass of water. "The obnoxious Kraut!"

"I hear you are referred to as the 'Kaiser'," David replied. "But, I don't listen to what other people say. I prefer to make up my own mind once I get to know someone."

Rhinehardt eyed him suspiciously. "We'll see," he said.

In the days that followed, David proved to be friendly and attentive and Rhinehardt came to look forward to seeing him when the shift changed toward evening. Often, after the other patients were settled in for the night, they would play chess while the other attendants watched television in the employee lounge or secretly napped in vacant rooms.

At the end of the first week, David began bringing leftovers from home that were gratefully accepted by the old man. On the night that he presented the old man with a plate of knockwurst, sauerkraut and fresh black bread, Rhinehardt was near tears with joy.

"Why are you so kind?" he asked between bites.

"It's only food," David replied, watching the old man devour the meal. "The food here is bad and you are much too thin."

CHAPTER 46

Plant turned a still vacant office into a command center, had several tables brought in and scrounged up enough chairs and phones to set things in motion. His secretary made a list of nursing homes within the first radius on a wall-size white board and taped an area map next to it with a carefully drawn ring indicating fifty–miles from the phone booth location.

Slowly, behind a background din of constant chatter, the nursing home names listed on white board were crossed out one by one until the administrative staff began leaving for the day and the task force was forced to shut down for the night. By then the makeshift call center resembled a back room telemarketing operation littered with empty soda cans and coffee cups, half-eaten donuts and empty pizza boxes.

"We deserve a couple of shots of red eye and a decent meal, don't you think, Mike?" asked Scully.

"What? You mean you've had enough burgers and pizza?" he replied sarcastically.

Donovan demurred and they stopped at an upscale restaurant called J. Alexander's on Hamilton Place Boulevard. "This is just what I had in mind," said Scully, taking in the atmosphere. "The tables are covered with linen. The waitresses aren't dressed in pink uniforms with nametags that say 'Ruby' and I'll bet they don't call you "honey".

After a couple of drinks, thick steaks and a good night's sleep, they were back to Police headquarters first thing in the morning to start again.

Slowly more names were crossed off the white board, then just after one o'clock Donovan noticed one of Plant's detectives waving frantically to get his attention. He held up five fingers to indicate line five and Donovan got on the line.

"I have Detective Donovan on the line Mrs. Macki," he said. "Mrs. Macki is the administrator at Mason's Forge Rest Home, Detective. Please go ahead, ma'am."

"Well, as I was telling you, we do have a resident by the name of Adolf Rhinehardt here," she said.

The command center grew silent as the other detectives finished the calls they were on and paused to listen.

"How long has he been a resident?" asked Donovan, putting the call on speaker.

"Well, let me see. Just a minute," her voice went faint as she called out, "Edna. How long has the Kaiser been with us?"

"About two years now," came an even fainter reply.

"About two years," said Mrs. Macki.

"May I speak with him, ma'am. It's very important," said Donovan, trying to maintain his composure.

"I'm afraid he isn't here, detective," she replied.

"Where is he? It's very important that I speak with him."

"Well, I can take your number and have him call you back when he returns," she said.

"Returns from where?" Donovan said, the impatience growing in his voice.

"Well, he's on an outing," she replied.

"Like a group outing?" asked Donovan.

"No. He's with one of our staff today. A nice young man. Even though it's his day off, he's taking Mr. Rhinehardt for a drive."

"Can you tell me his name, ma'am?" asked Donovan.

There was a pause. "Well, I don't know. We have a policy for that sort of thing and I shouldn't be giving out that sort of information," she sad in a maddeningly officious manner.

"Is he around thirty. Slender. Greenish eyes?" asked Donovan.

"Why yes."

"Is he new there?"

"Why yes."

"Would his first name happen to be David?"

"How do you know these things?" she asked.

"We need to talk with him, Mrs. Macki. You have to give me

his name and any other information you have about him. His place of residence."

"My goodness, what's this all about," she replied, surprised by the urgency in his voice.

"Is David's last name Geller or Abraham?"

"How can I be sure who you are?" she asked nervously. "I can't give out personal information about our employees."

"Can you at least tell me where they went?" Donovan asked almost breathlessly now.

After a slight pause she said, "Well, I guess that can't hurt. They're making quite a day of it," she replied.

"I need to know where!" Donovan almost screamed.

"I think he said they were going to drive through the Great Smokey National Park and have a picnic. Mr. Rhinehardt doesn't get around very well. He's in a wheelchair mostly so there is only so much he can do," she said.

Donovan opened the map and took in the vastness of the park. "Precisely where are you located?" he asked.

"Why we're off Tucaleechee Pike just north of Mason's Forge on 73," she replied.

He circled the area on the map with a pencil. "What time did they leave? Do you know what kind of vehicle?"

"I don't believe I ever saw what Mr. Abraham drives, but I can tell you they've been gone since late morning. David said not to worry if they came back late. He has a special surprise for Mr. Rhinehardt."

"A surprise?" said Donovan.

"Yes. They're going to a zoo."

CHAPTER 47

"How's the Kaiser, today? You ready to go?" David Geller asked, sticking his nose in the doorway of Rhinehardt's room at the appointed 11:00 a.m.

"Yah," replied the old man waiting in his wheelchair. He tried not to show his excitement, but knew it was obvious. He had bathed, shaved, groomed his mustache and even shined his shoes before dressing in his best slacks and shirt. Truth was, he had been ready for an hour before Geller showed up.

"Well, let's motor, Mr. Rhinehardt. The beautiful Smokey Mountains are waiting," said Geller.

"I almost didn't recognize you without your white uniform. It never occurred to me that you would be in regular clothes," said Reinhardt as Geller rolled the wheelchair up a homemade ramp into the back of the van that was now painted black. Overspray on the windows and chrome testified to the quality of hasty paint job done at Vincent's Discount Auto Paint for $189. Even the set of license plates he had stolen off a wreck parked in Vincent's back lot had overspray.

"Sorry, you don't have a window to look out," said Geller as he anchored the chair to the floor before climbing into the driver's seat and adjusting the rear view mirror so he could see the old man's face.

"It's like being locked up in a cattle car back there, isn't it?"

Geller grinned when he saw a look of apprehension suddenly appear on Rhinehardt's face and just as suddenly disappear.

They chatted amiably as the van pulled away from the nursing home and turned onto Tucaleechee Pike toward highway 73. "This is so nice of you, David. It is wonderful to be free of that prison they call a nursing home," he said, straining to watch through the front window as the beautiful Tennessee scenery went by.

"Oh," Geller replied with a slight smirk. "You deserve a day like I have planned."

Rhinehardt grew quiet for a few seconds and Geller saw another fleeting apprehensive look before responding.

"I haven't been in the mountains for years," he said.

"I think you'll still recognize them. They haven't changed much," Geller replied. "Unless of course you're older than the mountains are."

They both chuckled briefly. Geller focused on the road ahead. Before entering the park, he pulled into a convenience store along the road. "I have to make a quick phone call. Do you need to use the bathroom or can I get you something to drink? Coffee or a soda or maybe a bottle of water, Mr. Rhinehardt?" he asked.

"I'm fine," the old man replied. "Don't be all day."

Geller disappeared around the side of the building where a public telephone was located. He pulled a folded note from his pocket and punched in the number written on it. The phone rang several times before a woman answered with a heavy southern drawl.

"Funland Park and Zoo," she said.

"Hi. I'm the man who called a couple of days ago and arranged for an after hours private visit."

"Yes, Sir," she replied. "I remember you. You're the nice man with the elderly friend who's gonna die soon."

Geller grinned. "Yes, that's me. I'm calling to confirm that the night watchman is still planning to meet after closing time."

"Oh, yes. Lester's already spent some of the two hundred dollars you said you'd give him. He'll be waitin' at the back gate. You want me to scare him up to come to the phone?"

"No. Not as long as you're sure he'll be there," said Geller.

"Just like you said. The zoo will be spic and span. He'll have shooed everyone out, turned down the lights, swept the place clean, hosed out the zoo cages, fed all the animals," she reassured him.

"Except for Bruno," interrupted Geller.

Bruno was the enormous 700-pound grizzly bear and the zoo's main attraction.

"Yup. Bruno will be hungry enough to eat the butt out of a buffalo," she replied.

"Tell Lester we'll be there around midnight, maybe a little later," said Geller. "I'll be driving a black van."

"I'll do that very thing," she said in her breezy southern manner.

CHAPTER 48

Donovan looked up at the map that was now congested with clusters of colorful round dots indicating nursing homes in the immediate area and beyond. He found the dot next to Mason's Forge, placed the tip of his index finger on it and turned to face everyone in the makeshift command center.

"The good news is that we've identified the nursing home where Adolf Rhinehardt is living and that Geller is working there using the name David Abraham," said Donovan. "Damn good police work you guys."

A buzz began to grow in the room.

"I talked with the administrator. The bad news is they left together late this morning to go sight seeing in the Great Smokey National Park," said Donovan. "I need someone to contact park officials and alert them to watch for two men possibly in a van. One young, the other elderly and in a wheel chair. See if you can get other local law enforcement around the park to assist."

"Geller also said they were going to visit a zoo."

The room went silent.

"If he continues to murder his victims in the same ways they are believed to have murdered prisoners, that probably means he's planning to feed Rhinehardt to some animal around here somewhere," Donovan continued. "Alive."

Once again the room came alive with buzz. There was air urgency in his voice as he briefed the team about the conversation he had with the nursing home director.

"I don't have to tell you that we don't have much time. We don't know how he's going to do it or where, but it sure looks like he's planning on killing again today."

"Do we know what kind of van he's driving?" asked one investigator.

"We don't. He might still have the white Econoline, but I'd be surprised," Donovan replied. "Still, it's probably be a van if he's hauling Rhinehardt in his wheelchair, but there are all sorts of possibilities." He turned to Scully and nodded.

"All right, we have to start all over and replace the nursing home locations with zoos," said Scully. "This time we'll work out from a radius with Mason's Forge at the center."

"We need every zoo, wildlife park, circus or anywhere else Geller could find a large, hungry carnivore."

Donovan divided up the local detectives and FBI team members and assigned each different regional states in which to identify and investigate zoos.

"Let's start fresh," he said, erasing the white board. "List every place you find that has a carnivore big enough to eat a man. Call them, warn them, send them Geller's photograph, locate them on the map and write up a contact report–Scully will give you a simple format to follow so we're consistent. Names, numbers, addresses, types of animals, security, everything. Then call local law enforcement in that jurisdiction and bring them up-to-date. Ask them to provide additional security."

Chief Plant appeared in the doorway. "I heard," he said. "What do you need?"

"Can you hook me up with one of your guys who knows the area around the Mason's Forge Rest Home to keep me from getting lost in the hills again? Someone who likes to go fast. And we need someone in that jurisdiction to get a search warrant ASAP to shake loose everything the rest home has on an employee who goes by the name David Abraham," said Donovan.

The command center atmosphere was already electric by the time Donovan borrowed a Kevlar vest, checked his service revolver and rushed to the waiting cruiser outside. The excited young officer in the driver's seat who introduced himself as Gus Gaylord, turned on the light bar and peeled out of the parking lot with the siren blaring.

They turned onto the highway five minutes later and shot past car after car as each pulled to the side of the road like the Red Sea parting for Moses. They followed route I-75 north for 105 miles and finally turned off the lights and siren when they arrived at the Mason's Forge Rest Home an hour and seventeen minutes later. A Deputy from the Monroe County Sheriffs office was waiting in the parking lot, search warrant in hand.

"You guys work fast," said Donovan, introducing himself.

"This is pretty big doin's for us," replied the deputy from behind his dark aviator glasses. "Carl Stoops. Pleasure to meetcha."

"You too. Well, let's get to it," said Donovan leading the way into the front entry.

Donovan saw the nameplate reading "Edna Macki" on her desk in the small administrative office off the main entry. She looked very much like Donovan imagined. Plain featured with thin lips. Conservative blouse with a matching sweater, thinning brown hair parted down the middle with wispy bangs that hung on her forehead like a hayfork. A chain dangled from practical metal-framed glasses.

"Mrs. Macki," he called.

Edna Macki's eyes widened in surprise when she heard her name and looked up to see the three men staring at her, two of them in police uniforms. She rose timidly and walked around her desk and looked at the proffered shield. "Yes?" she said in a whisper.

"We talked on the phone. My name is Michael Donovan," he said. "I'm a detective from Eau Claire, Wisconsin. This here is Deputy Stoops."

"Pleased to meet you," she said, not knowing what else to say. "Is this about our Mr. Abraham?"

"Yes. Yes, it is. While I appreciate your discretion in maintaining confidentiality about your employees, Mrs. Macki, it is extremely important that we find him as soon as possible."

"Is he in trouble?" she asked.

"We want to talk with him. We believe Mr. Rhinehardt's life is in danger," Donovan replied.

"I'm sorry I couldn't tell you more. ... ."

Donovan cut her off. "We understand, Mrs. Macki. That's why Deputy Stoops has a search warrant issued by a county judge to relieve you of your responsibility of keeping David Abraham's personal information private."

Stoops placed the search warrant in her hand. She took a cursory look. "My goodness. I didn't mean to start a ruckus," she said.

"Not to worry," Donovan said in as comforting a tone as he could muster. "We just want to see Mr. Abraham's personnel file along with any information you have on Adolf Rhinehardt."

Edna Macki obediently pulled the requested information from a row of filing cabinets and returned with two folders. "I hope you understand that you shouldn't remove any of the documents, but if you would like copies of anything, let me know," she said before going back to her desk without waiting for a reply.

David Abraham listed his address as a rental cabin in a remote area known to Deputy Stoops about twenty minutes away. Donovan found a photograph of Rhinehardt in his file and asked Mrs. Macki to fax it to Scully at the Chattanooga Command Center.

They were outside putting on bullet-proof Kevlar vests when it dawned on Donovan how real the chase had become. No more guess work. He was getting closer to Geller now by the minute.

Donovan climbed in with Stoops in the lead car with Gus following behind as the police cruisers wound and climbed their way through a maze of steep back roads cut into the thickly treed hills. He tried to call Scully on his cell phone but there was no signal so he spent the time studying the copies of the documents Mrs. Macki had supplied. He studied the photograph of the mustached, unsmiling David Geller and wondered what he was doing that very minute. The work history appeared to be entirely fabricated except for his stint with the Israeli Defense Forces. He wondered if the nursing home even checked, but knew they hadn't.

Just as Stoops had said, about twenty minutes later they came to a small, green clapboard cabin sitting alone in a clearing at the end of a long driveway. Even though there were no signs of life and no vehicles, Donovan drew his police revolver from his shoulder holster as he got out of the car. Stoops followed suit. Inside the cruiser behind them, Gus unlocked a 12-gauge Remington shotgun from its' floor mount and joined them in a huddle between the cars.

"I doubt he's in there, but let's operate as if he is. I'll move in from the front and check the windows. Stoops, you check around back, okay?" Stoops nodded.

"Gus, you back us up from here and take in the entire scene. Holler if you see any signs of life. I'll signal when I'm going in and you come up. I'll go in low and you give that 12 gauge a workout if you need to. Remember, this guy is a highly trained killer and extremely dangerous. Shoot to kill if you have to but let's try not to shoot the old man or each other," said Donovan. Gus let go a soft, nervous laugh.

"Let's go," said Donovan.

Gus took a position behind an open cruiser door, settled the shotgun into his shoulder, sighted down the barrel and scanned the cabin for movement as Donovan stepped cautiously toward the first window to the left of the front door. The birds in surrounding pines went suddenly silent. Squirrels stopped scampering and froze in place as if somehow aware of danger.

Donovan could feel his heart beating as he closed in on the man he had been stalking for weeks. The sadistic killer he had known only from photographs and the mutilated victims he left behind. He looked toward Gus for any sign of warning, swallowed hard and peered in. Beads of sweat formed on his forehead as his eyes slowly adjusted to the dark cabin. The barely furnished interior emerged into view. A neatly made bunk extended into the room from a far wall under a hanging, pull chain lamp. In the rear was a tiny kitchen area with a small refrigerator. Next to it, a small square table on which sat a television with rabbit ears, an alarm clock radio and a small stack of papers.

The cabin appeared to be empty and slowly Donovan began to calm. Then suddenly a figure moved somewhere toward the rear and once again he felt the rush of adrenalin. His finger tightened on the trigger involuntarily. His breathing quickened. Then he realized it was Stoops looking in a kitchen window. "Jesus," he said to himself. "I've got to get a grip."

He worked his way to the cabin door, glancing back to see Gus with the shotgun leveled at the area just ahead of him. The door had three small windows set in a row. He looked in. Nothing.

He tried the knob. Locked. He signaled for Gus to move in. Gus nodded. Donovan reared back and drove his foot into the cheap hollow core door just below the catch. Splinters sprayed from the casing as the door flew open with almost no resistance and crashed into the wall inside. Donovan dropped to a knee, his 38 revolver poised in both hands. Simultaneously, Gus came up behind and swept the shotgun's black barrel over his back into the dark interior.

"Nobody home!" Donovan hollered loud enough for Stoops to hear.

Stoops ran around to the front of the cabin and the three of them went inside. "Its like a barracks," said Gus, lowering the shotgun.

Donovan holstered his 38 and scanned the spotless room. A pair of highly polished, military-style boots were lined up in front of the cot. Next to the kitchen sink sat a neatly stacked plate, saucer, bowl, coffee cup and glass in which stood the appropriate utensils.

"Doesn't look like he entertains a lot," said Donovan. He moved closer and sorted through an assortment of papers and mail on the table; two utility bills addressed to David Abraham, a couple of magazines addressed to the nursing home and a sporting goods supply catalog.

Stoops went through the cabinets and drawers in the kitchen while Gus went outside for a closer inspection of the area. Donovan's attention fell on the copier paper box on the floor. He set it on the table and lifted off the corrugated lid. What he saw inside was morbidly familiar. He removed the items one-by-one and spread them out on the table; an opened package of D-cell batteries with several missing, an open box of latex gloves, several feet of polyethylene rope, a box of 9mm ammunition, a sharpening stone and oil, several small canisters of propane, two rolls of duct tape and an empty box that had once held an Ultra II, Model A-4, 150,000 volt hand held taser.

Donovan saved the three red file folders for last. They were labeled Kurt Mueller, Dieter Eichel and Adolf Rhinehardt. The contents were virtually identical to those provided by the INS earlier. The only difference was that each cover page written and signed by Solomon Geller contained an entry scrawled in large bold letters with a blood red marker.

Dieter Eichel's read "GAS".

Kurt Mueller's read "STARVATION".

But, what he saw on Adolf Rhinehardt's cover was most disturbing of all. It read, "BEAR MEAT".

"It's Donovan for you, Scully. Line two," called the voice just loud enough to be heard over the buzz of ongoing telephone conversations in the command center.

"Hi, Mike. Where are you?" asked Scully.

"I'm at the cabin Geller is renting outside of Mason's Forge. We've gone through it and found all sorts of incriminating evidence; from an empty taser box to duct tape, but Geller is nowhere to be seen. It looks like he planning to feed Rhinehardt to a bear. What's happening there?"

"The park rangers are on high alert. State troopers and law enforcement from nearby departments are coming in to help," Scully replied. "We've sent out Geller's and Rhinehardt's photos to them and they're setting up checkpoints. There's damn near 400 miles of roads through the Smokey's so who knows."

"What about the zoos?" ask Donovan.

"It's a nightmare," said Brian. "We've contacted every city and roadside zoo we could find within a hundred miles of here. Memphis, Knoxville, Chattanooga, even a Safari Park on the other end of the state. I doubt Geller could get past the security at any of those, but the roadside zoos might be another matter."

"How many are there?" asked Donovan.

"Hard to tell. They aren't very well regulated. Plus, there are thousands of private parks outside the zoo system. Bear pits are not uncommon. Some are pretty bad. Those are the ones Geller is more likely to get into."

Donovan looked at his watch. It was 4:14 p.m.

"I don't have to tell you we're running out of time. Stay on the phones and keep me up-to-date. I'm going into the park to monitor things from there. If Geller is in the park and plans on taking the old man to a zoo from there, at least I have a chance of being in the vicinity."

Donovan instructed Stoops to move his cruiser out of sight behind the cabin and call for backup. "He doesn't know we're onto him so I expect he'll be back. Place some uniforms in the woods near the road and position a couple of cars close by on one of these side roads. They can block the drive if he pulls in or pursue him if he figures out you're here and takes off. Keep out of sight and shoot to kill. Geller is armed and very, very dangerous."

CHAPTER 49

Twilight was just beginning to settle over the mountains when Geller pulled to a stop at the end of the gravel road where it turned to asphalt. Ignoring the complaints of his passenger, he had turned off the congested main route through the park earlier to avoid the slow traffic and the crowded scenic overlooks. He didn't know that the slow pace of the traffic was caused by security checkpoints that were popping up all over the park looking for him.

He studied his road map and determined that the best route to the bear park was to the right for a half-mile or so where he could pick up another back road that led to an intersection with Highway 441 in North Carolina. He was unaware that this route led away from a security checkpoint at a park exit a short ways further.

It was dark when he arrived at the intersection and almost didn't see the barricade. There was just enough light to make out and stop for the "DO NOT ENTER – NATIONAL PARK MAINTENANCE ROAD" sign that he quickly moved out of the way. He drove through, replaced the barricade and turned south toward the town of Cherokee and their final destination. By eight o'clock, Rhinehardt began grumbling about being fed and to be let out of "this Goddamn box". By the time Geller stopped at the first roadside diner he saw nearly a half hour later, the old man was complaining about everything. The coffee was weak, the roast beef was grisly, the mashed potatoes cold and lumpy. "Southern cooking, my ass," he grumbled to the waitress who cleared the table.

"If you only knew it was your last meal," thought Geller as he gave Reinhardt his evening pills to take with his glass of water. He had cut the regular sleeping pill in half to put the old man to sleep or at least keep him quiet for the next three hours while they waited for the appointed time to arrive at Funland. Geller could already feel the first hint of the familiar tightening at the base of his skull.

It was nearly one in the morning when the Econoline pulled up next to a row of dumpsters at the side entrance to Funland. As he waited nervously, Geller could hear the distant calls of zoo animals in the night air. He watched the still sleepy old man in the rear view mirror and was about to get out and look around for the watchman when the rusting sheet-metal gate slid opened and he saw Lester for the first time. Rail thin with a greasy ponytail hanging down from a filthy baseball cap, Lester wore a black t-shirt and faded blue jeans with a huge key ring on his belt. His big smile was missing teeth here and there and made his mouth resemble the black and white keys of a piano in the dim light.

There was barely enough illumination from the single light pole to see inside but Geller could tell that Funland had seen better days. Lester waved him forward and he pulled in and parked. The headlights of the van threw harsh light on assorted junk that seemed to be everywhere–old tires, broken benches, rusting gears and various other parts from the midway rides. On top of a pile of weather-beaten lumber was a bent and faded sign advertising SNO CONES $1. All became dark again when Geller shut off the headlights, stopped the engine and got out. Lester slid the gate back in place, shook hands with Geller and found two crisp hundred-dollar bills in his palm. He smiled.

"Sorry, I'm a little late. Took a wrong turn," said Geller, covering for the extra time it took to waken the old man.

"Not a problem," Lester replied, folding the bills and sliding them in his shirt pocket."

"You don't mind being alone here at night?" asked Geller, fishing for reassurance that no one else was in the park.

"Hell, no, I like it. When the last one leaves, its' kind of like my own little kingdom. Nobody buggin' me or tellin' me what to do," he replied. "No kids screamin'. The only sounds I hear are the animals. When they get goin' some nights it sounds like a fuckin' jungle in here."

"Give me a hand here, will ya, Lester," said David, sliding open the van door. Inside waited the imperious figure of Adolf

Rhinehardt sitting in his wheel chair fast asleep again.

"Adolf?" asked Geller. "Wake up. I have a surprise for you."

Rhinehardt opened his eyes and lifted his head groggily.

"We're at a zoo!" said Geller as he and Lester pulled him from the van and set the wheel chair on the asphalt walkway.

"Why is it so damn dark. I can't see a thing!" the old man complained.

"He doesn't understand what's happening," Geller whispered into Lester's ear.

Lester nodded.

"Lester will turn more lights on in a while," David assured him as he grabbed his backpack from the van. "Now let's go see the animals. We'll start with Bruno. I'm sure he's eager to be fed."

"Oh, he's eager, all right. Had to listen to his complainin' for hours," said Lester, leading the way while Geller pushed a slightly confused Rhinehardt in the wheel chair several feet behind.

"What's Bruno?" asked Rhinehardt.

"The biggest, fuckin' hungriest grizzly you ever saw. Or have you seen big hungry bears before?" asked Geller.

A sudden, quizzical look appeared on Rhinehardt's gaunt face in the dim light.

"Lester, is it true what the Indians around here say about being eaten by a bear is the worst way to die? Worse than say... that tiger?" asked David as they passed by a huge Bengal tiger pacing in his cramped cage. He was beginning to feel the pain growing in his head.

"Yup. That tiger'll kill you first. Grab your throat and suffocate you. Bears don't kill people fast–they're too powerful to worry about you gettin' away. They jes pin you down and start ta eatin'," Lester replied. "Like a hungry cat gnawing on a fat mouse."

Rhinehardt grew increasingly uncomfortable as they passed the cages. It wasn't only the pungent smell of animal dung and urine. Something else wasn't right. Monkey's clutched the bars of their cages and screamed. A black panther, barely visible in the darkness except for his glowing eyes, stared threateningly as he paced back and forth.

Geller felt the pain begin to gather more intensely at the base of his skull now, felt himself begin to drift. By the time they stopped, the pain had grown and he began hovering, watching his other self take control.

"Well, this here's the bear pit," said Lester as they approached a large open chasm with high, roughly finished concrete walls on three sides and iron bars along the front. "The access door to feed him is down here inside a safety cage. Gotta go through two doors to get in or out. A precaution, ya know." He lifted the lever on an electrical box and the pit lit up like day.

"There he is," said Lester. Inside the pit was an enormous mass of darbrown fur. The huge animal seemed all teeth set in an enormous head made to appear even larger by his tiny, close-set eyes. His long, sickle-like claws clicked on the concrete and flashed in the harsh light as he moved menacingly toward them from the back of the pit. His head was down. He was stalking.

Rhinehardt could feel the panic rising in his chest. It was all too familiar. Was this really happening?

"That's his supper," said Lester, nodding to the slab of red meat on the other side of the bars as he sorted through his keys. He unlocked the first door that led into the small safety cage where there was a second door with a sliding panel large enough to drop chunks of horsemeat into the cage.

"Now all we gotta do is toss in that slab of meat and Bruno will come a runnin'," said Lester. He turned to Geller and saw the strange, dead look now in his eyes. "Say, are you okay?" he asked.

"I'll take it from here, Lester," Geller replied, grabbing the keys from the surprised watchman and pressing the taser to his neck. Instantly, 150,000 volts shot through Lester's body rendering him senseless. Geller caught him as he collapsed and laid him gently on the asphalt. It took five-seconds.

Rhinehardt was too shocked to react at first then struggled frantically to get out of the wheel chair. He tried to scream but all that could be heard was a whimper. With cat-like speed, Geller jammed the taser into the old man's neck and delivered the paralyzing jolt. This time he held it there several seconds longer.

Rhinehardt went rigid. His eyes seemed to explode with light.

He was only vaguely aware of the rubber ball being stuffed into his mouth or the duct tape winding around his head and securing his wrists to the arm rests of the wheel chair.

Before the shock wore off on Lester, Geller bound, gagged and blindfolded him. "I'm not going to hurt you, Lester," he told the terrified watchman as reassuringly as he could. "You just lay here quietly and don't make a fuss."

He removed the paddle lock from the metal lever on the door to the safety cage where the horsemeat lay and opened it. Rhinehardt's eyes grew wide with terror as Geller wheeled him into the small space as the putrid, sweet stench of human excrement crept into the air like a fog.

"Oh dear," said Geller. "You've shit yourself, Adolf. I hope Bruno won't mind. I doubt he's a fussy eater, but we're going to get you out of those soiled clothes anyway. Wouldn't want to ruin Bruno's appetite."

The effects of the stun gun were wearing off fast now and Rhinehardt watched Geller with a combination of dread and curiosity as he took the branding iron from the backpack. The old man quickly understood what was in store when a flaming jet of blue propane began to heat the brass numbers.

Geller set it carefully on the asphalt and turned to face Rhinehardt. "It takes a few minutes to heat properly," he said almost apologetically as he took out his knife. Rhinehardt cried and whimpered as his clothes were cut and torn away until he sat naked in the wheel chair.

"Makes you feel even more vulnerable, doesn't it," said Geller calmly. "Too bad we don't have a bigger audience for you to fully appreciate the humiliation you put so many others through. I would have invited a few Jews from the Majdanek death camp to watch you squirm but, of course, they couldn't make it."

Inside the pit, the ravenous bear moved closer in anticipation of his meal when Geller grabbed the huge chunk of horsemeat with both hands and threw it in Rhinehardt s lap. Seeing his dinner stolen, the ravenous creature became enraged and let go a terrifying roar.

"Don't worry," said a startled Geller. "I brought you something much better for your dinner, Bruno. He's on the thin side, but at least he's meatier than a half-starved Jew."

Fully recovered from the stun of the taser, Reinhardt's eyes grew huge and his chest rose and fell in frantic breathing. Flies buzzed and flitted excitedly around the raw meat resting in his naked lap.

"I'm glad you've come around so soon," said Geller. "I wouldn't want you to be late for dinner."

Reinhardt struggled helplessly–pleading with his eyes.

"A Jew a day. Isn't that what they used to say at Dachau when they fed the daily prisoner to the bears?"

Still holding the knife, Geller moved slowly behind the wheelchair. "Time to shave your head, Kaiser. Can't have hair in Bruno's food," he said and calmly began slicing off bloody handfuls from the old man's scalp.

"Grizzlies are interesting," he said as he worked. "I've heard they prefer the soft tissue around the lower legs and buttocks. They rip at it and take large bites, but it isn't enough to kill you and screams don't seem to have any effect on them at all. They just go about their business and eat. Was that your experience at Dachau?"

"Mmph. Mmph!" Rhinehardt shook his head wildly.

"Well, it was a long time ago. Perhaps you don't remember," said Geller satisfied with the butchered scalp. He stuffed the clumps of hair into a plastic bag and placed it in the backpack.

"My father met someone who was there at feeding time. In fact, she was supposed to have been dinner. Perhaps you remember. She's probably the only one who lived to tell about it. Her name was Eva Gerstner, Adolf. She was nine years old."

Rhinehardt's face took on a look of recognition as if a memory was coming back to him.

"They took her from her mother to their little zoo where there was a bear pit and they threw her in. She recalled the bear gnawing at the back of head and ripping the scalp off like you skin a chicken. Then he went for her arms. But, then the bear moved off and one of the camp doctors ordered her to be pulled out. He wanted to examine her. To see what a bear could do to a human being. He laughed when she told him she thought her brains were hanging out. Can you believe? He laughed."

Geller reached for the now red-hot branding iron. "I don't know what number you gave to that little girl," he said, turning off the flame and studying the glowing numbers. "But, yours is A18733."

The smell of the burning flesh seemed to excite the ravenous bear. A pinkish, gray tongue shot from his huge mouth and swept across his lips. He prowled closer as Rhinehardt's muffled scream filled the air. "Mmph. Mmmmph!"

Geller took the branding iron away and examined his work. The individual characters were perfectly seared into the old man's forehead in angry red welts. He set the iron down and cut the tape away that held the old man's arms to the chair. Finally, he tipped the chair over on its side and sent Rhinehardt sprawling onto the asphalt. The hungry bear moved closer still, his huge head swaying in anticipation. Strings of saliva falling from his waiting mouth.

"I'm going to open the cage now, Adolf," he told Rhinehardt who was lying in a quivering heap, trying with enormous effort to pull himself up on the bars.

"Mmmph. Ammph," he whined in a pleading mumble as he rocked unsteadily. His eyes begging Geller to spare him.

Geller threw the inner cage door open wide, then quickly scrambled out of the safety cage and slammed the main door closed. The bear moved closer still, his wet, flaring nostrils sniffing – taking in the scent of fear and fresh meat. Then, without fanfare, he sank his huge teeth into the old man's calf, jerked him from the holding cage and dragged him naked and flailing to the spot in the pit where he would feed.

Lester would later tell police that he heard Bruno rip and tear on the Reinhardt's flesh for at least twenty minutes after the muffled screaming stopped.

CHAPTER 50

Donovan was at a rest stop washing down a vending machine sandwich with a cup of bad coffee when the call came in from Scully on the police radio.

"What's up?" he asked.

"Looks like we have Rhinehardt, or what's left of him," Scully announced.

"Shit," blurted Donovan. "Where?"

"Roadside Park called Funland in a little tourist town called Cherokee in North Carolina."

"Geller?" asked Donovan.

"Long gone," Scully replied. "The only witness was the night watchman who says Geller made arrangements with him for a private night tour of the zoo and showed up with the old man around one in the morning. As I understand it so far, Geller subdued the watchman with a stun gun, bound and gagged him and let him watch while he shaved Rhinehardt's head, stripped him, then branded him before putting him in the cage with a huge and very hungry grizzly bear. Whole thing was over in a half an hour and Geller was gone."

"Do we know what he was driving?" asked Donovan.

"Black Econoline. No license number," Scully replied.

Scully gave him the particulars and directions to Cherokee.

※

Donovan arrived at Funland just as the sun rose above the bear pit. Combined with the odd silence of the animals, the warming morning light gave the murder scene an almost surreal calm. White plastic sheets covered the scattered body parts of Adolf Rhinehardt. The bright mounds reminded Donovan of the last remnants of melting snow drifts in Wisconsin. Curled up like a massive brown caterpillar in the far corner laid the massive hump of blood-stained fur that had been Bruno, his tongue hanging languidly from the slack, motionless mouth.

"We had to kill the bear," said the Cherokee Sheriff, already sporting dark glasses as if it was high noon on the beach. "Seemed a shame. He was just bein' a bear."

"Where's the watchman?" asked Donovan.

"Over yonder in a patrol car. He's pretty shook up," the sheriff replied.

"Can he talk?" asked Donovan.

"He can talk plenty. Can't shut him up. Guess some folks get like that. Musta been a sumbitch to see," the sheriff said.

Donovan surveyed the scene inside the cage again. "Musta been."

"What do we know?" asked Donovan.

"Name's Lester Gunn. He identified your boy, Geller or Abraham or whatever his name is all right."

"Geller," confirmed Donovan.

"Geller. The second we showed him the photo you sent he said, 'That's the guy.' He said Geller paid him to keep the zoo open for a private tour for the old man."

"Didn't Lester think that was odd?" asked Donovan.

"Sure did. Said it was pretty creepy, but for $200 he wasn't askin' too many questions," said the sheriff. "Geller and the old man showed up around one in the morning and Lester took him to the bear pit like he wanted. That's when Geller tasered him and wrapped him up with duct tape. Lester said Geller scalped the old guy, cut off his clothes, and fuckin' branded the poor bastard. You can take a look – his head is under one of those tarps. Anyway, he just fed the old guy to the bear–just like that. Went on for near twenty minutes."

"Vehicle?" asked Donovan.

"A black Econoline van. Few years old with a sloppy, do-it-yourself paint job," Lester said. He's a car guy – overspray everywhere."

"Plates?" asked Donovan.

"He didn't notice any on the front and never really saw the rear."

When the sheriff had related everything he had learned from Lester, Donovan called Scully who was already on his way.

"We're looking for a black Econoline now. Get word to the guys staked out at the Geller's cabin. He might to be showing up anytime."

※

Carl Stoops was sitting in the darkness of the foul smelling outhouse when he heard the radio squawk outside a hundred feet away. He finished quickly and followed the beam of his flashlight as he hurried along the path to the squad car that was concealed behind the cabin. In his haste, Stoops didn't notice the sound of the passing vehicle on the nearby road.

He answered the call slightly out of breath. "Base–this is Stoops."

"Hold on for Donovan," said the dispatcher.

"Stoops. Our man hit again in Cherokee, North Carolina early this morning. He's probably on his way back to the cabin. Could be there anytime. There's help on the way, but get ready and stay out of sight. And remember, Geller is armed and very, very dangerous."

※

David Geller slowed on the mountain road to turn into his driveway when he saw the fleeting glimpse of a flashlight beam near the cabin. Quickly accelerating, he continued past a hundred yards, turned down a logging road and parked. Gun in hand, he circled back through the trees to the rear of the cabin and saw a policeman in the dim glow of the dome light loading a shotgun inside the cruiser. If they found the cabin, they also found the files inside and knew the identities of his final targets. And they knew what he was driving. Knowing the area would soon be crawling with law enforcement, he returned to the van, took out his backpack, the cash hidden under the seat, his few personal belongings and drove it to a nearby promontory when he sent it off a cliff into the dense forest below.

By the time the morning sun struck the eastern slopes of the Smokey Mountains a short time later, Geller had disappeared.

CHAPTER 51

Network and local news crews from at least four different states converged on Funland by early morning and Donovan reluctantly returned to the spotlight. The press conference was a reporter's feeding frenzy, but he remained calm and answered questions with candor and professionalism while steadfastly refusing to comment or speculate on the prospect of possible future victims.

Within 24 hours David Geller was placed on the FBI's most wanted list and fingerprints positively identified what remained of Adolf Rhinehardt. Once word got out, Funland had the biggest crowd in its history. The main attraction was an empty bear pit with bright yellow crime scene tape strung around it.

The story of the serial killings with photos and biographies of Geller and each of the victims was page one in newspapers from coast to coast. It was also the lead story on virtually every network and local television news program for several days until a crisis in the middle east bumped it.

And David Geller had disappeared from the face of the earth.

It was no small relief to Donovan and Scully when their 727 touched down in Minneapolis. Tired and mentally exhausted, they drove back to Eau Claire without much conversation. Scully dropped Donovan at home where Tess was waiting with two fingers of Bushmills and his favorite dinner.

"Welcome, back Copper," she said, throwing her arms around his neck. "I missed you."

"You, too, Tess. It's good to be home," he replied, kissing her cheek.

"You okay?" she asked, studying his haggard face.

"Just pooped," he replied.

"I hope you're not to tired to eat. I made your favorite dinner," she said.

"What's my favorite dinner?" he replied.

"Whatever I say it is," she shot back, handing him the glass of whiskey.

He laughed out loud. "That's my Tess. Now I really feel like I'm home."

After a quick shower, Donovan joined Tess in the den where she was watching the evening news. "Anything new?" he asked.

"They just did a thing on how busy the police are everywhere responding to calls from good citizens who are turning in neighbors they had known for years simply because the had an accent or kept to themselves," Tess replied. "And it seems like every documentary on the holocaust and Nazi war criminals has been dusted off and running."

"Mind if we just listen to Sinatra or something, babe?" asked-Donovan.

"It would be a relief. I've got to check on the duck."

"Duck? I hate duck!" he scoffed.

"Okay. The pheasant or whatever it is. I forget," she said grinning.

"It's a good thing you got big tits," he teased.

The weeks passed by slowly after the initial excitement of Rhinehardt's murder. The public went back to their lives and Donovan continued counting down the days remaining until his retirement with increasing impatience in his inability to move forward with his pursuit of David Geller. Despite the fact that the van had been recovered and Geller's face was now familiar to the vast majority of the population, no progress in the investigation was made.

"He's changed his appearance by now and has a different vehicle," Donovan said to Scully over lunch at the Athena Cafe. "He could have a beard, long hair or none at all. Changed his hair color. Put on weight."

"He could be dressed in drag, for that matter," said Scully, biting into a butter burger.

"Maybe he retired," said Donovan hopefully.

"Not with two left on his hit list," Scully responded. "Based on his track record so far, he doesn't seem likely to give it up now."

"I checked on our Florida target. He's still being watched 24/7, but the local police have been grumbling about the expense. They don't see the point in paying an extra to guard an old man who doesn't even know who he is anymore."

"What about Mueller?"

"The FBI has pulled out and the Storm Lake Police Chief is complaining about the added expense," Donovan replied. "And Reverend Mueller is fit to be tied – he still insists he's not the guy."

CHAPTER 52

"Detective Donovan, this is Francis Brubaker at the INS."

"Morning," replied Donovan into the phone.

"I see you have another victim; Adolf Rhinehardt," Brubaker said.

"Afraid so," replied Donovan with a sigh. "The list you gave us is growing shorter and we can't seem to do a thing about it."

"That's why I called. Last week the Russians released new documents that were confiscated from the German's when they took Berlin. Most of them are military records that were thought to have been destroyed. Anyway, among the records were files on two different Kurt Mueller's who spent time in Krakow," said Brubaker. Donovan detected a slight nervousness in her voice.

"Yes, go on," probed Donovan.

"It looks like we had the wrong Kurt Mueller," she said ominously.

"Keep talking," said Donovan.

"The man you know as Reverend Kurt Mueller was stationed in Poland for a time all right, but, he was in North Africa at the time of the killings. So I started another search and found the new guy. Same age. German immigrant. Former soldier in the German Army. Living in Iowa same as the Reverend Kurt Mueller only this one was in Krakow when the murders took place," said Brubaker.

"God. Who would think there could be two of them?" Donovan said.

"Common name. There are thousands of former German soldiers who found their way here after the war, so I guess it isn't all that strange," said Brubaker.

"So who is the real Kurt Mueller?" asked Donovan.

Hearing the name, Scully looked up from the report he was reading to listen more intently.

"He's close by. According to the INS documents, he applied for a visa to the United States after the war claiming he was merely a foot soldier in the Wehrmacht. He was approved after establishing he had an uncle here he could live with who had a farm near Algoma, Iowa. Married an American citizen in 1955 and they took over the farm when the uncle passed away a year later. Aunt passed away shortly thereafter."

"The farm is about a hundred miles northeast of Storm Lake in Kossuth County," Brubaker explained as Donovan jotted in his notebook.

"Thanks, Brubaker. I'll keep you posted," he said, hanging up and turning to Scully. "Looks like we have the wrong Mueller."

Scully looked relieved. "There's another one?"

"Couple hours northeast of Storm Lake," Donovan replied. "Brubaker dug him up."

"I better make some calls," said Scully. First he contacted the Kossuth County Sheriff's Department, filled them in and was assured they'd keep an eye out for Geller and keep a watch on Mueller's farm. Then he called the new Kurt Mueller's home phone number.

"Hello," answered a gravely voice."

"Mr. Mueller?"

"What?"

"This is Detective Brian Scully, Mr. Mueller. I'm with the police department in Eau Claire, Wisconsin," he said, pausing to wait for some kind of response. When none came, he continued.

"Can you confirm that you are the same Kurt Mueller who served with the SS in Krakow, Poland in the years 1941 and 1942 during World War II?"

"Who did you say is calling?" asked Mueller edgily.

"This is Detective Brian Scully–with the police department in Eau Claire, Wisconsin."

"Why do you call me?" asked Mueller.

"If you're the Kurt Mueller I'm looking for, I'd like to drive down to Iowa and talk with you," Scully replied.

"What do you want to talk about?" asked Mueller, now

noticeably irritated.

"Can you confirm that you served with the SS in Poland during the war, Mr. Mueller?"

"That was a long time ago," Mueller replied. "I don't talk about the war now."

"It's important that I talk to you, Mr. Mueller. I have information you should know about," said Scully.

"I have done nothing. I'm just an old farmer. Leave me alone."

"I know. You're not in trouble with the law. I just want to talk with you."

"I said leave me alone. You have no business with me."

"It's about a possible threat to your life."

"A threat to my life?" asked the old man incredulously. "You must be joking."

"This is no joke, sir. I'll explain when I talk with you. I can be in Iowa tomorrow. Can you give me directions to the farm?" asked Scully.

After more cajoling and reassurance, Mueller reluctantly consented to a meeting and gave Scully directions to the farm.

"Jesus, what a jerk," said Scully, hanging up.

"Now who are you calling?" asked Donovan, as Scully punched new numbers on his phone.

"The FBI and the Storm Lake Police to fill them in," he replied. "To have them tell Reverend Mueller he's off the hook."

CHAPTER 53

The detectives crossed the state line into Iowa on Interstate 35 and headed west at Clear Lake onto Highway 18. Shortly after noon, they arrived at Mueller's battered, clumsily lettered mailbox and drove up a long dirt driveway to a cluttered barnyard.

"Reminds me of Ma and Pa Kettle's farm," said Donovan as chickens scattered away from the car.

"Whose farm?" asked Scully.

"Old movie," Donovan sighed, regretting another reminder of the gap in their ages. "Never mind."

Scully looked around at the clutter. "I thought Germans were neat-nicks," he said.

"Not this one," Donovan replied. He climbed out of the cool, quiet of the cruiser and was greeted by the noonday heat and the stench of manure. Pigs snorted behind a faded red barn and cattle bawled in a far off pasture. Clusters of corncribs and outbuildings in various stages of disrepair were everywhere.

On the other side of the car, Scully wrinkled his nose, removed his sunglasses, and surveyed the rundown farmhouse sitting in the shade of a congregation of towering elms. The roof was a patchwork of tarpaper and mismatched shingles. A brick chimney, slightly askew and seemingly without mortar, rose from one end. Long abandoned farm implements gathered rust in the overgrown yard.

An old man in worn, sun-bleached denim overalls and rubber boots appeared from around a grain silo carrying a pitchfork.

"Mr. Mueller?" called Donovan.

"You must be the fellas from the police," the old man replied, shuffling toward the car. He had sagging, bloodshot eyes and his leathery, weather-beaten face glistened with white stubble. Ragged white tufts of hair stuck out from under a battered felt hat and tobacco juice punctuated the corners of his mouth like wet, brown commas.

Donovan flashed his badge. "Mike Donovan," he said. "This is my partner Brian Scully. He's the one you talked with on the phone."

"You're a long way from home," said Mueller, turning to hurl a stream of tobacco juice at a foraging chicken and missing long. "I don't always get 'em," he said. "But, when I do, it really pisses 'em off."

"I'm sure it does," said Scully.

"You said something about a war crime?" he asked Scully, switching to a serious tone. "You're still fightin' the war, huh? That's over and done with for me. I've moved on and I think you people ought to do the same. Don't do nobody no good to linger on it. The dead are dead and there ain't a thing can change it now."

"Maybe we should go inside to talk, Mr. Mueller. It's sort of a long story," said Donovan.

Mueller led them into the simple farmhouse kitchen and offered to reheat the pot of coffee sitting on the stove. Donovan and Scully declined.

"Is there a Mrs. Mueller?" asked Donovan.

"No. The Mrs. passed on years ago," he replied matter-of-factly. "Haven't had a decent meal since."

They settled at the kitchen table and brought Mueller up to date on the killings and what they knew about David Geller. "So, you see, Mr. Mueller, there's good reason to believe that your life is in danger," Donovan concluded.

The old farmer sat quietly for a few minutes. "It has been a long time. How can this man know it was me?" he finally asked.

"Was it you?" asked Scully. "Did you shoot those children like they said you did?"

"Don't go there, Brian," admonished Donovan.

"Does it still matter now?" asked the old man. "It's done."

"Does it matter to you?" Scully replied, glaring.

"I followed orders like the others–did what I was told."

Donovan felt the tension growing and interrupted. "Look, it isn't our place to determine whether or not you're guilty of a war crime. David Geller believes you are and we believe he's coming for you."

"Let him come. I can take care of myself," growled Mueller indignantly.

"Maybe so," said Donovan. "But, I'd like to move you from here to someplace safe. Place you in protective custody where he can't get at you."

Mueller spit tobacco juice into an empty coffee can he kept on the floor by his chair and snarled. "I have a farm to run. Animals to take care of. I'm not going nowhere."

Donovan and Scully exchanged glances. "Then you'll have to get used to having company, cause we're going to have security here twenty-four hours a day."

"Do I have a choice?" asked Mueller in a manner that answered his own question.

"No. Mr. Mueller, you don't.

CHAPTER 54

It was back to old-fashioned police work. A deputy was posted at the farm to guard Mueller as he went about his daily chores. Deputies from other departments assisted Donovan and Scully in scouring the countryside showing photographs of Geller to filling station attendants, waitresses, grocery store clerks and anyone else with whom he might have come in contact. The photos were retouched to show him with various beards, mustaches, haircuts and glasses.

It was hot, discouraging work that produced no results until the detectives stopped at a modest, six-unit motel. "Dew Drop Inn" and "Vacancies" glowed in neon letters over the entrance to the tiny office. It was one of those ma and pa places off the beaten path that rented rooms to itinerant farm workers, truck drivers, the odd tourist and, during the season, pheasant hunters.

A morbidly obese woman in a faded sweat suit was pushing a cleaning cart toward a dumpster when they pulled in the parking lot.

"Jesus," said Scully, seeing her enormous behind undulating as she moved. "It looks like two pigs wrestling under a blanket."

She stopped and turned when she heard Donovan slam the door.

"You need a room?" she called, squinting in the sun.

"Police officers," he called. "Just need to talk."

She left her cart and waddled toward to the office. "What about?" she asked,

"I'm Detective Donovan and this is Detective Scully," he said, displaying his badge.

"C'mon in," she said, opening the office door.

She walked around the front counter and tossed a ring of keys on top of a half-finished crossword puzzle on the desk.

"Have you seen anyone resembling the man in this picture?" Donovan asked, handing her David Geller's military ID photo.

She held it under a desk lamp. "Don't think so. I'd remember.

We don't get too many people through here. Ain't exactly a hot spot for tourists," she replied.

"How about any of these?" asked Donovan, spreading the other photos along the counter.

"Why that's Mr. Ames," she exclaimed, excitedly pointing to a photo of Geller retouched with a thick black beard and mustache, grown-out hair and glasses. "He stayed with us for three days. But, why are you looking for him? Ain't no crime to be a bird watcher."

"When did he check out?" asked Scully, barely able to conceal his excitement.

"Yesterday," she replied.

"What was he driving?" asked Donovan.

"Some kind of van. You know, like plumbers and electricians drive," she replied.

"Can I see your register, please?" asked Donovan.

The woman set the registration book on the counter and opened it to the most recent date. She pointed a thick finger to a barely legible entry and rotated the book for them to see.

"Mr. Thomas Ames. 3429 Elm Street. New York," she read out loud. "Just wrote 'Chevy Van' under year and make of vehicle and 'green' under color."

Donovan tried to decipher the nearly illegible license number as best he could but decided it was probably stolen anyway.

"What can you tell us about Mr. Ames, Miss...."

"Humphreys. Thelma Humphreys."

"Miss Humphreys," he repeated. "Anything at all."

"Well, let's see. He was a quiet fella. Gone bird watching most of the day. Had a camera with one of those real long lenses and binoculars and the like," she replied. "He was by himself. Never brought anyone to the room as far as I know."

"Did he indicate where he went to watch the birds?" asked Scully.

"Every morning I watched him spread a big map out on the side of his van. I figured he was planning where he was going that day. Even went out at night a couple times. Musta been looking for owls or bats. Like that, ya know."

"State map?" asked Scully.

"Think so," she said.

"Could you see which areas he was most interested in?" asked Donovan. "Did he make any marks on the map. You know, circles or X's?"

"Yes, but I didn't really pay that much attention," she replied. "Seemed to me they were all over the place."

"Where did he take his meals?" asked Scully.

"I saw him bring in groceries, so I just figured he ate in his room. Saw him haul in a cooler, too."

"Did you see anything unusual when you cleaned his room?" asked Scully.

"I was never in his room to clean until after he checked out. He said he'd take care of it himself."

Scully asked to see the room while Donovan got on the car radio to inform local law enforcement.

"Geller has been seen at a motel outside a small town called Ayershire about forty miles west of the Mueller farm. He is probably somewhere in the area, probably driving a green Chevy van. He was last seen wearing a full black beard, mustache and glasses. He may be posing as a bird watcher."

Scully returned a few minutes later just as Donovan was done requesting the Sheriff's office to double the security at Mueller's farm and was about to call Agent Palmer at the FBI for assistance.

"Anything?" asked Donovan.

"He was very tidy. This is all he left behind," replied Scully, handing him a small plastic bag containing a single 9-volt battery. "It had apparently fallen behind the night stand. Could be for a taser. Then again, it could be from a vibrator."

"Well, let's have it checked for prints," said Donovan, turning his attention to calling the sheriff's office first, then the FBI where he was connected to Agent Palmer immediately.

"We'd really like to take this guy alive," said Donovan.

"I understand," said Palmer. "But, you have to understand that I can't put my agent's lives at risk. If he starts shooting, he's a goner."

"Well, look," Donovan replied. "We know he's coming but he

doesn't know we know. The local guys will set up a perimeter around the farm and Scully and I will baby sit Mueller in the farmhouse. If you can set up some kind of surveillance on the roads without being seen, maybe we can trap him before he makes his move."

Agent Palmer agreed to dispatch several agents to the Mueller farm from their offices in Minneapolis and Omaha. By the next morning, they would be hiding in plain sight posing as crews of linemen for the local power company.

Donovan was pumped. After all these months of running around the country after him, David Geller was coming to him.

CHAPTER 55

The deputy was watching the old farmer shovel pig manure into a spreader when the cruiser pulled into the barnyard. "Any place we can get this car inside?" asked Donovan, jumping out. Mueller stopped shoveling and pointed to an empty space in the machine shed next to the County Sheriff's Suburban.

"The man who wants to kill you was seen yesterday less than fifty miles from here," said Donovan.

Mueller didn't react at first, then sent a stream of tobacco juice at a wandering chicken. "Well, I guess maybe he is coming for me, after all," he blustered with unconvincing bravado.

"He's coming, all right," Scully called, returning from the shed.

"I want you to stay inside the house, Mr. Mueller," said Donovan in a tone intended to discourage debate.

"I gotta milk the cows," the old man responded. "Can't milk themselves."

"Milk 'em after dark and stay in the barn," Donovan replied, leading the way to the house. Once inside, Mueller disappeared and returned loading shells into the double barrel shotgun he took from a rack on the living room wall.

"Bad idea," said Scully.

"I have a right to protect myself!" Mueller snarled.

"And we have a right to do our jobs without being accidentally shot by the man we're trying to protect," Scully replied, taking the gun and removing the shotgun shells from both barrels of the old twenty-gauge.

Mueller turned in a huff and stood at the kitchen window looking out on the woods behind the house.

"And keep away from the windows," Scully added. "You make a nice target."

The old man slumped into a chair next to the kitchen stove and crossed his arms defiantly. "This whole thing is ridiculous," he grumbled. "The war was a half century ago. It's over. What's done is done!"

"It isn't over for David Geller," taunted Scully, noting Mueller's cool indifference was fading.

"You're too young to understand war," Mueller said dismissively.

The kitchen became uncomfortably quiet for several minutes then Scully started up again. "Did you do it?"

"Knock it off, Brian," warned Donovan just as he saw the Iowa State Police SWAT truck pull into the yard. He nodded to the deputy. "C'mon. Let's get these guys positioned. Brian, you stay and keep an eye on Mr. Mueller."

Scully watched them go, unwrapped a stick of Juicy Fruit and tossed the wrapper into the kitchen trashcan. He put his arms behind his head and stared into Mueller's eyes. "Well. Did you do it? Did you shoot those kids?" he prodded, trying to force a confrontation.

Mueller was growing weary of avoiding the arrogant young detective's attempts to intimidate him and took on a look of impunity. "They were warned," he said, as if to absolve himself of some trivial matter. Scully fought the urge to lunge.

"And more than once," said Mueller. "In the end they chose the time and the place of their own execution. I had no choice."

"They were starving," seethed Scully as his rate of gum chewing increased.

"They knew they shouldn't have gone outside the wall," said Mueller calmly. "I warned them, 'don't go out there', I said."

"But, you shot them," Scully retorted.

"Yes. I shot them," Mueller growled. "I had to. I had my orders."

"How did it feel?" a red-faced Scully asked in disgust.

"They were better off. It was fast and painless," Mueller said with a note of self-satisfaction. He seemed to enjoy antagonizing Scully. He liked fucking with his mind. "It was better than going to a death camp."

"You're a real piece of work," growled Scully, chewing his gum more slowly now.

"Come now, Detective Scully. We're not so different, you and I," said Mueller. "We follow orders even when they're disagreeable. I was told to shoot thieves. You were told to protect the life of someone you hate."

"It doesn't matter how you paint it. You're still a fuckin' Nazi."

"Take a walk, Brian," said Donovan, hearing Scully as he returned to the kitchen. "This isn't doing anyone any good."

"He's a fuckin' child killer and an asshole," fumed Scully, spitting the gum into his hand and tossing it in the trash as he walked to the kitchen porch door.

Donovan followed close behind and walked with him into the yard. "No more Fuckin' Nazi, child killer comments or you're gone, Brian. It's distracting and I'll be Goddamned if I'll let you fuck this up," he lectured.

Scully apologized grudgingly and agreed that a drive into town for groceries might help him cool off.

Donovan returned to the kitchen and was spreading an Iowa map out on the table and listening to the radio conversations when the deputy returned with a plat map that showed every section, road, pond and creek on the farm and in the immediate area. Together they plotted where the SWAT officers were posted.

CHAPTER 56

Wearing camouflage clothing and night vision goggles, the SWAT team spent a long and uneventful night out of sight in woods around the farm. When they came in for breaks, Donovan and a calm Scully offered them fresh coffee, doughnuts and sandwiches.

They were relieved and grateful when replacements appeared in the morning and learned that FBI agents posing as linemen had established three checkpoints on each of the roads that led to the farm. Donovan located them on the plat map and waited....

10:17 a.m.: The agent positioned at the top of the first pole at the checkpoint Alpha, furthest from the farm, reported a visual of a tractor on the horizon pulling a hay wagon. It turned off into a farm along the road.

10:22 a.m.: A white pickup appeared in view of checkpoint Charlie then continued toward Alpha. It was driven at a high rate of speed by three young girls and was quickly out of sight.

Donovan listened to the radio reports of cars and trucks passing the checkpoints for hours and was beginning to notice the effects of sleep deprivation when a new call came in.

11:02 a.m.: "Base, this is Checkpoint Bravo. We have a dark colored panel truck traveling east on HH toward the farm. Tennessee tags A2-957. Moving your way, Charlie. Do you copy? Over."

"10-4," came the reply from an agent atop of power pole a half-mile up the road. "We'll watch for him. Over."

Donovan was alert now. "Brian, bring Mueller in. He's out there mucking out the barn. Alert the deputy that we've had a possible citing."

Five minutes later Mueller was safely in the farmhouse. For the first time, Donovan saw that the old man was nervous and agitated.

"Charlie, this is Bravo. We lost visual on the target five minutes ago. Can you see him? You should have seen him by now," said the agent who made the first identification.

"Bravo, this is Charlie. Negative."

"He must have stopped or turned off somewhere in between us," said Bravo. "There aren't any roads on the map, but the whole area is heavily wooded with several openings wide enough for a truck. We'll take a look, over."

Fifteen minutes later the radio in the farmhouse squawked again. "Base, we have a visual on the truck. It's parked in a wooded area roughly a quarter of a mile from the main road. There is no sign of activity."

Donovan located the general area on the map. It was less than a mile from the farm. "Alpha and Bravo, you guys come in and set up a perimeter around the farm. Charlie, you guys move in around the vehicle. Proceed with caution. This guy is dangerous."

"Roger, that," blurted the radio.

Five minutes later the two power company trucks pulled into the barnyard. Donovan came out of the house and spread his map out on the hood of one of them. After orienting the agents to the spot where the suspect's truck was parked, he showed them where to take up positions around the perimeter of the farm and alerted the SWAT guys they were coming. "I'd like to take this guy alive, but if he fires, waste him. And, for Christ's sake, don't shoot each other."

Twenty, tense minutes passed. During that time, Donovan learned from the dispatcher that the tags on the truck were registered to a Milford, Tennessee owner named Brandon Shine. Neither the truck nor the plates were reported stolen.

By then, two FBI agents from Charlie unit had taken up positions near the truck and were waiting for the order to move in. Each had a truck door in their crosshairs. Still there was no sign that anyone was inside. Suddenly two rifle shots echoed through the woods in close succession.

"Was that you guys?" radioed Donovan.

"Negative. It seemed like it came from a ways away," an agent replied.

"Approach the truck with caution. He probably isn't in there, but go slow. The rest of you keep your eye on the origin of the shot," Donovan ordered. "And stay covered."

Agents Krause and Fitz slowly worked their way toward the truck and were within fifteen feet when another shot cracked in the air from directly ahead. In an instant, the bark of an oak tree exploded next to Krause's head. Both men dropped to the ground.

"You okay, Krause?"

"I'm okay."

"Can you see him?" called Fitz.

"No. But, I figure he's more or less straight ahead of us to the east," Krause replied, his heart pounding.

Krause crawled several yards through the brush, crouched low behind a large tree then slowly rose to scan the area with his field glasses. He barely got them to his eyes when another shot blasted through the woods. A powerful fsssst-sound rocketed past him and he felt a sharp pain in his ear. He swatted at it reflexively thinking a bee had stung him. When he did, a strangely warm, wet sensation covered his hand and he saw that it was red with blood.

"Fucker got me!" he called. "I've been hit!"

Fitz fired a burst from his automatic rifle in the direction the shot came from and sprinted for the cover of the van. "How bad is it?" he called.

"It's just my ear but it smarts like a sumbitch," Krause replied.

Fitz got on the radio. "Krause is hit. I'm at the truck. The target is somewhere out there ahead of us. Be careful. It'll be real easy to shoot each other."

Krause applied pressure to his ear with a handkerchief and waited for the ringing to stop. "What's in the truck?" he called out to Fitz.

Fitz opened the rear door of the panel truck and looked inside. There he saw a skinning knife, a meat saw, some rope and a tarpaulin on the floor heavily streaked with dry blood.

"I'm going over there, Brian. Keep an eye on Mueller," said Donovan.

Two minutes later he pulled to a stop behind the power company truck parked in the opening in the woods and got out. He put on a Kevlar vest and unlocked the shotgun from the floor mount. His hands shook as he stuffed shotgun shells into the magazine. Finally, he opened the trunk and took out a megaphone.

Walking into the woods until he saw the truck parked among the trees, he stopped behind a tree and called out. "Put your weapon down and come out with your hands on top of your head. You are surrounded."

"Fuck you!" came a voice from deep in the woods. "Put yours down and you come out."

"You don't have a snowball's chance in hell if you don't give yourself up," Donovan called. The agents began moving in.

"You plan on killing me?" came the voice.

"Not unless we have to," called Donovan.

"For huntin' a fuckin' deer?" came the reply.

Donovan froze. Did he hear right?

"Deer hunters don't shoot FBI agents," called Donovan.

"The FBI don't chase after deer hunters," the voice replied.

"Will you put down your weapon and come out or do we have to come for you?" asked Donovan.

There was a long pause then the voice called out. "I'm comin'! Don't shoot."

"Put down your rifle and place your hands on your head," ordered Donovan.

Slowly, a strange figure emerged from the brush wearing a Ghillie suit; an elaborate hunting outfit covered in ragged strips of camouflage cloth designed to blend in with the wooded environment and render the wearer virtually invisible. Within seconds he was swarmed by SWAT and FBI teams, thrown to the ground and handcuffed.

"You guys are pretty serious about your deer I guess," he said, as his head was uncovered to reveal man in his mid-twenties with long, stringy blond hair, blue eyes and a small mouth set in a wide jaw. It wasn't David Geller.

Donovan took the man's wallet from his pants pocket and found a Tennessee driver's license that gave his name as Brandon Shine, born 1972.

"You're Brandon Shine?" asked Donovan, comparing the face with the photo.

"Yep," he replied.

"You're under arrest, Mr. Shine. For resisting arrest, attempted murder, hunting without a license and probably a lot more."

"Attempted murder? I ain't tried to murder nobody," he protested indignantly.

"You shot one of our agents, Mr. Shine," said Donovan.

"I was just discouraging him. If I was fixin' to kill 'em, he'd be dead," said Shine boastfully.

The deputy read him his rights. He was placed in a Sheriff's van and taken to the county jail. Shine's van would eventually be towed away and examined to see if the blood really was from a deer, but Donovan had little doubt that it was. As it turned out, this was not Shine's first run in with the law for poaching. It was big business in Iowa with poacher's frequently coming from other states.

The SWAT and FBI teams had returned to their designated positions and a discouraged Donovan and Scully watched the van pull away under an appropriately sullen sky.

"We seem to have better luck catching poachers than serial killers," said Scully on their return to the farm.

"Yeah. With all that fuckin' activity, do you think Geller is on to us and maybe decided to wait for another opportunity?" asked Donovan.

"Maybe he's waiting for darkness. He did most of the them at night. Maybe he's planning his move for tonight, ya know?" Scully replied.

Mueller was in the living room asleep in his recliner next to three empty beer cans. While Scully and the deputy played gin with the old man's cards at the kitchen table, Donovan settled into a beat up lawn chair on the porch and thought about the poacher, Brandon Shine. He thought about Tess. But mostly he thought about Geller and wondered where he was and what he was doing that very moment.

Without really noticing at first, it grew eerily quiet. There wasn't a whisper of a breeze to stir the leaves in the giant elms, not a single bird in flight. Donovan's thoughts were interrupted when he heard Mueller's cows crossing the pasture toward the barn. He looked up to see the sky had turned a sickening green. Lightening flashed in the distance as the cows crowded nervously at the entrance to the dairy parlor even though it was hours before milking.

"Better wake the old man," Donovan said, opening the screened porch door. "He's got some anxious cows out here." Before the door could close, the lights went out and the old refrigerator stopped it's humming.

"Shit," said Donovan. "That's all we need."

"I best call in a welfare check," said the deputy, but before he could get to the radio it squawked.

"Unit 38. Please respond, over," came the scratchy voice of the dispatcher.

"Unit 38, 10-4," the deputy responded.

"We just received some information that Detective Donovan and his partner will want to know about," she said.

"Go ahead," said the Deputy.

"Reverend Mueller is missing."

CHAPTER 57

Donovan released the SWAT team and requested the FBI agents to shut down their operation and relocate to Storm Lake as soon as they could. That meant returning the borrowed power company trucks and finding different vehicles somehow in the middle of the remote Iowa farm countryside.

Donovan knew that the one hundred-ten-mile drive to Storm Lake was a race against time. For once he was thankful for Scully's lead foot on the accelerator. If Geller had Mueller, and he probably did, the Reverend might already be dead.

Angry, dark clouds were climbing over the distant horizon now. "I think we're going to get a ripsnorter of a storm," said Scully. He turned on the radio and pushed buttons until he found a weather report.

"A slow moving front is working its' way through northern Iowa accompanied by heavy rain and high winds. Meteorologists are cautioning people to stay at home close to a portable radio as conditions are ideal for the formation of tornadoes,"

Less than two-hours later, Donovan and Scully drove into Storm Lake in the darkness. Not a single light pole or neon sign lit up the night. The streets were empty, the stores dark. When they arrived at the main intersection in the center of town, the headlights of the car fell on a temporary stop sign weighted down with sand bags. Scully turned at the corner that led to the police station and saw it glowing in the distance under its own emergency power. They pulled into the parking lot and ran inside through the now lightly falling rain.

Chief Conrad Sorenson graciously took the toothpick from his mouth when he met them at the door. Next to him was a haggard-looking woman wearing shorts and an oversized Iowa Hawkeye sweatshirt. She appeared to be in her mid-fifties.

"This is Reverend Mueller's daughter," he said.

"I'm Detective Donovan and this is Detective Scully. Any word from your father?"

"No. Nothing. Do you think that man has him?" she asked nervously, not wanting to hear the answer.

"Can't say. It's possible he might have gotten lost or had car trouble, too. Tell us what you know," said Donovan.

"He left the parsonage early in the morning to attend a Christian Conference in Des Moines," she said. "I told him I'd drive him but he insisted.

"He always calls when he goes any distance from home, so when several hours passed and we hadn't heard from him, I called the conference hotel where he had reserved a room and they said he hadn't checked in," she said.

Donovan could see that she was slowly growing hysterical and asked if there was somewhere they could all sit down. "Maybe a glass of water or something?" offered Scully.

The chief led them down the hall to a small lounge with a couch and a couple of comfortable chairs.

"Anyway, I came here to file a missing person's report," she continued.

"I informed Angela that a missing persons report couldn't be filed for twenty four hours, but in view of the circumstances, I would wave that," interrupted the chief.

"We've contacted every law enforcement agency between here and Des Moines with his photograph and a description of his car. If it's out there we'll find it," said the chief.

"Do you have any idea what route your father might have taken?" asked Donovan.

"Dad preferred the slower pace of country roads to the highways," she replied with tears in her eyes. "He could be anywhere."

"I've plotted the most likely routes the Reverend would have taken and began the search," Sorenson said, pointing to a wall map. It was marked with grease pencils of varying colors.

"We have as many officers as we can spare looking for his car, but with the weather, we're spread pretty thin. There are trees down blocking roads everywhere," he said.

"There are at least 10 FBI agents on their way from Algoma. We'll reroute them south to give your boys a hand," said Donovan, looking over to Scully. "Let's make sure every one is spread out and not going over the same area again and again. We have to make the best use of the time we have before..." he stopped himself when he remembered the Reverend's daughter who was hiding her face in her hands on the couch.

"The weather is only going to get worse so let's move."

CHAPTER 58

Reverend Mueller was busily dusting his roses with insecticide in the last light of the day when the air was still and there was dew on the leaves. He looked up when he heard the squeal of the screen door and heard his daughter walk out on the porch.

"There's a phone call for you, dad," she said. "It's the police."

"Oh, bother!" he mumbled through his paper mask.

"We have good news for you, reverend," Mueller heard when he answered the phone. "You're off the hook."

The reverend felt enormous relief when he learned he was no longer considered the target of the serial killer. He had grown tired of explaining the constant presence of the police car parked on the street and was eager to get his life back to normal.

With his renewed spirit, but over his daughter's objections, he decided to attend the American Synod Christian Conference in Des Moines that he had cancelled earlier. He reconfirmed his hotel reservation, packed his bag and in less than an hour was backing his white Toyota out of the garage behind the parsonage.

Mueller looked forward to the leisurely drive through the beautiful Iowa farmland. Some areas as were level as a barn floor for miles, others as lush and rolling as a Grant Wood painting. He didn't tell his family that he sometimes got lost because he always managed to find his way with a little help from kind people who fell over backwards to come to the assistance of an elderly man in a clerical collar.

All in all it was a perfect morning as the aging car rolled lazily along until he turned south onto the loneliest of country roads and a green van suddenly appeared in his rear view mirror. It seemed to come out of nowhere and shot past leaving a cloud of dust in its wake.

The Reverend muttered a few carefully chosen words and pulled over to wait for the air to clear. When the van grew smaller and smaller and finally disappeared over the horizon, he started the Toyota again and continued on his way.

He had not gone far when, with a chuckle of mild amusement, he saw the same van with the hood raised parked along the side of the road next to a large stand of trees. Promising himself he would refrain from lecturing the bearded young driver, he pulled up next to the disabled vehicle and stopped.

"What seems to be the problem?" Mueller asked.

"Do you know anything about engines, reverend?" the man asked.

"Just enough to be dangerous," Mueller replied, getting out and walking over to the opened hood.

Just as he leaned in to inspect the grimy engine, the man grabbed him around his upper body and he felt an agonizingly painful surge of electrical current shoot through him before everything went black.

Amos Thoms looked back to check on the plow he was trailing as he bounced along on the ancient Farmall tractor chugging and climbing the gentle rise of the country road. He tugged the frayed visor of his baseball cap lower in the noonday sun as the familiar abandoned farmhouse appeared on the horizon. Years of incessant prairie wind had worn away the last vestiges of the once-stately house's white paint and sent the brittle asphalt roof shingles flying across the Iowa countryside. He wondered, as he often did, when the old Victorian would finally collapse alongside the chaotic heap of gray and faded red lumber that was once a fine barn. The farm had been the showplace of the large and wealthy Swenson family until they ran into hard times and left it to live in Ankeny years before.

As he passed by the entrance to the long, overgrown driveway that led to the far off homestead, Thoms noticed fresh tire tracks of flattened twin swaths through the long grass. He slowed the tractor's engine to a quiet idle, listened for the report of guns from hunters who sometimes stopped to plink out the last slivers of window glass in empty farmhouses with their 22's or, when they couldn't find anything else to kill, empty their shotguns on the pigeons that roosted there. When he heard only the soft hiss of the grass waving in the breeze, he decided the tracks were probably made by local teens that sometimes partied in the abandoned houses that dotted the countryside. Without another thought, he throttled up again and continued climbing the next rise toward a distant parcel of land he leased that was ready to be plowed.

CHAPTER 59

The rain was beginning to fall when the commandeered police cruiser stopped abruptly in front of a fallen tree on the dark country road.

"Can we get around it?" asked the FBI agent in the passenger seat as the wipers beat back and forth on the windshield.

"I'll take a look," the driver replied, raising the hood on his slicker and grabbing a flashlight. The rain seemed to fall harder as he walked around the car and aimed the beam at the base of the fallen tree. As he did, a pulse of lightning in the distance gave him the briefest of glimpses at something white and angular in the surrounding trees.

He climbed over the tree limbs as the rain pelted down on him and worked his way closer. Soon a white Toyota was clearly visible among the branches. He went closer, aimed the beam of flashlight on the plates and confirmed that the car belonged to Reverend Kurt Mueller.

He hurried back to the cruiser and motioned his partner to roll down his window. "That's it. Call it in, will you? I'll take a closer look."

He felt uneasy as he neared the car. He knew the kinds of things Geller had done to his victims and was prepared for the worst when he shined the light inside. To his relief, it was empty except for a small suitcase and other items you'd expect to find; a box of tissues, a map and several empty paper coffee cups. "Nothing here," he said to his partner who had joined him.

"I'll check the trunk," he replied. The doors were unlocked and the agent removed the key that was still in the ignition. He moved to the rear of the Toyota, nervously slid the key into the slot and turned it while his partner watched. The trunk released and lifted an inch. The agent stood back, swallowed once, held his breath and lifted the trunk lid all the way with a single, swift movement.

"We have the Reverend's car," the dispatcher bellowed down the hall. "But, no Reverend."

Chief Sorenson retrieved the dispatcher's hand-written note and circled the location on the wall map in grease pencil. "It's about twenty minutes from here," he said. "The agents who found it say to be advised that there are trees down everywhere."

"Remember, we're looking for a green van, now," said Donovan. "Or at least it was green. Ask your dispatcher to update the search teams out there, will you chief? We'll start searching the immediate area around the car and work our way out from there."

Sorenson didn't like being ordered around by an outsider and it showed. "Try and keep up with me. We don't need city slickers lost out here."

Donovan and Scully followed close behind the police chief's car as it raced down the rain slick roads. After a brief detour to avoid a downed power pole, they saw the flashing lights of the FBI agent's car and sped to it. They got out and negotiated their way around the downed tree to the Toyota. "Have you gone through the car?" Donovan asked.

"Just to look for the obvious. When we didn't see any sign of the Reverend and thought it best to wait for you and the crime scene guys."

"Thanks. Great work," Donovan replied, turning to the chief.

"Do you know who lives around here?" he asked.

"There's a plat book in my car," Sorenson replied.

Scully divided up the area with hastily sketched maps from the book while Donovan gathered together the search teams that had found their way to the scene. "I'll make this quick," he said as they huddled together in the glare of headlights.

"We checked with the power company. Electricity is out in most of the area. They say it's going to get worse before it gets better. Several tornadoes have touched down just a few miles from here, so be prepared to take cover. Detective Scully has prepared maps dividing the area into quadrants. You're looking for a green or dark colored van or any other suspicious looking vehicle. Check every farm, every home, every outhouse on your map and any others you see. Show Geller's pictures. If you find anyone who has seen him, the van, the Reverend or anything out of the ordinary, call it in immediately."

Scully passed out the maps while Donovan continued. "This is an extremely dangerous situation. Geller won't think twice about killing the Reverend, or you or anyone else who gets in his way. Plus, tornadoes are cropping up all around us. I know I don't have to say it, but if you see one coming toward you, get out of the car and into some kind of shelter–a ditch or culvert if you have to. Watch out for downed trees and avoid downed power lines, they're probably hot. Be careful. Okay?"

Everyone nodded and slogged through the puddles to their vehicles. Chief Sorenson returned to his office to "establish a command post", he said. Donovan and Scully watched as the flashing lights filed down the road into the night.

They got back in the cruiser. Scully fired up the ignition, turned on his flashers and put it in gear. Huge trees swayed like saplings in the headlights as they shot down the road toward the first farm on the map.

"I've been thinking," Donovan said. "Geller has used a different method to kill each victim, but all of them were taken from the Nazi handbook. I figure there are four likely methods remaining; first is shooting, but I doubt he'd shoot Mueller. He likes to inflict pain and shooting would be too fast."

Scully popped a stick of gum in his mouth as he listened– impressed with his partner's powers of observation.

"I thought about burning alive. The Nazi's often did that. It's slow and painful. Still, I think Geller wouldn't want to destroy his calling card serial number on the body," he continued.

"That leaves hanging, gassing or starvation. Any of them would fill the bill. Hanging can be fast or it can be slow and agonizing. I read in one of Solomon Geller's books that the Nazis used piano wire when they executed the Nazi generals who attempted to assassinate Hitler."

Scully unconsciously touched his neck.

"Gassing could be as simple as idling a car's engine in closed garage. Effective, but not painful enough. I think you just go to sleep and never wake up.

"Starvation could take days if he gives Mueller water. That would give us more time, so I'm hoping that's it."

※

Reverend Mueller was in total darkness and struggling to breathe as he drifted back to consciousness. He realized his head was hooded and his hands and feet were tied. Worst of all, what felt and tasted like a rubber ball was stuffed into his mouth. He fought a powerful gag reflex and forced himself to relax so he could breathe through his nose. Stay calm. Stay calm he told himself.

Jostled around and smelling exhaust fumes, he realized he was in some sort of vehicle and gradually the sequence of events that got him there fell into place. The van, hood open, stranded on the lonely road. Stopping. Offering to help the bearded young man. Then the excruciating pain and now here he was. It all made sense. Terrifying sense. This was the man he was told was looking for him. The killer. His mind racing wildly, he recalled bits and pieces of the conversation he had on the porch with the detective from Eau Claire.

Geller. The killer's name was David Geller and he was three feet away from him right now taking him someplace to be tortured and killed.

What to do? He tested the ropes that bound his hands. There was no give. His feet. The same. He tried to shake off the hood and managed only to loosen it slightly so that a suggestion of light flashed on the cloth in front of his eyes.

All he could do now was wait. No. He could pray. He prayed fervently again and again for intervention and when he was

emptied out, he prayed the first prayer his mother taught him–
"Now I lay me down to sleep, I pray the Lord my soul to keep. If I
should die before I wake, I pray the Lord my soul to take."

He lost his normal concept of time, but guessed it must have
been the better part of an hour before the van seemed to slow and
the road went from smooth to rough. Minutes later, it stopped and
he heard a door slam followed by the distinctive sound of a metal
sliding door opening. Suddenly his feet were cut free and he was
being dragged.

"Get up. You have to walk," ordered a gruff, faceless voice.

Mueller tried clumsily to stand, but fell. The man pulled him
roughly back to his feet. "This way," he ordered.

The Reverend tried desperately to keep his self-control as
he was led away. He counted seventeen steps through tall grass,
climbing three wooden steps, crossed a hollow-sounding porch
or platform in five, then took twenty-three more before he was
thrown to the floor inside some sort of building that smelled of
dust and decay.

The hood covering his head was jerked off and he found
himself in a dimly lit room inside a neglected, abandoned house.
He turned and looked at his captor.

"Do you know who I am?" asked Geller, setting a large
backpack on the floor and resting a rifle against a peeling, yellowed
wallpaper wall.

Mueller nodded nervously.

"Do you know what is going to happen to you?"

Mueller breathed hard and swallowed.

"You're going to die," said Geller, pulling him onto his feet
again and stringing a long rope between his tightly bound wrists.

"Did those children plead for their lives before they died.
Before you shot them, Sergeant Mueller?"

He threw the rope in the air again and again until it was draped
over a heavy brass light fixture high overhead. He pulled on it
several times until he was satisfied that it would hold. Mueller's
eyes grew wide as his arms were hoisted into the air until only
the toes of his shoes touched the floor. Then, without warning,

Geller flashed a large knife and pressed it into Mueller's neck. He swallowed again, squeezed his eyes shut, held his breath and waited for the pain of the first cut. When it did not come, he looked down to see Geller cutting his shirt away then slashing through his shoelaces and pulling off his shoes and socks.

"Before we finish with your clothes and give you a nice haircut, there are a couple of items of business," Geller said without expression.

Amos Thoms enjoyed the relaxing to and fro of plowing—passing pleasant hours in a lazy shuffle of random thoughts as he watched the dry stubble of the field curl and turn over on itself in long, black furrows. Suddenly a gust of wind lifted his hat and sent it tumbling into the sky. He throttled back and watched it sail across the field to land on the barbed wire fence along the road. It was then that he saw for the first time that the sky had been transformed from an azure blue to a dead, luminous green. A rush of foreboding washed over him. He had seen the sky like this before and knew it was often a warning of an approaching tornado. He turned his attention back to the field ahead that was still unplowed, eased up on the clutch and brought the idling engine back to a roar. He hurried now as he continued to watch the sky.

With the final pass done, he stopped to raise the plowshares and saw a towering bank of cauliflower thunderheads forming over a slate gray band on the horizon. Today he would not pause to admire his work but headed for home at full throttle.

It was just beginning to mist when he neared the abandoned farmhouse. He was surprised to see a light coming from a downstairs room and an unfamiliar dark van parked out back.

"I hope those kids have the good sense to get out of there before all hell breaks lose," he said out loud as he hurried by. It was beginning to rain when he turned into his barnyard and pulled into the machine shed. His wife rushed up to him as he was climbing down from the tractor.

"They said on the radio that a tornado has touched down and is moving in this direction!" she called over the thunder and light drumming of rain on the metal roof.

They ran for the house and the safety of the cellar. "I'll be right down," he said. "I have to call the police. There's someone at the old Swenson place. Probably some kids having a beer party or God knows what. Maybe the chief can chase them home."

"Don't bother, Amos," said his wife. "The phone is out."

They were huddled together in the tiny farmhouse root cellar when flashing red and blue lights appeared in the small, ground level window overhead.

"You sit tight, honey," said Amos, getting to his feet. He grabbed a flashlight, climbed the steps and saw Detective Michael Donovan banging on the door as he peered into the kitchen with a flashlight.

Amos threw open the door. "Come in. Come in," he called too loudly.

Donovan flashed his badge and asked, "Are you okay here?"

"So far. How bad is it out there?" he asked.

"It's going to get real bad," Donovan replied. "Heavy rain and high winds are moving this direction. Tornadoes have been spotted."

"I tried to call the police," said Amos. "I think there's some kids hold up in an empty old farm house near here. I saw a light. They're probably drinking beer or smoking weed. Doubt they know how serious this is."

"Did you see a vehicle?" asked Donovan.

"A dark van of some kind. I think they'd been there before. I saw tire tracks earlier in the day."

Donovan's heart was pounding. "Can you show me on this map where it is?"

"Lousy map," the farmer said, commenting on Scully's drawing. "It's the old Swenson place. Guess it would be about here. Maybe a mile and a half north."

He described the large Victorian house, the arrangement of decaying outbuildings and the collapsed barn. "Look for a dim light. I think they have a lantern going in there. Crazy kids."

CHAPTER 60

Naked from the waist up except for the clerical collar left around his neck like a ring toss, the slack, white skin hanging on Reverend Mueller's torso seemed to glow in the dim light. A cool breeze blew from the broken windows made him shiver.

Geller squatted in a corner caressing a black pistol in the darkness while he stared into the Reverend's gray eyes. "Know how you're going to die, Reverend?" he whispered menacingly.

Mueller met his stare–his wiry eyebrows silently pleading for his life while he struggled in a pathetic toe dance with his naked feet to push himself up and ease the strain on his shoulders and arms.

"I was going to shoot you like you shot those kids for wanting something to eat, but I've been thinking; you deserve more. After all, you are a man of God. Don't you agree?" he seethed snake-like.

"Maybe you would benefit from starving to death–going hungry like those kids until you'd risk your life for a crust of bread. I've talked with several Jews who managed to survive starvation in Dachau. They told me it was the worst way to go. After a while your body begins to feed on itself. First your mouth dries out and becomes caked. You get so thirsty you drink your own piss. Your lips crack, your tongue swells and your eyes sink. Your nose bleeds, your bladder burns like fire and you'll get the dry heaves, convulsions and cramping. Eventually your organs fail–lungs, heart, and brain–the works. Very unpleasant."

He stood and moved to a window. A flock of crows was settling into a stand of trees in a distant field. "Leave you here to starve; maybe that's what I should do after I finish with you. Just walk away and leave you to the crows." He stuffed the pistol in his waist and slid a knife from its scabbard.

Of course, all this takes more time than we probably have. I'm sure they're looking for you by now."

Geller flipped the knife in his hand, caught it expertly by the flat of the blade and threw it in one fluid motion, driving it deep into the wooden floor at Mueller's feet. The old man looked down at the knife then watched Geller remove the branding iron from the backpack and walk behind him. Mueller struggled to see but could only smell the propane and hear the striking of a match and the soft whoosh as Geller lit the flame. His heart now pounded wildly. He knew what was coming.

Lights flashing, searchlight scanning the terrain, the cruiser looked like a carnival ride moving along the dark country road.

"We should have come to it by now," complained a frustrated Donovan. Scully scanned the search light over a freshly plowed field, pausing on a beat up baseball cap caught in the barbed wire fence. "Let's go a little farther and turnaround if we don't run into it."

Five minutes further up the road, the rain became heavier and the wind was picking up. Scully turned the wiper blades on high. "Better go back. We must have missed it."

They turned around and were retracing their path when Donovan saw a faint light glowing on the horizon from a barely visible structure. "There it is!" he shouted. "That must be the house."

Scully slowed, scanning the edge of the road for the entrance to the overgrown driveway with his searchlight. Less than a hundred feet away they saw the twin tracks of matted grass just as Amos Thoms had described. Donovan got on the radio. "Dispatch, this is Donovan. 10-97–we're at the Sorenson farm and we're going in. Code 8–request backup."

"Stand down, Donovan. Do not engage!" They both recognized the voice of the Storm Lake Police Chief.

He and Scully looked at each other and shrugged. "Officious bastard isn't he," said Scully.

"10-9. Repeat last transmission," Donovan replied.

"This is Chief Sorenson. Do not engage."

"10-1. Cannot copy."

Suddenly, the farmhouse parlor was alive with flashing blue and red and white lights leaping in through the windows and jouncing frantically on the walls. Reverend Mueller's eyes widened. Geller hastily set down the flaming branding iron and scrambled for the rifle. He raced to one of the windows, fired a quick shot at the approaching police car then moved to another window and fired twice more.

"Oh Lord, I'm saved! Divine intervention," Mueller thought to himself.

"Down!" screamed Donovan at the crack of the first shot and the loud, hollow "thunk" of the bullet striking the cruiser's front fender. The detectives threw off their seat belts and slunk low just as two more shots shattered the windshield and tore into the car's interior.

Donovan's heart was pounding as he reached for the radio. "Dispatch, this is Donovan. 11-99. We need backup. Shots fired!" He gave directions to their location.

Rain spit through the bullet holes in the windshield with the pass of each wiper blade. Scully shut them off. They waited for more shots and caught their breaths. When it appeared the shooting had paused, Scully ducked low behind the steering wheel and backed the cruiser farther away from the house, angled it broadside and popped the trunk. Both detectives scrambled out the passenger door into the rain and duck-walked through the ragged, high grass. They were soaking wet when they reached the rear where they strapped on bulletproof vests and took out ponchos. Donovan grabbed the Vietnam era M16 assault rifle and 3 magazines.

"You're finally gonna get to shoot at a bad guy," said Scully as Donovan rammed home the 30-round magazine of .223 cartridges just as another rifle crack erupted and a side window blew out.

"Actually, I was thinkin' more about him shooting at me," Donovan replied, surprised and gratified at how calm and composed he felt. "What the hell," he thought. "This is what I trained for, what I had rehearsed in my mind a thousand times."

They threw on the rain ponchos, lowered the trunk and took up positions behind the car.

While Scully got back on the radio, Donovan leveled the M16 at the house and scanned the windows through the Colt 4 X 20 scope. All were dark except for those in a room at the far end of the first floor where a soft, dim light shown. He focused the scope on it and felt a rush of nausea.

"Jesus," he said to Scully. "Look at this!"

Scully clamored out of the car, took the rifle and held the scope to his eye. "Lower left window–where the light is," said Donovan.

Scully found himself looking at the nearly naked body of Revered Mueller. He swallowed hard. "Good God," he said. "He looks like a side of beef hanging in a slaughter house."

"Is he still alive?"

"Can't tell," Scully replied. "He isn't moving, but it's hard to see. The rain is getting heavier."

Another shot blasted through air, this time hitting the hood of the cruiser. Both men dropped down.

"It would help if we could turn off the lights, but I'm afraid our backup won't find us in this weather if we do."

Scully got back on the radio while Donovan scoped the house again looking for movement. Abruptly his concentration gave way to a flash of light and another salvo of gunfire from an upstairs window. This time the shot missed. Donovan quickly returned fire, but with less hope of hitting anything than needing to get it out of his system.

Scully was back in an instant. "Another unit is a nearby. I told them to stay on the road at the end of the driveway with the lights going so we can shut them down up here."

A minute later, flickering lights appeared far off in the darkness and grew brighter as the first backup unit covered the distance to the farm.

It stopped at the end of the driveway. Scully hurried to turn off his own flashers as another shot came from a different upstairs farmhouse window.

Donovan returned fire with a three shot burst then all went quiet as he saw two of the FBI agents running to the cruiser through the rain and darkness. They both carried assault rifles. One, who Donovan recognized as Agent Fitz, was also toting a small equipment case.

"The vic is strung up downstairs and may be deceased. We can't tell," said Donovan. "There's a light down there but it's dim and there doesn't appear to be any movement. Geller's been firing sporadically from the upstairs windows with what I'm guessing is a high-powered rifle."

Fitz produced a pair of night vision binoculars from the case and switched them on. "Let's see what we have here."

He brought the binoculars to his eyes and lowered them down again. "I have to get closer. Can't see through this stuff."

"We'll lay down some fire if he starts shooting again," said Donovan as they huddled behind the car. "But, only if it doesn't come from the far room. We can't risk the Reverend."

Donovan, Scully and the other agent leveled their rifles at the upstairs as Fitz sprinted into the downpour and disappeared. He was gone a minute. Then two. Then bright strobes of lightening lit the entire scene exposing his position.

From the darkness of an upstairs window, Geller saw Fitz less than fifty yards from the house. His military training made his action automatic and instantaneous as he fired three shots in rapid succession–barely missing the agent.

The response from below was immediate. A fierce barrage from the police assault weapons ripped through the window, tore through the walls and sent shattered wood and bits of plaster flying all around Geller. Before he could throw himself on the floor and cover his head, a wooden splinter from a window frame lodged in his eye socket. He pulled the splinter out and felt warm blood run from the open wound into his eye.

Fitz sprinted back to safety behind the cruiser when the firefight ceased.

"The Reverend's alive. He appears to be alert, but he's in a bad way," he said breathlessly. "Looks like he's hanging from the ceiling. His mouth is taped shut. He's naked as a jay bird from the waist up except for his collar."

"We gotta get him out of there," said Donovan. "Where the hell is the rest of our backup?"

"I'll see what the hold up is," said Scully, opening the cruiser door to get to the radio. He was back out in a minute.

"Trees are down blocking roads everywhere," he said. "They're coming on foot, but they're miles away and not certain where they're going."

"Shit," said Donovan, turning to Scully. "Do you think you can find the last farm where the guy told us about this place?"

Scully nodded.

"Well, go see if he knows how the house is laid out. Bring him back if he can help," ordered Donovan.

Scully hurried to the single waiting car and sped off. Donovan turned to Fitz who still held onto the night vision binoculars. "I think the rain is letting up. Train those things on the house and see if you can figure out what Geller is up to. If you locate him upstairs, maybe we'll be able to pin him there when we know what the floor plan is. Then we can go in after Mueller."

Fitz nodded in agreement.

"Let's see if I can get him to talk," said Donovan. He went to the trunk and took out the bull horn.

The gunfire from outside and upstairs was little more than background noise to Reverend Mueller now. He focused on the hissing of the branding iron behind him as the light from its flame cast a long shadow of his suspended torso on the wall. He stretched to the floor, grimacing from the painful knotting in his calves as he turned on his toes in a grotesque, halting pirouette until he saw the brass numbers glowing orange hot. He also saw that the flame was just inches from the wall where Geller had left it when the police arrived. To his horror, the old wallpaper nearest the flame was turning brown as it slowly began to scorch. He wondered if it would outlast the small bottle of propane before it caught fire.

Time was running out. Don't panic, he thought. Think. He tilted his head back to study the heavy brass fixture mounted to the high ceiling. Would his weight have loosened it? No, he saw. It held fast. Desperately he thrust his hips from side to side and brought his knees up as if to swing. The fixture swayed but held and he gave up exhausted and in despair.

Suddenly the amplified voice blasted into the house lifting his spirit and giving him renewed hope. "David," he heard. "This is Detective Donovan with the Eau Claire, Wisconsin Police Department. It's time to come in, David. It's all over. You can stop this now and no one else has to get hurt. Can we talk about it?"

Outside, Donovan waited for an answer. When none came, he turned to Fitz. "Do you think we might have nailed him when we returned fire?"

Before Fitz could answer, another shot cracked through the darkness into the cruiser's hood.

"Guess not," said Fitz.

"David. Reverend Mueller is not the man you think he is! Do you hear me? You've got the wrong Karl Mueller. Call out if you can hear me!"

Geller skulked from window to window as he listened, but held his response. Then, when a brief lull in the rain cleared his view of the cruiser, he fired a three shot burst into the driver's side door and heard a satisfying "thunk, thunk, thunk".

The three men dropped behind the car again. Donovan held the bullhorn to his mouth but stayed low. "David. I understand your anger. I talked with your mother. She told us everything. I know how everyone suffered. How your father suf...."

Abruptly, another shot blew out the search light on the driver's side sending shards of glass flying through the air. Donovan dropped back down and waited.

"David. Your mother would want you to stop now before an innocent man dies," called Donovan.

Nothing.

"David. Do you have a cell phone?" Donovan asked hopefully.

Nothing.

"David. I can call you and we can talk about this if you have a cell phone."

"There's nothing to talk about!" Geller called through the hiss of the falling rain.

"Step one," Donovan thought to himself. "Getting the perp to communicate."

"Yes. Yes, there is!" he replied. "You can tell your father's story to the world without anymore killing. I can help you!"

Three more rounds tore into the cruiser. "No one cared about getting justice when they had the chance and now it's too late," called Geller.

"Killing Reverend Mueller won't help. It will only destroy what you and your father accomplished. Let him go!" called Donovan.

"He'll go. But, not where you want!" called Geller.

"Let me bring you a cell phone, David. We can talk," called Donovan.

Geller's response was another three shot burst.

Donovan leaned back against the car, rested the bullhorn in his lap and wiped the rain from his face. Just then he saw the flashing lights of a squad car approaching and heard Scully on the squawk box. "I have Mr. Thoms with me."

"Keep him down there with you," he radioed to Scully. "It's like Pork Chop Hill up here."

"Say again?" requested Scully.

"Never mind," said Donovan.

"He's drawn a layout of the house. I'm bringing it up!" Scully squawked back. Two minutes later, Donovan and Scully were huddled behind the car together studying the soggy, hand drawn layout by flashlight.

"Mueller is hanging here in the parlor," said Scully as he oriented Donovan to the location in the drawing. "It's open to the dining room and connects with the kitchen. There are two sets of stairs to the second floor. The big main staircase and this smaller stairway that goes up from the kitchen pantry in the back."

"So Geller is moving from window and bedroom to bedroom upstairs along this hall," said Donovan, following the diagram with his finger.

"Yeah. He might not even know about the pantry steps. Thoms says they're very narrow and wind around a corner," said Scully, chewing nervously on a fresh stick of gum. "If I can get into the kitchen in back, I might be able to get upstairs that way and surprise him."

"Pretty risky," said Donovan.

"Look, Copper. We don't know when or even if backup will get here. We can't sit around and wait without trying something. That old guy hanging there can't last much longer even if we can keep Geller away from him."

"I hate this shit," replied Donovan, returning his attention to the drawing. "But, I guess we don't have a choice."

Scully took the Smith and Wesson 38 from his shoulder holster and looked it over even though he had checked the gun earlier in the day. He wished the revolver had more stopping power and could fire more than six shots.

"You set?" asked Donovan, patting him on the shoulder.

Scully looked over the floor plan one more time, made sure his flashlight worked and nodded.

"Don't be a hero–and get rid of that fuckin' gum before you go in. You reek," said Donovan.

Scully spit the rubbery wad several feet into the grass, took a deep breath and sprinted off. Donovan was grateful to see how quickly he was swallowed up by the night because he knew Geller couldn't see him either.

Scully paused when he neared the back of the house. Seeing no movement, he crept up to the van and shown his light inside. It was empty. He moved onto the porch and shined the flashlight through a broken window and saw the kitchen where Tohms had said it would be. Careful to avoid the remaining slivers of glass, he crawled in, crossed the room and quietly opened the pantry door. The old hinges squeaked softly. He froze and listened for footsteps but it remained quiet.

He swept his flashlight around inside; across musty stonewalls under tents of spider webs and along empty, rough shelves covered in dust and pigeon shit. Finally the beam rested on the tiny back staircase. With his flashlight in one hand and his Smith and Wesson in the other, he put his weight on the first step and began to climb –slowly–stopping at the least suggestion of a squeak and listening for footsteps overhead.

Reverend Mueller's eyes widened when he saw the first tiny wisp of smoke rise like an apparition from the wallpaper, then another and another. Suddenly, a small flame erupted and in seconds the wall was enveloped. Mueller gyrated frantically from side-to-side in a final, futile attempt to get free as the flames engulfed the entire far end of the parlor. With his mouth taped shut and air passing only through his nose, he turned his face away from the searing heat and struggled to breathe. Soon billows of thick, black smoke were racing across the ceiling chased by tongues of orange and yellow flames hungry for more fuel. Then, just as the hair on the reverend's knuckles began to singe, he felt his toes touch the floor – then the balls of his bare feet. Soon he was standing flatfooted. The strain on his arms and shoulders relaxed.

"Oh, God! Is the roof coming down?" he wondered as he continued to drop. Then he realized that the rope was melting!

He pulled down greedily with his remaining strength and slowly, almost gently, the rope stretched and he descended through the smoke to the floor where the air was clear enough to breathe. He lay there exhausted, desperately inhaling and, frantic for more, felt for the duct tape with the fingertips of his bound hands. With painful, violent jerks, he tore it from around his head, pulled the ball from his mouth and gulped in the air. The muscles in his cheeks relaxed and a wet breeze from the broken windows fanned his scorched flesh. Fire nearly surrounded him, but he was alive.

Geller was squatting in the darkness next to an upstairs window when he smelled smoke and remembered the branding iron. "Shit!" he said. He fired a burst out the window in the general direction of the cruiser, rushed into the hall and saw the thick black smoke pouring up the stairwell. Pulling his t-shirt up over his nose and mouth, he was about to descend into it when he heard Scully shout behind him.

"Police! Stop. Drop your weapon!"

Geller ignored the order. Scully pulled the trigger on his Smith and Wesson again and again. The first shot shattered the finial on a newel post. The second drove into the back of Geller's left thigh, and another tore a through-and-through hole in his side. Wounded now with blood in one eye and the other burning, he flailed blindly for the handrail and, fueled by adrenaline, launched himself into the smoking stairwell as Scully raced toward him.

Halfway down, Geller's wounded leg gave out and he plunged headlong the rest of the way to land in a heap in the hallway at the base of the staircase. He lay there writhing in pain when he realized that the air there was clear and he could breathe. Instinctively, he pointed the rifle up the stairway expecting to see Scully lunge down through the smoke, but he didn't appear.

Twenty feet away, lying under the roiling black cloud, Reverend Mueller saw Geller's knife imbedded in the floor. He crawled toward it on his elbows, held the rope that bound his wrists against the blade and began to saw. A strand at a time, the soft polyethylene separated as the heat increased and breathing became more difficult. His arms grew tired and his shoulder ached but he continued to saw until finally he was free. Blood rushed painfully back into his hands. Slowly the feeling returned. As the fire's roar grew more deafening and the heat intensified, he crawled through the feathers and pigeon shit and shards of glass toward the front door to escape. Weak and terrified, he struggled desperately an inch at a time toward the entry hall when he heard an unearthly cracking noise behind him and looked back to see the far wall and roof of the parlor collapse in a pile of blazing timbers. Suddenly the smoke and hot air trapped in the inferno rushed to the opening and, for one brief moment, the air cleared and the Reverend saw Geller, rifle still in his arms, huddled in a heap like a terrified lamb. In that instant the monster, the broken evil menace intent on killing him just minutes before, was made human and frail and he knew without understanding that he had to try to save him.

The Reverend lifted his eyes up into the flames and whispered, "God help me," and began to crawl. Geller saw him coming and fired the rifle aimlessly into the ceiling. Just then the old man was on top of him, wrestled the rifle away and tossed it into the fire.

"I'll help you," shouted Reverend Mueller.

"No! No! Get away!" screamed a wild-eyed Geller, kicking frantically at the old man.

Mueller cringed in pain as the blows struck then, with his last bit of strength, straddled Geller from behind, grasped him under his flailing arms and, digging the bleeding heels of his naked feet into the floor, began dragging him toward the front door an inch at a time.

Scully stopped shooting when Geller disappeared down the stairs. He scrambled after him, but just as he reached the staircase, flames exploded up the opening and drove him away. He pivoted and ran back down the hall as more and more smoke poured into the entire second floor. The flashlight was of little use now, forcing him to feel his way along the hall. By the time he reached the pantry steps, he was in total darkness. His breathing grew more rapid. He fought for air. His eyes burned. Soot invaded his lungs and he began to cough. Unable to see, he missed the first step and slid feet first to the landing. Something snapped in his ankle, but despite the pain that shot up his leg, he continued down to the pantry and hobbled back outside where he could finally breathe and see again.

Donovan saw Scully limping around the corner of the house on the porch.

"Back off! He's still shooting!" he shouted. Scully ignored him and was soon standing in the doorway watching Reverend Mueller struggling desperately to pull Geller outside away from the flames.

"Don't! Don't go in there, Scully!" screamed Donovan, rushing toward him.

"Gotta get the Reverend," Scully yelled. As the words left his mouth, the roof overhead collapsed in a thunderous crash taking the entry wall with it and filling the sky with a fury of flames. The blast drove Scully backwards off the porch. He landed in the singed, blackened grass as sparks rained down, melting holes in his poncho, catching his clothes on fire and burning his skin.

Donovan sprinted toward the blaze, swept the hot coals from Scully and beat out the flames with his bare hands. Throwing him over his shoulder in a fireman's carry, he raced back to the car a safe distance away where he settled him in the wet grass before collapsing in exhaustion.

Scully fought desperately to catch his breath. "Did you see? Did you see what he was doing?" he gasped between coughs. "He was trying to save Geller. The Reverend could have made it out, but he stopped to save Geller."

"I saw," said Donovan.

The flickering orange light of the fire danced on their faces as the two men looked at each other knowingly. They didn't speak–each was lost in his own confusion of thoughts.

Scully was still coughing violently and beginning to feel the sharp, searing pain of the burns when a battalion of fire fighters and EMT's from Storm Lake arrived.

Donovan waved his flashlight and screamed: "Over here.

Medical help–over here!"

While the fire fighters rushed to connect hoses to the tanker truck, two EMT's scrambled over to where Scully lay. One immediately administered oxygen while the other hurried back to bring the ambulance up.

By now flames were licking higher into the night sky in a final bawling, burst of energy. The powerful streams of water from the fire hoses seemed to have no impact. Suddenly, the house rumbled and cracked a loud warning and someone shouted, "Get back! The whole thing is gonna go!" In an instant, a thunderous crash split the quiet and echoed across the fields.

The once stately Victorian was gone.

"Best let her burn out," said the Fire Captain as billows of smoke and heat rushed out. "Shut down the pumper."

"There are two people in there," said Donovan.

"I'm sorry, but they're gone. Nothing more we can do now," he said. "Too dangerous to go in."

Donovan called into the Eau Claire Police Department and left a message for Chief Krumenauer that the chase for David Geller was over. He outlined the events, explained that Scully was being treated for smoke inhalation and minor burns and said he would call again with details. "Oh, yeah. And tell the chief we broke his police car."

He signed off, wiped the rain from his face with the wedge of his hand and walked beside Scully as the stretcher was carried away and loaded into the ambulance.

Before the door was closed, Scully lifted the oxygen mask from his face. "We lost him, Copper," he said.

"You gave it your best shot, partner," Donovan replied. "Remember, we got the bad guy. No one could have done more. Go get fixed up. I'll see you soon."

The ambulance doors closed and he watched them drive out of sight. He shoved his hands deep into his pockets and strode slowly away from the heat to the shelter of a dilapidated machine shed. Standing there in the darkness amidst the chaos of lights and rumbling engines, he tried to sort out the jumble of anger and sadness and frustration he was feeling. He thought about Reverend Mueller's astonishing act of forgiveness and he prayed for his soul. And when he was done, he prayed for David Geller.

Tess heard the strain in his voice when he called to tell her what happened. She offered to drive down, but Donovan declined and told her he would be staying until the bodies had been recovered in the morning when the fire had burned out. By then, maybe Scully could come home with him.

The Fire Captain allowed a search for the remains of Reverend Mueller and David Geller sometime before dawn. By then a long line of television crews from Des Moines, Minneapolis and Eau Claire had arrived and crowded into the barnyard. Thick cables spread like roots from a forest of satellite dishes towering atop trucks. Bright lights turned night to day. Donovan made a brief statement and described the final heroic moments of Revered Mueller and Detective Brian Scully, but refused to answer questions.

A short time later, as the first light of dawn spilled over the long, straight edge of the Iowa horizon, the fire chief found the weary detective leaning against what was left of his cruiser.

"We found them," said the Captain. "Want to take a look before we take them away?"

Donovan nodded silently and followed the Fire Captain to the charred, still smoldering rubble that had been the house.

"Not much left," said the Captain.

Donovan studied the charred remains of the two men. They lay side-by-side. Their arms seemed to be wrapped around each other in a final embrace.

"Take 'em away," he whispered hoarsely.

Cameras and lights came to life again as he watched the firemen carry the two black body bags to waiting ambulances– past reporters who spoke in hushed tones of death and heroes and endings.

At last, the long journey was over.

The End

Made in the USA
Charleston, SC
24 September 2013